SOMEBODY, SOMETIME

CHRIS KELSEY

Black Rose Writing | Texas

ISBN: 978-1-68513-714-4
LIBRARY OF CONGRESS CONTROL NUMBER: 2025945594
PUBLISHED BY BLACK ROSE WRITING
www.blackrosewriting.com

Printed in the United States of America
Suggested Retail Price (SRP) $19.95

Somebody, Sometime is printed in Chaparral Pro

*As a planet-friendly publisher, Black Rose Writing does its best to eliminate unnecessary waste to reduce paper usage and energy costs, while never compromising the reading experience. As a result, the final word count vs. page count may not meet common expectations.

PRAISE FOR CHRIS KELSEY

"5 Stars! *Where the Hurt Is* is western noir at its best ... Kelsey's Emmett Hardy is a flawed hero with a heart for justice and a voice that keeps the reader flipping pages."
–Cam Torrens, author of *Scorched*

"Really enjoyed *Where the Hurt Is* – it got me into the same type of head space as Jim Thompson, but a little milder. Great characters, awesome voice. Look forward to more from Chris Kelsey!"
–Joe Barrett, author of *Managed Care*

"The author's style, the banter, the suspense, and the plot are engaging and made this book impossible to put down."
–AJ McCarthy, author of *Cold Betrayal*

"*Ain't Nothin' Personal* is a riveting page-turner ... an engrossing whodunit ... "
–Literary Titan

"Chris Kelsey hits another home-run with this fast-paced and enthralling mystery starring Emmett Hardy."
–Sublime Book Review

SOMEBODY, SOMETIME

PROLOGUE

I didn't get around to looking for Carrie until she'd been dead for almost three years.

Actually, that's not 100 percent true. I'd long known where Carrie was, or at least where her earthly remains were interred: a Department of Corrections Cemetery near the Oklahoma State Penitentiary in McAlester, commonly known as "Peckerwood Hill."

Denizens of Peckerwood Hill are members of an exclusive club comprising inmates who die behind bars whose bodies go unclaimed by anyone on the outside. While Carrie was never an actual inmate in McAlester, or any other prison I know of, she probably would've ended up there if she hadn't been shot to death in the commission of her crime.

Carrie's crime was killing a candidate for the United States Congress, a fella named Burton Murray. There was no question of her guilt; I was standing ten feet away when she did it. One of my officers, Joel Carter, tried to shoot her before she could shoot Burt, but was a fraction of a second too late. Both Carrie and Burt died. Joel felt bad about it for a long time after—both for taking Carrie's life, and for being unable to save Burt's. I told him then and continue to say it wasn't his fault; he only did what the situation required. I'm not sure he agrees.

Burt Murray himself was a piece of work, a crooked former sheriff of our county whose crimes sent him to prison for several years, until he found a lawyer smart enough to game the system and secure his release. He'll come up in this account from time to time, maybe more than time-to-time, but this isn't his story.

These events occurred in the summer of 1976, right around the time people were painting fire hydrants to look like George Washington in honor of the United States' 200th birthday. All we knew about Carrie was that she'd appeared out of nowhere at one of Murray's campaign rallies, aimed an antique Colt Buntline revolver at him, and pulled the trigger.

If there was a political aspect to Carrie's crime, I expect you'd call this an assassination, but there wasn't anything remotely political about it; during my investigation, which was definitely unofficial, I discovered irrefutable evidence that Murray had recently shot her boyfriend to death. That's why she did it. Unfortunately, the law enforcement agencies conducting the official investigation did a piss-poor job of constructing a timeline of Carrie's activities leading up to when she shot Burt, so the case ended up being closed without a stated determination of motive.

We found out more about Carrie's boyfriend than we did about her. His name was Leon Qualls. As far as we could determine, he was Carrie's only friend and presumably the father of the child she carried in her belly on the day she died. Both were troubled; Leon had schizophrenia, and according to the one person I met who actually knew her, Carrie suffered from an intellectual disability, what they used to call mental retardation.

Like I said, this all happened in the summer of '76. In the immediate aftermath, I felt a compulsion to learn everything I could about her. Not just her last name, but where she was from, and whether she had anyone in this world besides Leon Qualls. When her body went unclaimed and the state buried her in Peckerwood Hill, I wanted to do something about it. I felt bad that she didn't have a family to mourn her death. It's like the words to that Dean Martin song: *"Everybody loves somebody sometime."* Someone must've loved Carrie. Leon did, but there had to be others, someone still alive who'd want to know her fate. At least, that's what I thought.

Unfortunately, with everything going on—Burt Murray shooting Leon, Carrie shooting Burt, my officer Joel shooting Carrie—I didn't have the time or the resources to dig too deep. Anyway, it was technically the Oklahoma State Bureau of Investigation's case, not mine. They came up empty, but I don't think they looked too hard.

Time marched on, and I thought of Carrie less and less. At one point, I devised a half-assed plan to retire on my 50th birthday and maybe move to the Bahamas or someplace else with a nice beach and lots of sunshine, but that one and a couple more birthdays passed without it happening. Nothing much has changed at all, as a matter of fact, except that I'm older, more out of shape, and still trying not to crave what used to be my daily excessive intake of Old Grand Dad bourbon.

Meanwhile, Carrie remained a nobody.

***

Before I go any further, I should introduce myself. My name is Emmett Hardy. I'm the police chief in Burr, Oklahoma, a small town in Tilghman County in the western part of the state, snug up against the border of the Texas panhandle. Oklahoma has two counties pronounced the same but spelled differently—"Tillman" versus "Tilghman." I'd explain why, but it would take too long and doesn't have much to do with the story.

Burr had a pretty big oil boom starting back around '73 and '74 when the Arab oil embargo took hold. By the middle part of the decade, however, it became apparent that whatever oil was left had already been spoken for. The rich guys got richer, and the newcomers with lint in their pockets and dreams of hitting the jackpot moved on to the next boom town, leaving Burr in even worse condition than before.

These days, we have too many bills to pay and not enough money to pay them. It's all the town can do to keep up with its utility payments. Things have gotten so bad that last summer the town council ordered us to only cool the station to 78 degrees. I reckon that's better than having no air-conditioning at all, but it's still quite a comedown from previous years, when we kept it on 68 from April to October.

But you've got to do what you've got to do. It'd be a heck of a thing to have the town's bank foreclose on our police station, especially since the bank president hates me and would like nothing better than to see me working out of my pickup. We're not there yet, although I did have to lay off a part-time officer who'd been helping us out on weekends.

The town government and fly-by-night oil speculators aren't the only ones who've suffered. Lots of local businesses went under, too, including the town's two hardware stores, Otasco and Western Auto. For a while, we had two full-service gas stations: Wes Harmon's Sinclair, and a Conoco run by a fella whose name I've forgotten since he wasn't here very long. He sold the station to the folks who run the UToteM convenience store chain. It still has gas pumps, but they're self-serve, and with prices the way they are, I'll be damned if I'm going to pump my own gas.

A new McDonald's opened, which was good, but it ended up running one of our other drive-ins out of business. Burger Mart had been around since I was a teenager. I guess I took for granted it would always be a permanent part of the town landscape, like our red, white and blue water tower, or the *Welcome to Burr, Home of the Patriots,*

1948 and 1949 Oklahoma Class D Football Champions sign on the highway leading into town. I was wrong.

To make matters worse, there's now talk about McDonald's shutting down. Makes me wish they'd never come to town in the first place.

For a while, Burr had its sights set on being another Alva or Elk City. Not anymore. We'll be lucky if we can even get back to what we used to be, which frankly wasn't all that much.

Crime all over the state has gotten steadily worse in recent years. That's put a strain on both the state police and the Oklahoma State Bureau of Investigation, which is probably why, when it comes to serious crime, they've been more willing to let me take on more of the heavy lifting than before. For a while, I enjoyed being left alone to do things my own way; I don't like being bossed around, least of all by the know-it-alls frequently employed by state law enforcement. However, after investigating a few cases on my own, I began to look back fondly on the days I was the water boy and not the quarterback.

About my investigative skills, I used to tell folks I was no Sam Spade. I'm still not, but I've gotten better. Or maybe the crooks have gotten stupider. There aren't many Einsteins among them, that's for sure. We don't get the sort of master criminals you see on the TV detective shows. The murderers we deal with tend to shoot first and make up half-assed excuses later. Jealous boyfriends, racists who kill out of pure hatred, and psychotic ex-convicts rate pretty high on our list of offenders. Lieutenant Columbo never has to face off against guys like that, but I do, and let me tell you, it's not one hell of a lot of fun. To beat that type, you've got to roll around in the muck with them. I get some satisfaction from putting guys like that away, but with every killing I investigate, the dirt gets a little harder to wash off.

There are no white hats in the sewer.

Occasionally, a corrupt politician does something dastardly, Burt Murray being a prime example. I never felt dirtier than I did after he was killed, except in this case, it wasn't the victim I felt sorry for. Burt had already killed a number of innocent people, including Carrie's boyfriend. It was them I felt sorry for. The fact that Carrie was pregnant when she died piled an extra layer of hurt over the entire episode.

Afterward, when things quieted down, I promised myself that one day I'd put everything aside and dig into Carrie's past, find her family, and get her moved out of Peckerwood Hill into a proper cemetery. Yet for almost three years, I barely raised a finger.

Then one day I got a phone call.

CHAPTER ONE

If I live to be 100, I'll always remember the date: March 13th, 1979, the day the Chicago Police arrested Roger Dale Stafford.

The previous summer, Stafford allegedly killed a married couple and their young son on I-35 outside Purcell, a little town 30 or 40 miles south of Oklahoma City. I say "allegedly" because, as I begin this, he's yet to be convicted. But from what they say, it promises to be one of those open-and-shut cases.

Roger didn't do it all by himself; his wife, Verna, pulled over to the side of the highway, pretending to have car trouble, while Roger and his brother, Harold, hid in the tall grass by the side of the road like the snakes they were. When the aforementioned family stopped to help, the brothers jumped out, shot them to death, and drove off in their vehicle.

The Staffords weren't done. Three weeks later, they robbed, then executed six employees at an Oklahoma City steakhouse. Four of the dead were teenagers.

Six days later, in an example of justice being mysteriously served, Harold Stafford crashed his motorcycle in Tulsa and was killed.

My wife Karen believes it was a case of the universe meting out justice. She calls it karma.

Call it what you want, but karma didn't nail Roger Dale and Verna. They lived on. Their trail never did heat up, really, until Roger anonymously dialed the OSBI and fingered Verna and Harold for the killings. The cops looked into it and discovered that Harold had died several months earlier. At the funeral home, they found Verna listed among the mourners. They traced her to Chicago. She led them straight to her husband.

As I read about Stafford's capture in the newspaper that morning, I noticed a piece about jury selection in another notorious case: the murder of three little girls in the summer of 1977. Someone broke into their tent on their first night of Girl Scout camp and raped and murdered them. The authorities think they've got their man. I hope they're right.

I bring this up partly to make a point: Big cities don't have the market cornered on moral depravity. When it comes to psychos per capita, Oklahoma's up there with the worst. The Girl Scout murders and those perpetrated by the Staffords have made most Oklahomans as jumpy as spit on a griddle. Yesterday, you could almost hear the collective sigh of relief across the state when news came that the Chicago police had caught that piece of garbage.

Me and my wife Karen—sometimes I call her Red, owing to the color of her hair—talked about it over breakfast the next morning.

"Where's that guy from anyway?" she asked as she chomped her Cheerios.

"Don't talk with your mouth full," I said, my own mouth full of buttered toast. "It says here he was from Alabama originally."

"Alabama, huh?" she said drily. "Well, he's going to die an Okie."

"I expect you're right." I set aside the paper. I'd read enough about mad-dog killers for one day.

I've been calling Karen "Red" for about as long as I've known her, which, if I ever stopped to count, must be thirty years or more. Except for a few years when I was in the Marines during the Korean conflict and a brief time when I lived in New York City, Burr's always been my home. Karen moved here when she was a sophomore at Burr High

School, so by the universal rules of small towns everywhere, she's a newcomer. We initially bonded over the fact that we both played saxophone in the Burr High School band, and were good friends for years, but there was never anything romantic between us. Back then, I was still enamored of a girl I'd been in love with since I was a small boy. I never could make that gal like me in the same way I liked her. In fact, her shunning me was the biggest reason I joined the Marines straight out of high school. I guess I figured it would break her heart if I got killed in combat. That's a really dumb reason to join the Marines, I know, but men that age tend not to be very smart. The North Koreans didn't kill me, and neither did the Red Chinese, but coming home on leave and finding out that gal had married my worst enemy almost did.

As for Red, she married a fella we went to school with, but it didn't work out. When I came home and took this job, she was newly divorced and desperate for work. I hired her to be our dispatcher. She and I picked up our friendship right where we'd left off, but nothing in the way of romance bloomed until we were both in our late 30s. That was twelve or thirteen years ago. We've been together ever since.

In the intervening years, I promoted her from dispatcher to uniformed officer, and then finally to assistant chief. Nepotism tends not to be an especially big deal in towns like ours.

(By the way, she hasn't played the saxophone since she got out of high school, although I still pick up my horn from time to time.)

Anyway, about that telephone call:

We'd just finished breakfast and were washing dishes when the phone rang. Red picked up. "John, how are you?" she said. "Yes, he's right here. Hold on a minute. Emmett, it's for you. John Smith."

I met John back in '76, right after Carrie died, when I was first looking for someone who'd known her. John had recently graduated from the University of Oklahoma with a degree in Physics. However, in the course of his studies he realized working in a nuclear power plant or making hydrogen bombs wasn't what he wanted to do with his life. Instead, he settled into a job working the graveyard shift at the Sunshine Store, a convenience store in Norman, located near the university in a neighborhood called Campus Corner. Campus Corner was—and still is—a tame, Made-in-Oklahoma version of a bohemian neighborhood, *ala* New York's Greenwich Village. Open 24 hours a day, the Sunshine Store was Campus Corner's de facto center of activity, especially during the overnight hours.

Thanks to John, it also became a haven for Carrie and Leon. With nowhere else to go, the pair would hang out in the store and keep John company. They never had much money, so John would slip them food and coffee, paying for it out of his own pocket or writing it off as spoilage. After a while, he grew attached to them. Especially Carrie.

I took the phone from Karen. "Hey, John."

"Listen, Emmett," he said in a hushed tone, "I've discovered some things about our girl I think you'll want to know about."

"What?"

"I can't talk about it over the phone. Is there any way you could drive here?"

"I suppose I could," I said. "You still at the Sunshine Store?"

"Nah," he said. "I'm teaching science at Noble Junior High School." Noble is a small town a few miles south of Norman.

"That's fantastic," I said. I'd always known John was too smart to be wasting his time selling beer and girlie magazines. "I reckon I could drive down this morning if the boss doesn't have any objections." I looked at Karen. She shrugged.

"I know it's a lot to ask, having you drive all the way here and all, but I think you're going to want to hear this," he said. "I eat lunch between 12:10 and 12:45. Think you could make it by then?"

"I'll give it a shot."

He told me where to find his school, and we ended the call.

Red asked, "What was that all about?"

"John has something he wants to tell me about Carrie."

Of course, Red knew who I meant. "Why couldn't he tell you over the phone?"

"He didn't say. He's changed jobs, by the way. He's teaching junior high school science in Noble."

"So that's where you're driving. To Noble."

"If you don't mind."

"I think between Joel and me, we can keep the heathens at bay."

I'd already gotten dressed for work, so I went into the bedroom and changed into a pair of Levi's, a plaid flannel shirt, and the square-toed brown Dingos I'd only recently adopted after the decades of torture I'd inflicted on myself by wearing pointy-toed cowboy boots. I took my off-duty weapon—a Colt .38 Police Special—from the nightstand drawer, put it in its holster, and stuffed it into my left boot. It used to be I hardly ever carried a gun, even on duty, but after a number of close calls, these days I always carry at least one. Sometimes I'll even carry a backup. Today, I reckoned the little snub nose would be plenty.

I didn't feel the need to pack a bag; the plan was to drive there, hear what John had to say, then drive right back. I kissed Red goodbye, grabbed a Tab from the refrigerator, then stepped onto my front porch. It was a little chilly, so I went back inside, grabbed my red, white, and blue Burr Patriots windbreaker off the coat rack next to the door, gave Red another goodbye kiss and hit the road.

Given I was already on my second Tab of the day, I knew I'd have to void my bladder in another ten minutes, which is about how long it takes to get from my house to Wes Harmon's Sinclair. Wes has been telling customers his restroom is out of order; he says people keep vandalizing it, and it costs him too much to keep it in good repair. I still get to use it, though.

These days, I tend to plan my trips around where I know there are public restrooms.

***

Even though I sometimes felt a stab of guilt for not fulfilling my pledge to get her out of that prison cemetery, in recent months I'd been thinking less about Carrie. Other concerns had taken precedence, in particular my feud with Burr's new mayor, a dyed-in-the-wool John Birch Society member who uses my politics to undermine me with the town council. I'd also been dealing with staffing issues brought about by the slumping town economy.

Someone has to fill in for the fella we had to let go, which means Karen, Joel, and I seldom get a day off.

Talking to John brought back a little of that guilt, although thanks to those newspaper stories about Stafford's capture and the Girl Scout killings, I probably would've thought of Carrie that day, anyway.

The best thing about long drives is that they give me a chance to listen to music. On the drive to Noble, I plugged in my cassette of *Live at the Sands* by Frank Sinatra with the Count Basie Orchestra. I listened to it two or three times. The lead-in to the trombone solo on "I've Got You Under My Skin" always gives me goosebumps.

I'd driven through Noble a few times over the years without having much of a reason to stop there. Like most other small towns in this state, the highway running through it—U.S. 77, in Noble's case—doubles as Main Street, with a small web of side streets branching off and crisscrossing each other. Downtown comprises the usual fixtures: a feed store, a bank, a diner or two, and an Oklahoma Tire & Supply store. The sign outside the First State Bank said the temperature was 49 degrees, warmer than it had been when I left home, but the wind was awful. Driving into town, I thought it might blow my truck into a ditch. The drive took longer than I thought it would; by the time I arrived, there were only about ten minutes left in John's lunch break.

The school building was a long, one-story, dark-brick building located a block or two off the main drag. There were no vacant parking spaces in front, so I ended up parking in back, next to a separate barn-like building, from which there emanated music vaguely resembling "Stars and Stripes Forever" but which might also have been "Pop Goes the Weasel."

A polite little boy led me to the principal's office. The principal was a distinguished-looking middle-aged woman who reminded me of that actress from the *Thin Man* movies I used to love when I was a kid. I introduced myself and told her I was there to see John Smith. She asked to see some ID. I produced my driver's license. She gave me directions to his room: "Down the hall, last door on your right."

"Anyone ever tell you that you look an awful lot like Myrna Loy?" I asked.

"I used to get that a lot when I was younger," she replied with a smile. "These days, not too many people know who she is."

John's door was open. He sat at his desk sorting a stack of papers, putting them into a small box, and placing it in a desk drawer. He jumped when I knocked.

"You made it!" he said. "How're things in Hooterville?"

"Arnold Ziffel sends his best." Hooterville is the fictional town on the TV show *Green Acres*. Arnold is a precocious pig and, without a doubt, the show's smartest character.

John chuckled. "Come on in."

His classroom had a certain smell you only find in schools and sometimes libraries. Books and paper, and mimeograph ink. A hint of Elmer's Glue. Desks were parked in uneven rows; I squeezed into one in the front. Its ancient wooden desktop was covered in semi-obscene scrawls. For a split second, I was transported to a moment 35 years earlier, where, in a room a lot like this one, I exchanged shy smiles with the prettiest girl in Burr High School.

It's funny the things you remember.

"So what's the big secret?" I said.

"Sorry I had to bring you all the way here, but I couldn't talk about this over the phone; my boss was listening, plus, I figured this is something you'd want to know about as soon as possible."

"That's fine," I said. "So what have you got?"

He lowered his voice. "Someone told a friend of mine about something big that happened to Carrie not long before she died." He walked to the open door and closed it, like he didn't want any bystanders listening in.

"First of all," he said quietly, "I found out Carrie's last name. It's Fitzjarrald, only it's spelled weird: F-I-T-Z-J-A-R-R-A-L-D."

I knew Fitzgerald as JFK's middle name and as the last name of the fella who wrote *The Great Gatsby*, but I'd never seen it spelled like that.

"That's great," I said. "But you could've told me that over the phone."

"Yeh, but that's not the most important part."

"Ok, what is?"

Urgently, he said, "Listen, Emmett, you have to promise me you won't talk about this with anyone. Not even your wife."

The thought of keeping something from Red almost but not quite made me smile. "Ok, I promise."

He took a last look around for eavesdroppers, then said in a near whisper: "A friend of mine, someone I trust, told me yesterday about a conversation she had with one of her clients. The guy says he witnessed a young woman being tortured and raped about four years ago. He didn't name names, but he described her as having a red birthmark on her face. He also claimed he saw her being burned on the chin with a soldering iron."

That took me a second to digest. "Four years ago would've been '75."

"Which is the year before she died," said John. "And get this: The guy said the man who did it was Carrie's rich uncle."

I'd always suspected Carrie's life had been hard, but I'd never thought she would've had a rich uncle.

"Did this guy give your friend a name?"

"No," he said, "but I think I know who it is. And his last name is *not* Fitzjarrald."

"Did your friend tell you who it was that told her about this?"

"No, she wouldn't tell me. But I think I know who he is, too."

The bell rang, and suddenly the sound of stomping feet and overstimulated young voices echoed in the hallway.

"So who are we talking about, then?" I asked.

He threw a nervous look at the classroom door. "I can't tell you without explaining who he is—who *they* are—and that's going to take some time."

At that, a chubby little guy in a Farrah Fawcett t-shirt strolled in like he owned the joint. He walked up to me, pointed at me and indignantly declared: "That's my desk!"

"Sorry," I said and made to get up.

The kid crooked a thumb at me. "Who is this guy?" he asked John.

"This is Mr. Hardy, and he's a friend of mine."

He looked me over. "He's too old to be your friend."

"Sit down, Mike," said John, stifling a laugh. To me, he said, "Can we get together later?"

"I guess we could if I stayed in town tonight." I didn't love the idea of driving home after dark.

"I'd let you stay with me, but the place is a mess."

I could've tried to assure him of my indifference to his lack of housekeeping skills, but I sensed that wasn't his only reason for not offering. "Don't worry about it," I said.

"The Sooner Arms is cheap and clean," he said. "It's on Main Street or Lindsay in Norman; I forget which."

"Sounds good. I'll check it out."

"Here. Take this." He reached into his shirt pocket and pulled out a business card with his name, address, and phone number. "Call me around six."

"Sounds good," I said. I made for the door, fighting a tide of agitated kids coming in as I was going out.

"By the way," he added, shouting over the commotion, "I'm writing a book about her."

"You going to let me read it?"

He smiled. "Maybe tonight I'll give you a sneak preview."

I was almost out the door when he stopped me. "Hold on, Emmett. Could I see that card for a sec?"

I waded through the sea of kids and handed him the card. On the back, he wrote down a name and address. "This is a social worker I've been meaning to talk to. I think she might've helped Carrie and Leon at some point. Since you've got a free afternoon, would you mind looking her up and seeing what she has to say?"

Already, I could see this snowballing into something bigger and more complicated. By getting back into it, I might be biting off more than I could chew. Yet, by reaching out, John had sparked something in me, something I reckon I'd lost. It had been a long time since I'd felt good about something I'd done.

I told him I'd be glad to. We shook hands one more time, and I made my escape.

CHAPTER TWO

The name on the back of the card said "Linda Shadid." Underneath, John had written, "Dept. of Human Services," with a Norman address, which I took to mean she was a social worker. I've always admired social workers; I got a close-up look at the good work they do a few years back during a stint in a VA hospital meant to help me quit drinking.

Norman is only a few miles north of Noble on U.S. 77, meaning that a trip to Ms. Shadid's office shouldn't have taken more than a few minutes. Unfortunately, there had been a wreck near where 77 intersects with another highway, so traffic was bumper-to-bumper.

As I inched forward, I noticed a large billboard on the side of the road. It featured a giant-sized picture of a fella in a bright red cowboy hat pointing at the camera. Underneath the glowering face, it said, in big red, white, and blue capital letters: "ONLY YOU CAN SAVE OKLAHOMA'S CHILDREN! VOTE YES ON STATE QUESTION 339!"

I recognized the fella as Billy Joe "Cha Cha" Mulvaney, an ex-college-wrestler-turned-politician, and one of Oklahoma's favorite sons. Like most everyone else, I also knew what State Question 339 was: a campaign by politicians—mostly Republican, but some Democrats—to shut down all the striptease clubs in the state.

In fact, we do have an inordinate number of such establishments, which is kind of funny when you consider how Oklahoma prides itself on being godlier than the Pope, the Dalai Lama, and the Archbishop of Canterbury all rolled into one.

Back in the 1950s, Cha Cha Mulvaney was a national wrestling champion at one of our major universities, which in Oklahoma means he was as much of a celebrity as any non-football-playing athlete can be. Unfortunately, before his senior year, it was discovered that the slightly used Cadillac he drove back and forth to basket-weaving class had been given to him free of charge by a local car dealer. The revelation cost Cha Cha both his amateur status and his national championship trophy.

As near as I can remember, he dropped out of school and disappeared for a time before making a comeback as a professional wrestler. Like most pro wrestlers, Cha Cha turned himself into a live-action cartoon character; playing off his nickname, he wore an orange, black, and red leather mask, purple leotards, and a colorful Mexican-style blanket.

Unfortunately, a drag racer named Shirley "Cha Cha" Muldowney began to gain renown and eventually became more famous than he was. Rechristening himself "The Crazy Cowpoke," Cha Cha Mulvaney adopted a costume of sequined chaps and clingy orange and red tights that rode up to reveal more of his anatomy than good taste would allow. Fortunately, his Crazy-Cowpoke days were mercifully short; by then, he was nearing retirement on account of being hit on the head too many times by folding metal chairs.

Once retired, Billy Joe Clyde started calling himself Cha Cha again. He embarked on a career requiring less brainpower, which is to say, he was elected to a seat in the Oklahoma State Senate. As I understand it, he owed his win to the machinations of a wily campaign manager and the fact that a surprising number of Oklahomans do not typically discriminate against brain-damaged individuals when it comes to deciding who to vote for.

Word is, Cha Cha's going to run for Governor as a Republican next year, which, I expect, is why he decided to be the face of the anti-stripper campaign. His support of State Question 339 is a perfect way to ingratiate himself with religious zealots, a sizable percentage of whom consider strip clubs to be portals to hell.

After the better part of an hour, I came upon the cause of the traffic jam. A little-bitty chocolate brown Volkswagen Beetle had been mashed almost flat in a collision with a semi-tractor trailer. I drove by in time to see a body covered by a sheet loaded into a hearse.

For the moment, I forgot all about Cha Cha Mulvaney and State Question 339.

***

The Norman office of the Oklahoma Department of Human Services was located in the kind of plain-Jane red-brick building you might drive by for years without even noticing it was there. As I opened the door of my truck to get out, an empty Fritos bag flew out of my cab and was swept away by the wind. I tossed my fedora onto the front seat to keep it from suffering the same fate.

Inside, the office was divided into a rabbit's warren of cubicles. I asked the receptionist if I could talk to Linda Shadid. She called out, "Linda!" and pointed out a woman at the far end of the room. The woman she pointed to saw me, smiled, and waved me over. I threaded my way back to where she was. "Linda Shadid?" I said. "That's me," she said, standing and offering her hand.

Her chestnut-colored hair was cut in a short, blunt style, like Dorothy Hamill's, the figure skater who was all the rage a few years ago. A pair of silver starfish dangled from her ears, and a small piece of polished turquoise hung from a silver chain around her neck. She was small, not much more than five feet tall, if I were to guess. Her work area was messy; manila folders were scattered about, and white document boxes were stacked on the floor. Pinned to the walls of her cubicle were snapshots of happy people mugging for the camera.

She pulled a chair from the adjacent cubicle and rolled it to hers. "Take a seat," she said. "How can I help you?"

I told her where I was from and what my job was. "I was hoping you might be able to give me some information on a young woman who was involved in a case of ours from about three years ago."

"Is this young woman in some kind of trouble?"

"Well, she's dead, so—"

She nodded grimly. "What makes you think I can help?"

"Honestly? I'm not exactly sure. A friend of mine asked me to look you up. He thinks you might've tried to help this gal."

"What's her name?"

"Well, when all this happened, we only knew her first name. Carrie."

That sparked a look of recognition. She asked, "Did she have a red birthmark on her face?"

"Yes, and a burn scar."

"I think I know who you mean. How did she die?"

I described the case in enough detail to give her a good idea of what happened—basically, how we suspected Carrie shot Burt Murray because, as we later discovered, Burt had killed her boyfriend.

"I remember when that happened," she said when I'd finished, "but I had no idea the girl who did it was a former client."

"I tracked down a fella who knew her a little bit, a guy named John Smith. He was working the graveyard shift at a convenience store on Campus Corner—"

"The Sunshine Store," she interjected.

"That's right, the Sunshine Store. That's where Carrie and Leon used to hang out. Basically, what little I know about her, I learned from John."

"That's where I met her, too," she said thoughtfully. "If you don't mind my asking, what is she to you?"

"Good question," I said. "After she died, I wanted to find out who she was, which in a roundabout way led me to John. He told me what he knew—mainly that she was homeless, probably abused, and mentally handicapped. John and I got to be friends and decided to work together to try to track down her next of kin, although he's done most of it by himself. He quit the Sunshine Store a while back. Now he's teaching science over at Noble Junior High. This morning, he called me and asked me to drive down. He said he'd discovered some information about Carrie but couldn't tell me what it was over the phone. We were supposed to meet during his lunch break, but I didn't make it in time, so I'm meeting with him tonight. He did tell me her last name, which I didn't know before."

She opened a file cabinet and thumbed through some folders until she found the one she was looking for. She pulled out a form and pushed it across her desk so I could see. "After I met her, I came back to the office and started an application for emergency housing. All I knew at the time was her first name; we made an appointment for her to come in the next day, and I figured I could fill out the rest. I left it on my desk overnight so I wouldn't forget. Unfortunately, she didn't show up."

"If it helps, her last name was Fitzjarrald," I said, then spelled it out for her.

She wrote it on the form, then set it aside.

"So what's your ultimate goal here?" she asked.

"Originally, John and I wanted to get her moved from that prison cemetery in McAlester—"

"Peckerwood Hill," she said.

"You know it?"

"Of course. So, is that still your goal?"

"I reckon so. Both John and I would like to see her moved out of there to someplace decent."

"And to do that, you need to locate her next of kin."

"Exactly," I said. "Listen, the fella she shot wasn't one of my favorite people, which is not to say I wanted him dead, although I reckon he more or less brought it on himself by killing Carrie's boyfriend. It's just that Carrie seemed like such a pitiful figure; John and I figure this is something we can do to honor her memory."

"That's laudable," she said. "I'd like to help, but there's not much information I can give you. Just by telling me her last name, you doubled what I knew. I only met her that one time at the Sunshine Store. Carrie was like most of my clients—poor, with no roof over her head."

I asked, "Do you mind if I take another look at that housing application?"

She showed it to me again. It was dated June 15th, 1976.

Ten days before Carrie died.

I asked, "When you met her, did you ask about her family?"

She shook her head. "I didn't get any names, if that's what you mean, although she did say she'd been living with her parents and an uncle who had thrown her out. She seemed a little scared of them."

"But no names."

"No names. I went back to the Sunshine Store several times over the next few days, looking for her, but I never saw her again. I even asked the person working there if he'd seen her."

"John?"

"It might've been," she said. "Whoever it was said he hadn't seen her in a while."

I tried to think of something else to ask, but came up empty.

"I expect John might look you up himself, one of these days," I said. "He's writing a book about Carrie."

"Fiction or nonfiction?"

I laughed out loud. "I reckon it would have to be non-fiction, wouldn't it?"

She smiled sadly. "Not necessarily," she said. "Sometimes fiction can tell a deeper truth." She looked at her watch. "I'm sorry, but I've got a meeting."

We stood and shook hands. "It was a pleasure to meet you, Emmett. Let me know what you find out. I'll look into it myself if I get a chance."

I gave her my business card. "Give me a call if you find anything," I said. "If I'm not there, ask for Mrs. Hardy. She's my wife. I'll definitely get the message."

She saw me to the door. On the way, I asked if any of her colleagues might know something about Carrie.

"A week after I saw Carrie, I was transferred to the Oklahoma City office. I asked another caseworker to follow up, but he never did."

"Would it do any good to talk to him?"

In a clipped tone, she replied: "No, he was fired some time ago."

I suggested Carrie probably wasn't the only person she'd tried to help who wouldn't let herself be helped.

"It happens more often than you'd think," she said. "People assume if you're homeless, you'll snatch up any help at all as soon as it's offered. But it's not that simple. Homelessness is usually a symptom of their troubles, not the sole cause."

I understood that. We've had our share of drifters come through Burr, especially when I was a little boy, during the Great Depression. For many of them, not having a roof over their head was the least of their troubles.

I said, "I reckon you hear sad stories like this all the time."

"Not all of them are this dramatic," she said, her voice suddenly tired, "but yeh, I hear plenty. It's tough."

I said, "I don't know how you do it."

She replied, with a sardonic chuckle: "Sometimes I don't either."

CHAPTER THREE

My next stop was the motel John recommended, the Sooner Arms. It was too bad he didn't feel like he could ask me to stay at his place; it would've given us more time to talk and saved me a few bucks, to boot. But I didn't hold it against him. Apart from working on Carrie's case, we didn't know each other all that well.

The Sooner Arms was one of those old-time motor courts, like the Bates Motel from the movie *Psycho,* except the Sooner Arms was located on a main drag and not out in the middle of nowhere. The skinny little gray-haired man at the front desk even reminded me of a much older Norman Bates. I crossed my fingers I wouldn't get knifed in the shower and checked in.

My room smelled like a wet ashtray, but at least it was clean. I called Karen to tell her I'd be staying in town overnight. She started to kick until I explained why, then she agreed it made sense. When I was done talking to her, I turned on the TV. Evidently, the Sooner Arms did not subscribe to cable, so I was limited to three over-the-air channels, two of which barely came in. The one with halfway decent reception was showing a rerun of *The Andy Griffith Show*. After a few minutes of listening to Floyd the Barber drone on about how modern technology was ruining his profession, I decided to take a nap.

But before I could switch off the TV, a commercial came on that demanded my full attention. A camera zoomed in and out on an overstuffed, star-spangled, jiggling bikini top. In big yellow letters, the words *HENNY PENNY'S: For the Discriminating Gentleman!* flashed on and off as silly rock music blared in the background. An address and the words *Girls! Girls! Girls!* flashed on the screen.

Then suddenly it was over.

It went by so fast, I almost thought I'd imagined it.

Before I could turn off the set, another overexposed boob appeared on the screen: Billy Joe Clyde "Cha Cha" Mulvaney, the fella I'd seen on the billboard that morning while I was waiting for traffic to clear.

"Fellow Oklahomans," he said solemnly, "My name is Billy Joe Clyde 'Cha Cha' Mulvaney, and I'm asking you to make our proud state safe for the worship of Jesus Christ and off-limits for perverts and degenerates." He then added, with a smile and a wink: "Do ol' Cha Cha and the kids of Oklahoma a favor. Vote yes on State Question 339." *VOTE YES ON 339!* flashed on the screen, in the same bold yellow letters as on the strip club ad, followed by the words: "Paid for by Oklahomans For Oklahoma."

Like the billboard I'd seen earlier in the day, I reckoned the commercial was a way for Mulvaney to out-holier-than-thou anyone who dared run against him for governor in 1980—although, to me, seeing it back-to-back with the strip club ad seemed to emphasize how absurd the whole thing was.

My philosophy has always been: If you want to rid the state of perverts and degenerates, vote 'em out of office.

I switched off the TV before anything else could distract me. I slept for a while, waking up a few minutes past six. I worried I might've missed my chance to meet with John, but when I dialed his number, he picked up.

"Are we still on for tonight?" I asked.

"Most definitely," he said. "Would it be alright if we met where my fiancée works? I'd really like you to meet her."

"Where does she work?" I asked, thinking she was probably a waitress or something like that.

"It's called Henny Penny's."

"You're kidding."

"I am not."

I generally go out of my way to avoid such places, not because I'm offended by naked women—although I do find strip clubs pretty depressing—but mostly due to my checkered relationship with alcohol. It also didn't seem to be the most appropriate place to discuss what we had to discuss.

"Emmett, you still there?"

"John, I'd love to meet your fiancée, but don't you think we'd be better off doing it another time?"

"Oh, come on, Emmett," he said. "We'll just pop in and out. 20 minutes, tops. I'll introduce you really quick, then you and I will go someplace quiet to talk."

"I'm not sure it's such a good idea, John. You know I don't like being around a lot of drinking—"

"Then have a Coke!" he said breathlessly. "Emmett, I promise: You're going to love this place. It's like Walter Mitty's, only classier."

Walter Mitty's is another Norman strip club, located, by coincidence, around the corner from the Sunshine Store. I'd never been there, either.

"Well, I guess that'll work," I said, "as long as we can go someplace quiet afterward."

"Great. I'll be driving a yellow Ford Maverick with a white vinyl top."

"I'll be driving the same piece of crap Ford pickup I had the last time you saw me."

"Sounds good," he said. "See you in a few minutes."

***

Henny Penny's was located in the parking lot of a medium-sized shopping center, but was a separate building of its own. Its cinder-block exterior was painted Pepto-Bismol pink, with life-sized silhouettes of naked women stenciled on the walls. Over the door was a neon sign featuring a cartoon rendering of a sexy chicken in a bikini. It looked like Marilyn Monroe if Marilyn had been part-woman and part-Rhode Island Red.

John arrived soon after and parked next to me. He wasn't kidding about his car; it was as yellow as a New York City taxicab. He hopped out, as happy as a kid on his first trip to Six Flags. "Buddy, you are going to love this!"

I had my doubts.

My experience with strip clubs was limited, if at least a little bit noteworthy. Back in the early '50s, when I was a Marine MP stationed in Seoul, I went into a couple. And Butcherville, a small town adjacent to Burr, used to have one. I never went on my own accord, but Butcherville didn't have its own police force, so I was frequently called there to adjudicate disputes between disgruntled patrons.

My most memorable strip-joint experience occurred in the summer of 1963 when I was attending a police convention in Dallas. One evening, a bunch of my fellow cops convinced me to go out with them to eat some barbeque. Unfortunately, the place they took me— a disinfectant drenched eyesore called the Carousel Club—was known less for its ribs and more for its strippers. Of course, I was still drinking at the time, so I got good and hammered. About all I remember is a portly gentleman with a receding hairline who kept buying us drinks.

A few months later, I was watching on TV as that same fella shot Lee Harvey Oswald in a Dallas parking garage.

Turned out his name was Jack Ruby, and he owned the Carousel Club.

That about covers my prior experience with strip joints.

At Henny Penny's, you had to pay at a glass booth before going inside; according to John, the building had once been a movie theater. A pretty young gal in a tiny purple-and-gold bikini took our money. "Hey John!" she said through a tinny speaker. "Where've you been? Haven't seen you in a couple of days."

"Grading papers," he said. "Misty, meet Emmett. This is his first time."

"Welcome to Henny Penny's, Emmett!"

Her cheeriness was as counterfeit as a three-dollar bill scrawled in crayon on a sheet of toilet paper.

I reckon girls in her line of work have to be that way.

Misty said the price for the two of us was 40 dollars, which I thought was exceedingly high. I started to pull out my wallet, but John insisted it was his treat." While he paid, a redheaded fellow with a terrible case of acne opened the door to the box office, squeezed inside, and grabbed Misty's rear end. She looked about to bite the guy's head off, until she saw who it was. Smiling, she gave him a playful tap on the shoulder of his pink polyester suit and said, "Stop it, Mike!"

"Just came to cop my nightly feel!" he said, then exited the way he'd gone in.

Misty passed my membership card through the slot and told us to make sure the guy at the door stamped our hands before we went in.

I asked John, "Who was that fella?"

He shook his head and made a face. "That's Mike Fike, the manager."

"Kind of handsy, isn't he?"

He snorted. "I guess rank has its privileges."

"Listen," I said, "You sure you can afford this?"

He slapped me on the back. "Don't worry," he said. "Most of that was your membership fee. A onetime expense. Next time it'll only cost you a five-dollar cover. Factor in the free buffet, and it's a pretty good deal."

"Alright, then, thanks."

"You're welcome," he said. With a sly grin, he added: "Of course, if you want a table dance, you'll have to pay for it yourself."

I wasn't sure what a table dance was, but it sounded like something I should avoid.

The lobby floor was covered in burgundy carpet. The wallpaper incorporated burgundy and gold stripes, but the burgundy in the wallpaper was of a slightly different shade from the burgundy in the carpet. Evidence still remained of its movie theater past: Display windows that once would've held posters of coming attractions now displayed photos of semi-naked women with the Henny Penny's sexy-chicken logo splashed across their chests.

The buffet was located at the former concession stand. It featured food guaranteed to harden your arteries—fried chicken, macaroni and cheese, French fries, biscuits and sausage gravy. In other words, my soul food. I suggested to John we fill our plates. "Let's get a table first." I reluctantly agreed.

I followed him across the shag carpet to a second set of heavy wooden doors. "My friend, you are in for a treat!" he said, then opened the doors like he would the entrance to Shangri-La.

Maybe to him it was.

I was assaulted by a dense cloud of tobacco smoke, the stench of stale beer, and a blast of music so loud, my first impulse was to find the nearest ashtray, tear off a couple of used cigarette filters and jam them as deep into my ears as they could go.

Unlike the strip clubs I'd been in before, like Jack Ruby's Carousel and the one we used to have in Butcherville, the music wasn't made by live musicians; it came from a record player, or a jukebox hidden somewhere out of sight. The lighting was bright enough so that the all-male clientele could see what they'd come to see, but dim enough so they might not be recognized if they ran into someone they knew.

Next to the door, just five feet or so from where we were standing, stood a large, ill-natured looking fella wearing a black leather motorcycle jacket and thick-soled combat boots. His oily hair was parted in the middle. In the back it reached almost to his waist.

John saw me looking at the guy out of the corner of my eye. "That's Joe the bouncer," he said—too loud, as it turns out. "Stay away from him."

The bouncer looked our way and swaggered over, his hands jammed deep into in the pockets of grease-stained blue jeans. He looked us up and down with his head tilted back like he was trying to see out from under a blindfold.

He stuck his face close to mine—too close for comfort—and, in a loud voice, asked, "You got a problem?"

My first instinct was to say something like, "Yeh, you're ugly-ing up the joint something fierce," but that would've been counterproductive. Instead, I smiled all friendly-like and said breezily. "We're just here to say hi my friend's fiancée."

Without taking his eyes off me, he said out of the corner of his mouth, "Hey, John."

"Hey, Joe."

Joe stuck a finger in my face. "I'll be watching you," he growled.

"With all these pretty ladies around?" I said. "That'd be what I'd call a waste of time and energy."

He seemed about ready to slug me but thought better of it. He said to John out of the side of his mouth, "Chastity's around here somewhere," then gave me one more murderous look before returning to his post beside the door.

"Geez, Emmett, I told you to stay away from that guy!"

"I can't very well stay away from him when he's sticking noses and fingers in my face."

John shrugged. "I guess."

I scanned the room.

The room's past life as a theater was obvious. The floor slanted forward gradually. Where the screen used to be, there was a bar. Behind it was a stage. A short runway led from one to the other, allowing the dancers to strut their stuff inches away from men drooling into their cans of Coors. The side walls were lined with semicircular booths. Between them, in the middle, were about a dozen small tables, most with two legs sawn off so they'd sit level. Here and there, a women disrobed on one, while being ogled by a man old enough to be her father.

So that's what a table dance is, I thought.

Two women in exaggerated modes of undress emerged from the ocean of pulchritude and approached us. One was short and buxom, and wore furry red bikini panties with a yellow Jayne Mansfield wig. At the sight of John, she squealed, "My baby!" and wrapped herself around him like a boa constrictor.

The other gal was more conservatively dressed, although she still showed off more skin than I reckon her male relatives would have approved of. Unlike John's girlfriend, her hair was cut close to her head, almost like a man's crew cut, and dyed platinum blond. I thought it looked pretty good. She smelled nice, too; I'm pretty sure she wore the same perfume as Karen.

"Emmett Hardy, this is Chastity, my fiancée," said John. "Chastity, this is my friend Emmett." Chastity giggled and mock-curtsied. The woman with the short hair held out her hand and shouted—you had to shout to be heard over the music—"Pleased to meet you, Emmett. I'm Destiny. May we show you to a table?" She offered her hand. I took it, thinking we were going to shake, but she held on and led me away.

Suddenly, I felt concerned about my clammy palms.

We settled into one of the semicircular booths. Destiny slid in on the left, Chastity on the right, so they met in the middle. John scooted in beside Chastity while I sat next to Destiny.

A waitress wearing much the same uniform as Chastity and Destiny—which is to say, mostly her birthday suit—approached and asked us what we wanted to drink. John and Chastity unlocked lips long enough to order—a Miller High Life for John, a martini for her—then resumed making a spectacle of themselves. Destiny ordered a bourbon and Coke, which, it so happens, is what I used to drink back in the day. I ordered a Tab. The waitress said the only sugar-free soda they had was Diet Rite. I asked if she could put a slice of lemon in it; sometimes when I do, I can fool myself into thinking I'm having a real drink.

Suddenly, Chastity squealed, "I'm up!" John scrambled from his seat to let her out, then offered his arm, which she accepted as gracefully as the Queen of England.

Before they could get to the stage, that Mike fella, the one in the pink suit, gave Chastity a smack on her rear end. John shouted something—I couldn't hear what—and shoved the guy. For a second, I was afraid I might be drawn into my first barroom brawl in a while. I looked over to where I'd last seen the bouncer, but fortunately, his attention had been drawn elsewhere.

I looked back and saw Fike was now clowning around, trying to make John and Chastity laugh. He cracked John up, but Chastity still seemed upset.

Fike then vanished into the crowd, and John and Chastity resumed their procession to the stage.

Destiny ignored the folderol and used John and Chastity's absence to make a move on me. She snuggled close and, as intimately as the noise would allow, said, "It's cold in here, don't you think?" In a way it sounded sexual, but because she had to practically holler it into my ear, it seemed more like a business proposition, which in a way I guess it was. I almost suggested she put on some more clothes, but decided not to. Instead, I inched away from her a little bit. She smiled.

"So you're shy, huh?"

"Shy and married."

"So are most of the men here!"

"Ah!" I said. "That might be true, but unlike these other yahoos, I'm a one-woman man."

"Why'd you come, then?" I couldn't believe I was the first man to prove immune to her charms, but she seemed genuinely puzzled.

I said, "I came with John so I could meet his girlfriend."

She made a face like she found my explanation hard to believe.

The waitress returned with our drinks. Destiny's bourbon and Coke passed under my nose, and for a moment, I felt a yearning for my old friend, sour mash. I squeezed the slice of lemon into my Diet Rite and took a sip, but after getting a whiff of Destiny's drink, it didn't do the trick. The waitress walked to the stage, sat John's beer in front of him and handed Chastity her martini. Immediately, Chastity began incorporating it into her act. I'm not much on modern music, but I'd guess the title of the song she was dancing to was "Love to Love You, Baby," since those were the only lyrics. Every few seconds, John take a sip from his beer, without ever taking his eyes off his beloved.

Back at our booth, I tried to think of a way to get rid of Destiny without hurting her feelings. Not that there was anything wrong with her—she was pretty and nicely built, and of course she smelled nice—but the attraction presented by a beautiful, mostly naked woman half my age nuzzling my ear was something I didn't need, especially on top of the temptation to drink. Twenty years earlier, before Karen and I got married, things might've been different. Now, however, betraying the trust of the one person in the world who means the most to me, wasn't on my Top Ten list of things to do.

Yet Destiny still seemed to think I was only playing hard to get. She downed her drink in a few swallows, leaned close, and purred in my ear: "Emmett, do you like to party?"

"Isn't that what we're doing?" I said in a voice I could swear I'd outgrown when I was twelve.

She ran her hand along the inside of my thigh. "Well, there's partying, then there's *partying*."

I gently removed her hand. "No offense," I said, "but I reckon this Tab is about as much of a party as I can handle."

She gave me a long, appraising look. "Diet Rite," she said with a small grin, no longer trying to be sultry. "They don't serve Tab." She put a few inches between us and gave my knee a sisterly pat. "That's fine, cowboy," she said. "How 'bout you buy me another drink?"

If buying her another drink wasn't the *least* I could do, it was definitely the most I *should* do. I started to hail the waitress, but Destiny stopped me and said she'd get it herself. She scooted past me and out of the booth. Instead of heading to the bar, she disappeared through a door to the side of the room. I figured I was off the hook, that she'd decided I wasn't worth her time.

By then, Chastity's dance had ended. She'd put a few of her clothes back on and sat on John's lap at the bar. I wondered what her boss might think about one of the dancers fraternizing with a customer, but while John got plenty of envious stares from fellow voyeurs, no one tried to break them up. I sat by myself and waited for them to remember I was still there.

To my surprise, Destiny returned, carrying another bourbon and Coke and wearing a slightly more modest outfit than before.

"I'm a little surprised you came back," I said. "I'm sorry, but places like this aren't really my thing." Afraid I'd offended her, I then rushed to say: "Not that there's anything wrong—"

She held up her hand and said, "Don't worry about it." From somewhere on her person, there materialized a pack of Virginia Slims menthols. She offered one to me, which I declined. She lit one up herself, took a deep drag, then exhaled a long plume of smoke. "It's nice to go a few minutes without being pawed," she said, reaching over to pat my knee again. "As long as you buy me a drink or two, we'll be fine."

Destiny was a nice enough gal, but I didn't drive 200 miles to hang around a strip club and buy a woman who wasn't my wife expensive drinks. John told me we wouldn't be there any more than 20 minutes, but we'd already been there longer than that and he seemed in no mood to leave. I could leave any time, of course, and I did think about it. But I still hoped at some point we'd go someplace else and talk, and that maybe he'd even let me read some of the book he was working on.

So I stayed put, in the company of an exotic semi-naked woman with a bleach-blond crewcut who happened to be drinking my favorite beverage—bourbon and Coke—and wearing the same honeysuckle-scented perfume my wife wears when she's trying to get me hot and bothered. If I was going to stay, I might as well have company. If

Destiny left, other girls would come, and I'd have to go through the same rigmarole all over again.

All things considered, I'd rather keep buying her drinks.

I did, however, feel like I should offer her an out.

"You know," I said, "you don't have to sit with me. I know you can make more money flirting with some of these other fellas."

With a sly look, she said. "Emmett, do you know how much I made in tips last night?"

"A lot?"

"Right," she said. "A lot. Enough to pay my entire rent this month, with plenty left over. And it's a nice place, believe me."

I whistled. "That's pretty good for one night."

"I'm saying, some nights I like to find a nice guy who's not going to treat me like a piece of meat. I let him buy me a couple of drinks, then sit back and relax." As if to demonstrate, she leaned back and draped her arms along the top of the booth. "Tonight's one of those nights."

"Maybe I should try relaxing, myself."

"It's good for what ails you."

The sound system began blasting Bill Monroe's "Cotton-Eyed Joe." It sounded out of place until I realized it had gotten the whole room a' hootin' and hollerin'. Onstage, two gals in brightly sequined chaps, cowboy boots, and not much else were dancing together, naked-hillbilly style.

"How do you know John?" I asked Destiny.

She shrugged. "Chastity's my roommate. John's her boyfriend. He's around a lot," she said.

"John's a good fella."

"Seems to be. It's too bad—"

I waited for her to finish. She didn't. "What's too bad?"

"I feel sorry for John," she said. "He's a bit of a lost soul, don't you think?"

I'd thought that about John since the day I'd met him. "I'm hoping he's found himself, working as a schoolteacher," I said, without mentioning my concern that marrying a stripper might not be conducive to his mental health.

I didn't need to.

"Chastity's using him," Destiny said flatly. "She can be a charmer, and she's as cute as hell, but she's also a taker. She's always late with the rent; always borrowing money and forgetting to pay it back. John buys her things," she said, widening her eyes for emphasis. "She likes it. A lot."

"She must make more money than he does, right?"

"Of course, but most of it goes up her nose."

My heart about stopped. "Drugs?"

"Cocaine, heroin." She turned and faced me. "Listen, cowboy," she said; the glowing tip of her cigarette danced. "I'm only telling you this because I like John and don't want him to get hurt."

"What about Chastity? You don't want her to be hurt, do you?"

"I like Chas, I do. She can be so sweet, it's impossible *not* to like her. I've tried to talk to her about the drugs, but she's like a brick wall. Not to mention that she's involved with some bad people." She shook her head. "Really, John has no idea. Absolutely *no* idea."

"Does he know about the drugs?"

"Yeh, but he thinks he can reform her."

"Could he?"

"Perhaps, if she wanted to reform. But she doesn't." She shook her head.

For a few seconds we watched the happy couple, still seated at the bar at the front of the stage. With Chastity perched on his lap, chattering away, the expression on John's face was one you might see on someone who hit the million-dollar jackpot on a Vegas slot machine.

"You think they're in love?" I asked Destiny.

She thought for a moment. "John definitely is," she said. "Chastity might think she is, but I'm not sure she knows what the word means."

Hearing a story about John being on the wrong end of a one-sided love affair seemed too consistent with what had always impressed me as his general lack of self-regard. I wrestled with what to do. Should I tell John what he's up against and risk breaking his heart, or should I let him make his mistakes and hopefully learn from them?

I decided a strip club was no place to develop a plan of action regarding such an important matter. I switched lanes in search of something less depressing.

"How'd you get into this line of work?"

She threw back her head and guffawed. "That's what they all ask!" Shifting into a kind of redneck patois, she added: "'What's a nice girl like *you* doing in a place like *this*?'"

Not for the first time that evening, I felt embarrassed. "I don't mean to offend you," I said. "It's that you seem smart enough to do anything you want. Why this?"

"Listen, cowboy—"

"Please," I said. "Call me Emmett."

"Alright, Emmett. One: I'm doing this because I *want* to do it, since it's going to make it possible for me to do anything I want with the rest of my life. Two: Both my parents were teachers, like John. They worked their butts off all their lives and never got ahead, not even a little bit. On nights like last night, I make more than they made in a month."

"So it's for the money, then. I can respect that."

"Oh, it's for the money, but probably not like you mean. I'm doing this to pay for school."

"Working your way through college?"

"I know," she said with an embarrassed smile. "It sounds like a bad joke; 'the stripper working her way through college,' but it's what I'm doing. I'm a senior economics major at OU. I'll get my bachelor's degree in May. I'll start working on my MBA next fall."

"What's that?"

"Master of Business Administration," she explained. "It's the kind of degree you get when you want to run a business."

"What about Chastity?" I said. "Why's she here?"

"There is no 'after this' for Chastity. If John thinks he's going to be her knight in shining armor, he's in for a surprise. Chastity's only ambition is to get high, buy nice clothes, and drive a nice car. She'll be doing this until she dies. Which might not be that far in the future, at this rate."

None of this was easy to hear. "Do you think I should warn him about her?"

She shrugged. "You can try. I doubt it would make any difference. Chastity's got him wrapped around her finger. Sex tends to do that to a man." With a semi-deprecating smile, she added, "But not you, Emmett. *You're* above all that."

I laughed. "I'm not above it. I'm just a one-woman man, is all."

"I thought that one-woman man thing was a myth," she said. "You know, like Bigfoot."

"You want to hear about Bigfoot?" I said, "I'll tell you—"

Abruptly, the music stopped. Fluorescent bulbs lit the room as bright as day. For a second, there was one of those perplexed silences that have their own echo. Startled, men and dancers alike shielded their eyes from the bright light. The skimpy outfits men had been drooling over now looked tattered and sad. Overweight bald guys stared wide-eyed at the girls perched on their laps, as if they'd materialized out of thin air. Makeup that, moments before, had seemed so alluring now looked like it had been slathered on with putty knives.

"Gentlemen and *ladies*," a uniformed cop yelled with a sneering emphasis on the latter, "Henny Penny's is closed. Customers can make their way to the exits. Employees, stay where you are."

"Well," I said to Destiny, "it's been nice talking to you." Even in the bright light, she looked better than most of the others. Maybe it was that short hair-do and the fact that she wore hardly any makeup.

"Looks like you picked the wrong night to visit," she said, more annoyed than concerned. "Our monthly bust. I should've known it was coming soon. I haven't seen any of the bigwigs all week."

"Bigwigs?"

"Yeh, politicians, mostly." She ground out her cigarette. "They always manage to not be here when we get busted."

A cop approached our booth and signaled for her to get up. I moved aside and let her out. "It's been fun, cowboy," she said. The cop, obviously a self-styled hard ass, leered. Destiny held out her hands, wrists together, and said, "Aren't you supposed to cuff me?" The cop's eyes roamed, lingering over the predictable places. In a Mae West voice, Destiny said: "I suppose it's better to be looked over than overlooked."

The cop clearly didn't know what to make of her. "Don't worry, baby," he said. "You're not going to jail. You're getting the rest of the night off."

"This ain't my first rodeo, bucko," she scoffed, then strutted across the floor and disappeared behind a door that said *Dancers Only*.

CHAPTER FOUR

I found John outside milling around in the dark with the other expelled degenerates.

Maybe that's an overly harsh characterization, considering I'd been amongst them.

"At least we didn't have to pay our tab," he said.

Unfortunately, I'd paid cash as I went.

The whole group of us watched a pair of cops emerge from the club and escort a handcuffed fella to a patrol car.

"I'm guessing that's the bartender," I said.

"Yup," replied John. "They probably sent in a kid with a fake ID. They used to do that to me at the Sunshine Store—send a kid in to buy beer. It never worked with me, but not everyone's as careful as I was."

A second pair of cops emerged with a fella dressed in a bright pink suit: the manager, Mike Fike.

"I saw that scuffle you had with him," I said, nodding in Fike's direction.

"Fike thinks being the boss means he's allowed to feel up all the girls. I very much do not like it when he does it to Chastity."

"It looked like you two made up pretty quick."

"Yeh," he said vaguely. "I don't know."

He'd already tuned me out. His eyes were glued to that front door, waiting for Chastity to appear.

But she didn't, not right away. We shuffled our feet in the chilly night air, watching as almost every vehicle in the lot drove away.

Finally, the only ones left were John's hunk of junk, my hunk of junk, and a little Karmann Ghia parked some distance away.

"Is that Chastity's car?" I asked, nodding at the Karmann Ghia.

"Yup," he said. "Nice, isn't it?"

I agreed it was, then Chastity then flounced out the front door. I almost didn't recognize her. Gone was the Jayne Mansfield wig; her real hair was light brown with golden highlights, and cut short; not as short as Destiny's, but way too short to make into a ponytail. She wore a long-sleeved, tight purple sweater that showed off plenty of cleavage, and a pair of high-waisted blue jeans. Her high heels weren't as tall as the stilettos she danced in.

If you saw her for the first time, you wouldn't guess she was a nun, but you probably wouldn't have guessed she was a stripper, either. She was an attractive gal. For the first time, I was starting to understand what John saw in her.

"Ok, John," she said. "I got off early and I'm hungry. Where y'all takin' me to eat?"

John put his hands together as if in prayer, then, in a voice as stilted and artificial as Burt Lancaster's in *Elmer Gantry*, said: "Brother Emmett Hardy, do you believe in miracles?"

"Uh, no, John," I said. "I don't."

"That's alright," he said, "because miracles believe in you."

"I think you've got that wrong. Shouldn't it be: 'Do you believe in God?' and when I say 'no,' you should say: 'That's ok, because he believes in you?' Isn't that how it goes?"

He blew a semi-raspberry. "Details, details," he said. "What I'm talking about is a culinary miracle so delicious, so unbelievably scrumptious, it's been known to convert the vilest heathen into a committed follower of our Lord, Jesus Christ. A food so delectable—"

Chastity broke in. "John," she said, "are you talking about a Denco Darlin'?"

John threw his hands high and shouted, "Hallelujah, sister! Thou hast hit-eth the nail-eth on the head-eth!"

At the top of her lungs, Chastity howled, "NO, JOHN, NOT DENCO'S!" then threw her purse on the ground and kicked and stomped on it.

"Come now, m' lady!" said John. "The Denco Darlin' is a national treasure! Our friend Emmett should partake while there's still time!" He made a mock-disgusted face. "Look how old he is! Have you ever seen a man still drawing breath who was any closer to the grave?"

I chuckled. Chastity bent over angrily and stuffed the contents of her purse back where they belonged.

"What do ya say, Emmett?" asked John.

"You're the boss."

Chastity growled like an incensed chihuahua, but she wasn't about to let her anger get in the way of cadging a free meal. Forgetting she was still mad, Chastity yelled "Shotgun!" as we piled into John's car. That left the backseat for me.

I opened the door, and a small mountain of empty fast-food containers spilled onto the asphalt. I picked it all up, shoved it back inside like Chastity did with the contents of her purse, and got in. As I sat down, something jabbed me in the backside. I felt around and discovered that a semi-fossilized chicken bone had ripped through my jeans.

Now behind the wheel, John clapped his hands. "You two ready to eat?"

"*No!*" hollered Chastity. "Please! Take us to McDonald's or Taco Mayo. Any place but Denco's!"

"Denco's is fine with me," I said, trying to be accommodating. I'd heard Denco's mentioned a few times over the years, but never in complimentary terms. Its prime attraction seemed to be that it stays open after everything else in town closes. From what I'd heard, the Denco Darlin' was borderline inedible. I'd never actually been there, however, and at the moment, I was so hungry I'd have gone anywhere and eaten anything, although I reserved the right to draw the line at a Denco Darlin'.

Chastity continued to whine on the drive over, which inspired John to keep insisting Denco's was the Statue of Liberty of late-night eating establishments. Eventually Chastity cooled off and John stopped defending his choice of restaurants.

By way of making small talk, I said to neither of them in particular: "Too bad about the bartender and the manager being arrested."

"Oh, don't worry," said Chastity. "The dancers took up a collection and sent someone to bail them out. They're probably home already."

The idea of her workmates being sprung from jail seemed to cheer her up. She spent most of the ride talking about one of the dancers' boyfriends who had a rock and roll band but made his living digging ditches, or maybe it was washing dishes. If the story had a point, I'm not sure what it was.

Denco's was housed in a small two-story brick building. A sign facing the street—hand-painted, by the look of it—read "Denco Café." Another sign, this one lit up from the inside, promised Mexican fare.

Inside, a counter ran half the length of the dining room. A few battered dining tables with mismatched chairs occupied most of the space. The place was mostly empty. A couple of college kids sat at the counter; a gray-haired fella with a stubbly beard occupied one of the tables. He wore a grass-stained sleeveless undershirt, an orange Speedo, and rubber beach sandals with mismatched socks.

Denco's was not The Algonquin.

All I could think of to say was, "It's smaller than I thought."

"That's why it's good we got here early," said John. "It'll be packed in a couple of hours."

Chastity kept yakking away. She was cute and even entertaining if you didn't try too hard to understand what she was saying. The story about the stripper's guitar-playing boyfriend segued into one about a local celebrity who'd visited Henny Penny's earlier in the week. I didn't recognize his name, but Chastity seemed to think he was a pretty big deal. She only stopped when our bored-to-tears waitress came to take our order.

One last time, John urged me to order a Denco Darlin'.

"Yuck!" Chastity said. "Don't listen to him, Emmett."

"What is a Denco Darlin', anyway?" I asked.

Chastity reached across the table, grabbed my forearm and gave it a squeeze. "Trust me," she said. "You don't want one."

In a monotone, the waitress explained: "Macaroni baked with chili, melted cheese and two fried eggs on top." She snapped her gum. "You want it?"

"If you're smart," said John, "you'll order the 'Lookin' at Ya' version, with the eggs sunny-side up." He made his hands into binoculars and held them up to his face. "You know—like *eyes!*"

His pitch might've been more convincing if he were selling something like filet mignon, which the Denco Darlin' most definitely was not. "I don't much like having my food watch me while I eat it," I said. I ordered a cheeseburger instead. Chastity ordered a steak, well-done. John ordered a Denco Darlin' and pretended to be insulted that we hadn't followed his example.

Chastity announced she needed to use the little girl's room. As soon as she was out of sight, John said, "Don't talk about Carrie in front of Chastity."

I sighed. "Isn't that why we're here? To talk about Carrie?"

"Do me this favor. We'll talk about Carrie after I drop Chastity off."

Before I could argue, Chastity came back, rubbing a finger under her nose like she was getting over a cold.

I didn't like seeing that.

She sat down, all revved up, talking a mile a minute about how this or that girl she worked with was "a cow," or how she'd gotten so drunk the night before that she fell off her high heels. I cut in with an occasional "Really!" and "Don't that beat all!" but mostly I tried to not look bored while thinking how this entire trip had been a wild goose chase. John, on the other hand, nodded and smiled at everything she said. I've seen new parents who didn't fawn over their first child as much as John fawned over Chastity.

I thought for a second about cancelling my order, calling a taxi, and having it take me back to my car, but that would've guaranteed failure, so I sucked it up and hung in there.

The best thing I can say about my hamburger is that it was edible. The same cannot be said of the fries, which in the mouth felt and tasted like rubber. Chastity's steak didn't look too good, either, but she slathered it with ketchup and somehow managed to get it down.

Of course, John had something to prove, so he made a big show out of enjoying his.

"Should've had a Darlin'," he said, shaking his head sadly.

"I'd rather eat shoe leather," I said.

"I think I *did* eat shoe leather," said Chastity.

After we finished eating, John wanted a cup of coffee, but Chastity was in a hurry to go. John drove us back to Henny Penny's so Chastity and I could pick up our cars. The club was dark, and the parking lot was empty except for Chastity's car and my pickup.

We stopped alongside her Karmann Ghia. It wouldn't start, which inspired some colorful language on her part. John and I each tried and failed to get it going.

John said, "That's ok, baby, I'll give you a ride home and we'll deal with this tomorrow."

"Can't I go home with you?" she said in a pouty voice.

"Not tonight," he said. "Emmett and I need to have a talk."

She stomped her feet like an angry toddler and ended up breaking one of her heels. She picked it up and waved it in John's face. "There!" she shouted, her voice taking on a manic edge. "I hope you're happy!" She hobbled over to the Maverick, got in the front seat, and slammed the door.

Sheepishly, John said, "Listen, Emmett, I'm in big trouble if I don't let her stay with me tonight. Is there any way we can meet tomorrow instead?"

"I don't know, John. I left Karen and Joel shorthanded. I should really be getting back."

"One more day, Emmett. I've got lots to tell you. You won't be sorry."

Chastity rolled down her window. In a sing-song-y little girl's voice, she said, "*John*, I'm really, really *cold!*"

He turned and waved. "Hold on a sec, baby!" He turned back to me. "Really, Emmett," he said with some urgency. "I've been writing all this down. I'll show it to you tomorrow."

"I don't know," I said. "I'm staying tonight because I've already paid for the room, but there's a good chance I'll need to drive back in the morning." I paused. "I'll call you tomorrow and let you know."

"Alright," he said resignedly. "You still have my card, right?"

I opened my wallet and looked to make sure. "Yup, I've got it."

"Great," he said. "Hopefully, I'll see you tomorrow. If I don't, I'll put the manuscript in the mail."

"Ok," I said. "I'll call and let you know." I was still leaning toward going home, but the a note in John's voice gave me pause.

Maybe he sensed that. Suddenly, with no warning, he gave me a big hug. "You won't regret it, Emmett." He smiled happily and got in his car. Before he could shut the door, I heard Chastity say, "Why'd you hug him? That's so *gay!*"

He started it, drove a few feet, then stopped and rolled down his window. "You know she was from your part of the world, right?" he said, smiling mysteriously.

"Burr?"

"No, but somewhere close," he said, then rolled up his window and drove away.

CHAPTER FIVE

Once again, that night's ten o'clock news dealt mostly with the capture of Roger Dale Stafford. They showed film of him being hauled off to jail—a skinny little redneck with greasy hair and a mustache too big for his face. He shaded his eyes from the glare of the TV lights and mugged at the cameras. For the first time in his miserable life, he was being treated like a big deal, and he intended to milk it for all it was worth. Disgusted, I shut off the TV.

I still smelled like cigarette smoke from Henny Penny's, so I decided to take a shower. I hadn't expected to stay overnight, so I didn't have a change of clothes, but I reckoned that being clean was its own reward, even if just for a few hours. I went into the bathroom and saw that they hadn't given me any towels. I went out to the front desk. The same old fella who'd checked me in that afternoon was still on duty, watching the end of the 10 o'clock news on his little black-and-white TV.

"Keepin' you busy?" I asked.

"Yup," he said, his eyes glued to the screen.

"I was about to take a shower and realized there were no towels in my room."

He disappeared silently into an adjoining room and returned with a stack of linen.

"Thanks," I said as he handed them over.

"Uh-huh," he said, then went back to watching the news. He wasn't much of a talker, this fella.

I returned to my room and showered without checking the bathroom wall for peepholes. I did make sure my door was locked, however.

I felt better afterwards. I crawled under the covers naked and fell asleep.

My wife Karen has crazy dreams: cats talk, telephones grow eyes, turnips turn into spaceships.

In contrast, mine tend to be more literal.

That night, I dreamed Roger Dale Stafford killed Carrie.

But it wasn't the Chicago cops who tracked him down.

It was me.

***

I woke up intending to go home. John could either mail me that manuscript, or call me from his own phone to say what he had to say.

But I wanted breakfast first, so I went to the motel office, hoping someone there could suggest a place. I expected to see someone different, but the same little old fella from the day before was behind the desk. He was still watching his little black and white television, but this time the show was Captain Kangaroo.

"Don't you ever sleep?" I said.

"Yup," he said.

So much for small talk.

"I don't suppose you'd know a good place to eat breakfast?"

"What kind of food ya like?"

It shocked me to hear him string so many words together.

"Regular breakfast food, I guess."

"There's Denco's,"

I smirked. "Anyplace else?"

"Been to Denco's, have ya?"

"Yeh, last night."

"Didn't like it?"

"Not too much."

"There's Mary's."

"Where's it at?"

"Down the street towards the university."

God forbid, I make him talk for too long and exhaust himself. I thanked him, then went outside and looked. Sure enough, there it was, a couple of hundred yards away. I decided to walk.

I'd just gotten underway when several police cars passed, sirens blaring.

I thought, *Dunkin' Donuts must be having a two for one sale.*

On the outside, Mary's is one of those old-timey diners that look like an oversized Airstream camper with the wheels removed. There weren't any empty parking spots, so a couple of cars and a semi tractor/trailer had to park in the back.

As I walked in, a small chime jingled over my head. The room smelled like bacon and fried onions. I decided I was going to like Mary's.

The jukebox was playing Buck Owens' *Act Naturally*. A skinny brunette waitress bounced from booth to booth, while a tall, wide-bodied woman with hair the color of Lucille Ball's held forth behind the counter. Both women wore white dresses, white stockings, white shoes, and red-and-white-checked aprons. The waitress's nametag said, in tiny letters written in ball-point pen, *Hi, I'm Blanche.*

Her folks must've wanted her to be a waitress when she grew up.

The woman with the Lucy hair was tall and made to look even taller by her bouffant hairdo. She wore enough makeup to make up for Blanche's lack. Her nametag read, in thick black letters written in magic marker: *Hi, I'm Mary.*

The booths were all occupied, so I sat at the counter. A few stools down sat a fella in a greasy red and white Peterbilt cap. He said something that made Mary laugh, which caused her jowls to shake. She saw me sit down, came over and handed me a menu. "Coffee?" she said.

"Y'all got Tab?"

Hands on hips, she leaned forward and peered at me like she couldn't believe her eyes. "I'm sorry," she said, "I thought I was serving a grown man, not a danged fashion model."

I chuckled. "I'm not much of a coffee person."

"Suit yourself," she said, "but we don't have Tab. Just Diet-Rite."

"That'd be fine."

I perused the menu. She returned with my soda and asked if I was ready to order.

"How're your biscuits and gravy?"

"Best in the state."

"I guess that's what I'll have."

She snatched the menu from my hands. "Sounds like a plan, rubberband man," she said, then hollered back to the kitchen: "Heart attack on a rack!" which I reckon is diner lingo for biscuits and gravy.

By now, Buck Owens had segued to Kitty Wells and *It Wasn't God Who Made Honky-Tonk Angels*. Mary belted it out in a rough approximation of Kitty's nasal twang. The guy in the Peterbilt hat asked her if she was a honky-tonk angel. Mary tweaked his nose and said, "Uh-uh, I'm a honky-tonk devil!"

I sat back and enjoyed the show. The next song up was Merle Haggard's *Okie from Muskogee*. Somehow, Mary managed to get everyone in the place to sing along.

Except for me.

When it was over, she came over and said, "What's wrong, handsome? Too stuck up to sing?"

"Trust me. You don't want to hear me sing."

"So what you're saying is, you're no Merle Haggard."

"I believe that's fair to say."

She gave me an exaggerated wink. "Don't worry about it, sweet cakes. You're better looking than he is."

Originally I'd intended to wolf down my meal then hit the road, but I enjoyed the food and atmosphere so much, I ended up lingering over another glass of soda. The breakfast rush ended. Slowly, people filed out. Finally, the Peterbilt guy left, leaving me alone with Mary and Blanche, but not for long. He returned almost immediately, and huddled with Mary. I couldn't understand what they were talking about, only a few words:

Henny Penny's and *murdered in their bed.*

The hair on the back of my neck stood up. John. Chastity.

"Excuse me," I said, "but would you mind if I asked what y'all are talking about?"

"I just heard on my police scanner that some fella and his girlfriend were shot to death last night," said the Peterbilt guy. "They're saying the gal was a dancer out to Henny Penny's."

My blood ran cold.

"Have they given their names?"

"I ain't heard none yet."

"You know where it happened?"

"A house near OU, off Boyd."

I dropped a twenty on the counter and ran for the door. Mary called out, "Sugar, you forgot your change!"

But I was already gone.

The little chime over the door tinkled on my way out.

CHAPTER SIX

The drive to John's was a nightmare. I thought I knew where it was but kept getting lost. Finally, I found his block, but it had been barricaded by the police, so I had to get out of my car and walk. I checked the address against the card he'd given me. This was it, no doubt about it.

Several emergency vehicles were parked in front: patrol cars, a Ford Crown Victoria or two—probably unmarked police cars—and an ambulance. Yellow crime-scene tape barred entrance, but uniformed personnel walked in and out.

I ducked under the tape and walked to the front door. A square-jawed fella wearing a police uniform blocked my path.

"I'm sorry, sir, but you'll have to wait across the street."

"Excuse me, but is it true that a man and a woman were killed inside?"

"I'm not at liberty to say."

I was on the verge of losing my mind. "Listen," I said, doing my best to keep my cool, "the guy who lives here is a friend of mine. If he's been killed, I want to know. I was with him and his girlfriend last night."

He nodded along as I spoke. "Ok, sir, stay here and let me go talk to the detective in charge. What's your name?"

"Emmett Hardy."

"What was that? Emmett Kelly?"

"No. Hardy. Emmett Hardy."

"Ok, Mr. Hardy. I'll be right back."

The officer walked up the steps and into the house. He was in there for a few seconds, then came back. "This way," he said. I followed him into the house. Just inside the front door was a man who seemed to be in charge. "Mr. Hardy," said the officer, "this is Detective Blanchard."

We shook hands. "Officer Corcoran tells me you might've been the last person to see the victims alive," he said gruffly.

"I think I might've been."

Blanchard was a few inches shorter than me, about 5'8" or so, and about my age: early 50s or thereabouts, with a chubby face and a sparse moustache over a pair of lips that looked like they'd been stung by a swarm of bees. He wore a light blue polo shirt tucked into gray pants. His paunch extended over his belt like an over-inflated basketball, and the crotch of his slacks hung almost to his knees. He held a suit jacket draped over his arm. A sweat-stained dark gray fedora was pushed to the back of his head.

"Where was it that you saw them?" he asked, squinting over a pair of half-moon glasses.

"I left them in the Henny Penny's parking lot around 10:00 last night."

"What do you mean, 'left them?'"

"I mean, we'd been there earlier, before we took John's car to go someplace to eat."

"Where'd you go?"

"Denco's."

He smirked. "Officially, it's called Denco Café," he muttered. "You have my sympathies."

"Thanks," I said. "So when we were finished eating, John drove us back to Henny Penny's so his girlfriend and I could pick up our cars."

"Henny's was raided last night," he said. "Was the girlfriend working?"

"I guess you know that she was a dancer."

"We do."

"Yes, she was working last night, until, like you said, it got raided."

"So you saw them at Henny Penny's but never came here?"

"No, I've never been here before. I don't think he's been living here that long. He gave me his business card, which is how I knew where it was."

I showed him John's card.

He eyed me suspiciously. "You know we'll find out if you're not telling the truth."

"I know you will," I said. "I am."

He crossed his arms and tilted his head to one side, peering at me over those glasses like a schoolteacher trying to catch a kid in a lie. "If you weren't here, how'd you hear about the crime?"

"I overheard a couple of people talking about it in a diner this morning while I was eating breakfast. The place was Mary's, over near—"

"I know where Mary's is," he snapped. "How'd they know about it? We were just called to the scene an hour ago."

That would explain the parade of cop cars I'd passed on my walk to Mary's.

"One of them was a truck driver," I said. "He heard it over his scanner."

"I see."

"By the way, I'm a cop myself," I said, hoping it might merit at least some consideration. "I'm Chief of Police in Burr, over in the—"

"I know where Burr is," he said dismissively. "You'll know the name of the victims, then."

"John Smith. He teaches school in Noble. His girlfriend's name is Chastity. I only met her last night."

He nodded and pulled out a small notebook and pencil. "Let's go back to the beginning," he said.

"It's kind of a long story," I said.

"I've got time."

I hadn't expected to be confronted like this, but I really couldn't blame him. For all he knew, I could've been the killer returning to the scene of the crime.

I described the evening's events, beginning when I met John at Henny Penny's, where he introduced me to Chastity. I told him about being in the club when it was raided, and again how the three of us went to Denco's—I'm sorry, Denco Café—then back to the Henny Penny's parking lot. "Her car wouldn't start, so she went home with John. I drove back to the hotel where I'm staying."

"So her car should still be parked at Henny Penny's, is what you're sayin'?" he said in a less hostile tone. I thought maybe he was becoming more receptive to the possibility of my innocence.

"Right," I said. "A yellow Karmann Ghia."

"We'll check that out," he said. "You're sure they came straight here?"

"Honestly, I have no idea. They seemed in a hurry to get home, but I can't say for sure."

"Uh-huh," he said, still scribbling. He took a moment to read what he'd written, then asked, "To your knowledge, did either of them take drugs?"

"Chastity did."

"So hold on a minute," he said. "You say you just met this gal last night, but you know that she takes drugs. How would you know that?"

"Her roommate told me last night, plus I noticed her rubbing her nose when she came out of the ladies room at Denco's, like she'd just snorted something."

"Uh-huh," he said, continuing to jot things down. "What's this roommate's name?"

"Destiny. She's a dancer at—"

"I know who Destiny is," he said. "We're going to need you to come in and make a formal statement. How about three o'clock this afternoon?"

"That's fine," I said.

"I'll have one of my officers take down your contact information. You live here in Norman?"

"No, I came to Norman to visit John. Like I said, I live in Burr, over in Tilghman County, the one spelled with a—"

"I know how it's spelled," he said.

I couldn't tell whether he suspected me or not, but I could've done without his arrogant tone. So far, he struck me as a self-important clown.

He wouldn't be the first cop I've met who fits that description.

He stuffed the pen and notebook back in his pocket. "Sit tight for a minute. I'll send someone over to take down your contact info."

He turned and disappeared down the hall.

I looked around while I waited. From where I stood in the entryway, I could see into both the living room and the kitchen. In the living room, books had been pulled from bookshelves onto the floor; furniture cushions had been cut open and stuffing scattered about. The kitchen floor was covered in dry cereal and pasta dumped out of their boxes.

Whoever did it was looking for something.

Officer Corcoran appeared at my side. I gave him my home address, and my work and home phone numbers. He didn't ask where I'd stayed the night, which I thought was odd.

After he finished writing it all down, he asked in a friendly voice, "What brings you to town?"

"I was here to visit my friend."

"The fella who lives here?"

"Yeh."

"Gee, that's tough," he said. "It's a good thing you didn't stay with him."

It hadn't occurred to me that if John had offered and I had stayed with him, I might also be dead. Again, it struck me as strange that he didn't ask where I *had* stayed, but I didn't bring it up.

"Do you have any idea what happened?" I asked.

"Maybe they surprised a burglar," he said, looking around at the mess. "It sure seems like whoever did it was looking for something."

"John was a junior high science teacher," I said, "I don't think he had much in the way of valuables."

"Probably not," he agreed. "Detective Blanchard thinks it's more likely the gal was the target."

I was surprised he'd say that, but I kept it to myself. If the killer had been after her, wouldn't he have done it at her house?

Most of the police activity was occurring down the hall from where I stood. People walked in and out of a room that I assumed was the crime scene.

My mind turned to Roger Dale Stafford, and how there had been no rhyme or reason to what he'd done.

Is that what this was about? A random murder by some psycho who needed beer money?

I stumbled out the front door and onto the grass. The air was chilly, but the sun shone bright; it brought tears to my eyes, not that I needed help on that count. People gathered in small groups behind the yellow tape. I couldn't hear what they were saying and didn't care to.

I thought again about Corcoran saying it was probably a botched burglary, then how he changed his tune and said Blanchard believed Chastity was the primary target. Both couldn't be true, especially considering they'd been killed at John's house, not hers. The mess told me the killer was looking for something specific.

I remembered my last conversation with John and how he'd practically begged me to stay in town overnight so we could meet. "I've been writing all this down," he said. "I'll show it to you tomorrow."

Writing it all down.

That's when it hit me.

The killer wasn't some bum trying to score beer money.

John had discovered something he wasn't supposed to know and gotten killed for it.

The killer was looking for John's book.

I raced back into the house and down the hall towards John's bedroom. Corcoran appeared from around a corner and blocked my way. "Mr. Hardy," he said, "you don't want to go back there."

"You're right," I said. "I'm sorry, I just wanted to ask Detective Blanchard a question."

"He's busy," said Corcoran. "Tell me and I'll ask him."

"Ask him if they've found something that looks like a book manuscript."

Corcoran went into the bedroom. Blanchard came out seconds later. "What's this about a book manuscript?"

"John and I were writing a book together," I said, which might have been true in the broadest sense, but was mostly a lie. "I wanted to see if it was still here."

"Is that why you were in town visiting, to work on a book?"

"Yes," I said, again, not being entirely truthful.

"We didn't find anything like that," said Blanchard. "Don't you have your own copy?"

"Oh yeh, of course. I wanted to see if he'd done any more work on it since yesterday."

He looked at me suspiciously. "We didn't find nothin' like that," he said. "We'll let you know if we do."

"Ok, thanks."

I could only hope he was as good as his word.

****

I had trouble processing all that had happened. John and I weren't especially close, but we had developed a friendship of sorts that began when he helped me on the Murray case. His death didn't hit me as hard as a close friend or relative's would have, but it hurt all the same.

Thinking about how much had changed over the last 24 hours almost made me dizzy. Yesterday, I was sitting in a little kid's desk in a junior high school classroom, talking to John. He claimed to have lots of information about Carrie, but was only able to tell me was her last name and that she'd been raped and tortured at one point by her uncle, who had a *different* last name. He was supposed to fill in the rest last night, but instead, his girlfriend's car wouldn't start. She guilted him into letting her stay at his place, which turned out badly for everyone. All he managed to tell me was that Carrie was raised somewhere near where I live.

Now John and Chastity were dead. So were my hopes of ever knowing what he wanted to tell me.

All I wanted to do was track down members of Carrie's family so we could move her out of that prison cemetery. That's it. You wouldn't think it would be so hard. I'd always thought John wanted the same thing, nothing more, then yesterday I discovered he's writing a book about her life.

I'm not a religious person. It follows that I don't believe in heaven or hell, or the idea of an eternal soul, so why is it I felt moving her out of that cemetery was so goddam important? In life, I never knew her, except to watch her assassinate one of the worst people I'd ever known.

Is that why I was doing this? Because she'd killed a guy I hated?

Now, John and his girlfriend were dead, too, meaning that, so far, all this wild goose chase had accomplished was to get people killed.

"I tell you what I *should* do," I mumbled to myself as I walked back to my car. "I should just forget about this whole thing."

I should, but I knew I wouldn't.

CHAPTER SEVEN

I've always been more stubborn than a mule. I guess I inherited it from my mama.

I remember in the months before the 1940 presidential election, when Franklin Roosevelt was running for the third time. If he won, he'd be the first President to serve more than eight years; even George Washington stepped down after two terms. If he lost ... well, as my parents saw it, we might as well flush the country down the toilet.

It happened that one of our neighbors hated FDR the way a slug hates a saltshaker, and erected a billboard on his property that said: NO THIRD TERM! I forget the fella's name, but I do remember he was old and bitter and lived all by himself.

Both my parents, but especially my mama, considered that sign to be downright un-American. In our household, FDR was a living saint, and my folks weren't the only ones to feel that way. Roosevelt was a hero to a lot of Oklahoma farmers laid low by the Dust Bowl and the Great Depression. The New Deal had literally saved many of their lives.

The sign was so big you could see it from the highway. My mama took it as a personal affront, and made it her mission to convince our neighbor to take it down.

Several times a week, she'd march over to this old fella's house with a box of chocolate chip cookies under her arm. She was a hell of a baker, and I reckon this guy had a sweet tooth. Sometimes she'd even take me along, wanting to instill in me the power of gentle persuasion, a lesson I'm not sure I ever did learn. At first, those visits played out the same way: Mama would knock on his door. He'd open it a crack and ask what she wanted. She'd smile and say something like, "Good morning, Mr. So-and-So, how are you this fine day? I just made a batch of cookies, but I made too many and I thought you might like some." The fella would grumble thanks and try to close the door, but somehow she always managed to get him involved in conversation. She'd say something nice about his garden, which was his pride and joy, or ask how his grown children were doing. Before you knew it, they'd be chomping down on cookies and chattering away like old friends—at which point she'd bring up the subject of that sign, then explain calmly and patiently all the ways we needed to stay the course and re-elect FDR.

Long story short, by the time the election rolled around, not only had that fella taken down the sign, my mama had turned him into one of the biggest Roosevelt supporters in Tilghman County. When FDR died in '45, no one was more upset than he was.

Unlike my mama, I don't bake, and I don't possess her talent for changing people's minds. The art of gentle persuasion she'd mastered was lost on me; I can't help but let my contempt shine through when I encounter someone too stupid to see the truth.

But I am stubborn.

I drove around for a while, without knowing where in hell I was going or what I was going to do. Mostly, all I could think about was the absolute horror John and Chastity must've felt in their final moments. That's something I tend to dwell on at times like this, especially after a situation I experienced a few years ago, when the same thing almost happened to me. If a couple of women hadn't ridden to my rescue, one of whom was my wife, Karen, I'd have been killed for sure.

All this would've made more sense if John had been killed back when he worked the overnight shift at the Sunshine Store. You hear about things like that all the time: some guy in a ski mask robs and kills a store clerk for whatever money is in the cash register. That's essentially what Roger Dale Stafford did, walking away from killing those steakhouse employees with a grand total of $1,500.

Divided by the number of victims, that comes out to $250 apiece.

Life is cheap.

John would have been justified in thinking he'd put his death-defying days behind him. Schoolteachers don't normally suffer violent deaths.

Yet he did.

Life doesn't make a bit of sense.

I thought I should call Red and tell her what had happened. She didn't know John all that well, but he'd been to dinner at our house a time or two, and I knew she liked him.

I'd just started to head back to the Sooner Arms to do that very thing, when I flashed back to John shuffling a sheaf of papers when I walked in on him the day before. At the time, I didn't think anything of it. Now, it occurred to me that maybe those papers were the book. Even if they weren't, he could have stashed the manuscript in a desk drawer. I remembered the typewriter on his desk. It made sense that he'd work on it at school whenever he had a spare minute. Blanchard's boys were bound to be nosing around his classroom, looking for leads. If I wanted to get my hands on that book, I'd better get to it before they did.

I forgot about calling Karen for the time being and decided to pay another visit to Noble Junior High.

I got there just as the lunch period was ending—almost exactly 24 hours after my first visit. Unlike the day before, all was silent. Everyone, teachers and students alike, walked the halls like zombies. The receptionist remembered me from the day before. "John's friend," she said, stifling a sob. I asked to speak to the principal. She rose from her desk and knocked on a closed door. "Mrs.

Hollingsworth," she said, "John's friend from yesterday would like to speak with you."

"Send him in," said Mrs. Hollingsworth.

I knocked softly and entered. Yesterday, I thought she looked like Myrna Loy. Today, she looked like any woman who's lost someone dear to her heart.

She rose from behind her desk and extended her hand. I took it.

"I assume you heard," she said.

"I have. I'm numb."

"We all are," she said. "We would've called off school today, but we got the news too late." She dabbed at her eyes with a wadded-up Kleenex. "You must be devastated."

"I'll miss him. John was a good man."

"Amen to that."

"I was at his house this morning and spoke to the detective running the investigation," I said. "Blanchard was his name. I don't suppose he's been here, has he?"

"Not yet, but I spoke to him," she said. "He said he'd come by this afternoon."

I asked how they'd gotten the news.

"We were worried when John didn't show up for his first class this morning, since he's usually here by the crack of dawn. We called his house. The person who picked up said, 'Smith residence,' which I thought was strange. I told the person who I was and asked for John. He put me on hold, then another man came on the line and said he was sorry to have to tell me this, but John had been killed." She tossed the wadded-up tissue aside and snatched a fresh one from a box on her desk. "I couldn't believe it," she said, wiping her eyes. "None of us could. Who would want to hurt John? He was such a sweet man. So good with the kids."

"I don't know if John mentioned this to you," I said, "but he and I have been working together on a book."

"John told me he was writing a book about a friend of his who died," she said. "He didn't tell me he had a co-author."

"I was mostly helping him with research."

"Were you also a friend of this person?"

"Well, I actually never met her, but the way John talked about her made me want to help. I asked Detective Blanchard if they'd found anything that looked like a book manuscript, but he said they hadn't. I thought maybe John had been working on it here when he had a spare minute."

"We could check his classroom if you like."

"I'd appreciate it."

I followed her down the hall. Voices were subdued throughout the school. Occasionally, a sob would pierce the quiet.

John's classroom was empty. "We decided to have John's students meet in the gym today," Mrs. Hollingsworth explained. She gestured toward his desk. "I suspect what you're looking for is in there."

The typewriter was where it was the day before, on a small table set at an angle from the desk. "Do you remember if John did a lot of typing?" I asked.

"Just lately he'd be typing away before classes start. When it was quiet you could hear it all the way in the office."

That could mean he'd been working on the manuscript, which might also mean the manuscript was here somewhere.

I shuffled through a pile of papers on his desk. All I found was homework waiting to be graded.

I opened a side drawer. On top, was a small box the length and width of a sheet of typing paper, and a couple of inches deep. I opened it. On the top page was typed: *Carrie's Story, by John Smith and Emmett Hardy*.

Bingo.

I felt a rush of adrenaline, then thought: *Why would he give me credit?*

"This must be it," I said. I glanced at the first page:

I first met Carrie on a Summer night in 1975, it said. *Little did I know that one day I'd be writing a book about her life.*

I thumbed through the rest. There weren't many, perhaps 20. I rummaged through the rest of the drawers, then searched his shelves. I didn't find anything else.

It wasn't the full-length manuscript I'd hoped for, but maybe it would tell me what I wanted to know.

"Take it," said Mrs. Hollinsworth. "John would've wanted you to finish it."

I was glad to hear her say that, but the last thing I wanted to do was impede an official investigation.

"I'd better just make a copy and leave the original for Detective Blanchard."

"That's no problem at all." She led me back to the front office. A xerox machine sat in the corner. "Help yourself," she said.

I hurriedly made copies, put the originals back in the box, and handed it back to Mrs. Hollingsworth.

"Looks like it's your baby now," she said with a wistful smile.

I could feel Detective Blanchard hot on my heels, and I didn't want to cross paths with him. Not yet, anyway.

"I'd best be going," I said.

"I'll show you out," she said. On our way, we passed a restroom. Inside, a girl could be heard crying her eyes out. "I'm sorry, but I should see to that," said Mrs. Hollingsworth.

"That's fine," I said. "Thank you so much for your help."

"You're welcome," she said. "By the way, did John have a publisher?"

"Not yet," I said without really knowing. I assumed he would've mentioned it if he did.

"You'll find one," she said. "John was so smart and talented. Maybe it will be a best-seller."

"Wouldn't that be something?"

She gently placed a hand on my shoulder. "John was lucky to have a friend like you."

Feeling like an impostor, I said, "John was a good friend to have."

***

Driving back to Norman, I thought less about *why* John and Chastity had been shot, and more about *where* they'd been shot. If Chastity was the primary target and John just an innocent bystander, as Blanchard seemed to think, why were they killed at John's place? I reckoned the killer could've followed them from Henny Penny's, but when John dropped me off after dinner, the parking lot was empty except for her Karmann Ghia and my pickup. I'm pretty sure I would've noticed any suspicious vehicles.

Maybe they were *both* the primary target. Maybe someone was afraid of what they *both* knew, and wanted them *both* dead.

Had that occurred to Blanchard? Maybe, maybe not. Should I have shared my thoughts with him? Probably. Would things have turned out differently if I had?

I'd have to say yes to that, too.

But when it came right down to it, I didn't believe there was anything I could say that would make a bit of difference in how Blanchard would approach his investigation. He was going to do what he was going to do.

Just like *I* was going to do what *I* was going to do.

I told you I was stubborn.

CHAPTER EIGHT

I wanted to put distance between myself and Noble Junior High School. Blanchard or someone on his team might pull up any minute. I pulled away as quick as I could manage without drawing attention to myself.

After a few minutes, when I thought it safe to think about something besides not being seen, I considered what I'd said to Mrs. Hollingsworth—that John was a good friend to have. He was. I liked John a lot, but when I said it, I was thinking mostly about his relationship with Carrie. John had been one of the few people who were kind to her when she was alive, giving her free food and coffee when he could, for example, and allowing her and Leon to spend cold winter nights in the warmth of the Sunshine Store instead of outside on the street.

But it was really after she died that he did the most work on her behalf. I believe he felt guilty that he hadn't done more for her while she was alive. After her burial in that prison cemetery, he and I spoke of wanting to find her next of kin so they could claim her body and give her a proper resting place. Yet while I'd taken an almost-three-year break from the task, he had apparently never stopped digging.

He discovered enough that he wanted to bring me back into the loop. But aside from a second-hand story about Carrie being sexually assaulted and tortured, he never got the chance to tell me what he'd discovered. Don't get me wrong, that episode was upsetting on its own, but if there was more, I wanted to hear it.

Now John and his fiancée were dead. I strongly suspected that what he discovered—whether about her rape and torture, or something else—had been the motive. The question was: What was I going to do about it? Was I going to sit back and let the Norman Police Department and perhaps the State Bureau of Investigation handle it? I should, but I didn't necessarily want to. I may have developed an overestimation of my own abilities, but I can't help it; when the rubber meets the road, I feel I can do a better job.

Detective Blanchard seemed competent enough, but there was something about him I didn't trust. Hopefully, I'd get a better read on him when I went to the station to deliver my official statement.

Maybe the manuscript would clear everything up. If John spelled out in plain English who assaulted Carrie, or who had a vested interest in making sure that information was kept under wraps, then that person would jump to the top of any competent investigator's list of suspects.

But what if Blanchard wasn't competent? What if he was lazy or just didn't care? I can't stand by in a situation like that, even if it means butting into things that technically aren't any of my business.

Maybe I was wrong and they were killed for a different reason.

Hopefully, I'd know more after reading the manuscript.

***

The first thing I did after getting back to my motel room, even before looking at the manuscript, was call Red. Cindy, our dispatcher and receptionist, picked up.

"Cindy, this is Emmett. Is the boss there? I need to talk to her real quick."

"Sure, hold on a sec."

Red came on the line. "What's up? Are you on your way home?"

I just came out with it.

"John's dead."

She gasped. "My Lord," she said. "What happened?"

"Someone broke into his house last night and shot him in his sleep."

Silence.

"Do they know who did it?"

"Not yet."

Another pause.

"Do *you* know who did it?"

"Not yet."

"I'm not even going to ask if you're going to look into it yourself."

"I might. I was the last person other than the killer to see them alive, so I'll have to be involved to some extent."

"What do you mean 'them?' Was someone else killed, too?"

"They shot his girlfriend, too."

Another pause. "I just can't believe it," she said. "I'm absolutely stunned."

"Me too."

"Do the police have a motive?"

"An officer I talked to this morning said the detective in charge thinks it's a burglary gone bad, but that doesn't exactly ring true. The girlfriend's roommate told me the girl was a drug addict, so it might have something to do with that."

"Could it have anything to do with Carrie?"

"It might," I said. "John was writing a book about her. That's why he asked me to come here. Don't ask me how, but he discovered her last name was Fitzjarrald." I spelled it out for her, then added, "I'm thinking the killer might've been after something John had written."

"You think that there was something in it that the killer didn't want anyone to know?"

"Maybe. One of the few things John had a chance to tell me was that a few months before she died Carrie had been raped and tortured."

She groaned. "That would qualify. How'd he know about this?"

"A friend of his—I'm pretty sure it must've been his girlfriend, Chastity—was told about it by a client."

"What was she, a hairdresser?"

"No, an exotic dancer," I said. "There's something else, too: The fella who told Chastity about it said the rapist was Carrie's uncle."

She paused. "So you think John was going to expose this person, and that's why he was killed?"

"Again, I don't know for sure, but it's possible somebody discovered John knew about it and killed him to keep it from being known."

"Maybe the person who did it found out that John's *girlfriend* knew, and he killed *her* to prevent it from being known."

"Yeh," I said. "I guess that's possible."

"How much work on the book had John done?"

"Let me check," I said. "I've got it right here."

"*You've* got it?" she said. "How'd *you* get it?"

"I went to John's school, told the principal that he and I had been working on a book and asked if I could go through his desk and look for it. I found it and made a copy."

"That's some nice stretching of the truth, there."

"A little bit, maybe," I said, "although for some reason John gave me co-author's credit on the title page. Here, let me look ..."

I opened the box and thumbed through the pages. "There are only fifteen pages," I said. Not an encouraging sign.

"I'll let you go, then. Call me back after you read it."

"Wait," I said, "I'm not done. The detective on the case wants me to hang around for a while."

"You're not a suspect, are you?"

"Not that I know of," I said, "but I was with them the night before the murder, so I reckon they haven't written me off completely. How are things going there?"

"Well," she said hesitantly, "Joel caught Jeffrey Weeden, Betty and Russell Weeden's boy, peeing into Charles Hilton's gas tank." She laughed weakly. "I don't even know why I told you that."

I chuckled. "Well, I asked. I reckon if that's the worst thing to happen, y'all can handle things without me for a little while longer."

"I think we can," she agreed. "This town's getting duller by the day."

I gave her the motel's phone number and my room number. We exchanged a few mushy sentiments and said our goodbyes.

I picked up the pages and started to read. It didn't take five minutes. When I finished, I read it again, just to make sure I hadn't missed anything. To say I was disappointed is an understatement. Essentially, it was just a recounting of the events of June 25th, 1976, the day Carrie shot Burt. Everything on those pages, John had learned from me. If he'd discovered something else, it wasn't recorded there. The only thing new was her last name, which he'd already told me, and there was no explanation about how he'd discovered it.

I called Red back and gave her the bad news.

"There must be more *somewhere*," she said. "Was the manuscript typed or handwritten?"

"Typed," I said. "What difference does it make?"

"If he typed it, he was probably working from notes he'd written out by hand."

I hadn't thought of that. "So you mean this might be like a second draft."

"Right. An author doesn't just write a book off the top of their head. They put it down in rough form, sometimes by hand, then write it over and over until they get it right."

After all the reading I've done, it's funny that I'd never considered the actual process.

"That would mean that somewhere else there might be another, more complete copy."

"I wouldn't be surprised."

I felt good for about half a second, before it dawned on me that even if she was right, my chances of getting my hands on it were remote at best.

I said as much to Red.

"It'll turn up," she said. "Just you watch."

"I wish I could be as sure as you are."

"Trust me. John will have found a way."

The only other possibility I could think of was negative—that the killer had found what he was looking for when he trashed John's house.

"I wish I could be as sure as you are," I said.

"When am I ever wrong?"

We said our goodbyes and finished the call.

I then called John's school and asked Mrs. Hollingsworth if the police had been there. She said they'd arrived shortly after I left, packed the contents of John's desk in boxes, and taken it all away. I asked if she might've gone through John's things before they arrived. With the tiniest hint of indignance, she said, "No, I didn't go through his things. I didn't think the police would approve. I did tell Detective Blanchard you two had been writing a book together."

"What did he say to that?"

"Nothing, really. He just kind of laughed."

I expected he'd have something more to say about it when I saw him that afternoon.

***

In fact, when I gave my statement that afternoon, it was the first thing he asked about. The red and white box containing the original typed pages sat on the desk in front of him. He tapped it and said, "What is this I hear about you going through John Smith's stuff?"

"John and I were working on a book together," I explained. "I didn't have a copy, and I knew you guys would probably confiscate whatever was in his desk, so I made a copy."

"Did you take anything else?"

"No, I made a copy and left the original. I knew you'd want to see it." I pulled the pages from where I'd stuffed them in my boot and made a show of handing them over.

"Keep it," he said, tapping the box again. "We've got the original. Are you ready to give your statement?"

"Sure."

Blanchard called in the stenographer. He asked some questions. I answered them in about the same amount of detail as I had when we'd spoken that morning. When he asked about my whereabouts between the hours of ten last night and two this morning, I told him I was in my motel room except for when I visited the office in search of towels. Strangely, like the officer I'd talked to on the scene earlier, he didn't ask me the name of the motel. My confidence in the competence of this particular batch of local yokels dipped a few more degrees.

We finished and the stenographer left the room. Blanchard asked for my fingerprints: "Purely for the purpose of eliminating you as a suspect," he said. I probably shouldn't have gone along with it, but I did. I'd never been to John's house prior to that morning, so there was no chance of finding my prints at the crime scene.

We finished with that and sat back down. I asked him if he'd found anything resembling notes for a book amongst the material from John's classroom.

"Just this," he said, nodding at the box on his desk. "Why? You think there should be more?"

"I thought there would be," I said. "Maybe I was wrong."

He leaned back in his chair and started tapping a pencil on the edge of his desk. *Tap-ta-tap-tap, tap-ta-tap-tap.* For several uncomfortable seconds, he stared at me over his spectacles.

"You know, I've got to tell you," he said. "I don't like this. Not a bit."

I didn't know what he was talking about. "What don't you like?"

"You come in here and tell me you're writing a book with this fella, this friend of yours, who's just turned up dead." *Tap-ta-tap-tap. tap-ta-tap-tap.*

Beneath the calm voice and manner was a note of menace.

"Then you tell me you're a cop from some little shitass town, which I suspect means that you've got a hard-on for city cops, and would like nothing better than to show us how dumb we are and how smart you are. Have I got that about right?"

I bit my tongue damn near hard enough to draw blood.

I've never made any bones about disliking a lot of men in my profession, and Blanchard seemed like a prime example of the type I have particular disdain: a petty tyrant averse to hard work who'd rather get it all over with than get it right.

However, engaging in a pissing contest with a bargain-basement Sgt. Joe Friday ran a distant second to discovering who killed my friend.

"I apologize if I gave that impression," I said, calmly but with my jaw clenched. "Obviously, this is your case. If I can help you out, let me know, but if not, I'll butt out."

He grunted, "Alright then."

"So I'm free to go?"

"Yeh, I guess," he said, like he'd forgotten me already. "Drive careful going home, and if we need you for anything, I'll let you know."

I supposed I should be grateful he didn't consider me a suspect. I got out fast, before I could say something that might give him reason to reconsider.

***

I drove back to the motel, as mad as a jar of hornets. After settling my bill, I stopped by Mary's, hoping to pick up the change for the twenty I'd left that morning. I would've let her keep it, but I was running low on both cash and gas and I didn't know anybody in Norman who'd cash one of my checks.

Lucky for me, neither Mary nor the truck driver who gave me the heads-up about John and Chastity was there, so I was spared having to explain why I'd left in such a hurry.

When I told the cashier why I was there, she opened the register and pulled out an envelope. "You must be 'Good-looking guy who can't sing'."

I chuckled. "Why do you ask?"

"That's what she wrote on the envelope," she said and showed it to me. I told her to thank Mary for me.

Next I needed gas. I pulled into a Conoco station. The attendant pointed out a puddle of fluid collecting under the car. "I know," I said. "Leaky radiator."

"You should get that taken care of," the attendant said.

"You're right, I should."

Ever since I bought that truck, it had just been one thing after another. A week ago, it was the universal joint, which I'd put off getting fixed. Now it was the radiator. I told myself I'd take it to Wes Harmon tomorrow, then put it out of my mind.

Karen wasn't expecting me home for at least another day, so I thought maybe I'd surprise her by getting home early—then I remembered it was "Ladies' Night."

About a year ago, Red started hosting a group of girlfriends on Thursdays to watch a certain TV show that's apparently all the rage; don't ask me what it's called. I thought they might skip it this week, given the events of the day, but I couldn't be sure. The gas station had a pay phone. I called home.

Someone who was not my wife picked up on the third ring. "Karen's Roadkill Café," slurred a drunken female voice. "You kill 'em, we grill 'em." In the background, I could hear a jumble of female voices singing, *Stand by Your Man.*

Karen serves wine at these shindigs, one of many reasons I tend to work late on Thursdays.

The operator said, "Collect call from Emmett Hardy, will you accept the charges?"

The drunk lady said, "Sure, I'll take it. Karen, it's yer hub-sund."

Red came on the line. "Emmett?"

"Who was that?" I asked.

"Cissy Crooks," she yelled over the noise in the background. "You remember her. She works at the TG&Y Family Center."

"I thought she was more of a church lady."

"She likes her wine, too. Are you still in Norman?"

"Actually, I called to tell you I'm on my way home."

"What was that?" she shouted over the background noise.

Loudly, I said: "I'm on my way home!"

"Oh, you are? Good! They let you go, huh?"

"Yeh, I'm not important enough to worry about. I should be home in an hour or so."

"Alright, I'll shoo away the girls before you get home."

"You don't have to do that," I said, hoping she would.

She did.

CHAPTER NINE

I walked through the door and found Karen on our couch, arms crossed, eyes shut, with Mr. Paws, our cat, asleep on her lap.

I guess I closed the door a little harder than necessary and it woke her up. Mr. Paws rushed up to me and meowed in the peculiar, siren-like way he does when he's hungry. "Don't you ever feed this poor guy?" I said.

"He likes it when his daddy feeds him," she said in an approximation of how a cat might sound if it spoke English.

I went into the kitchen and opened a can of cat food. Mr. Paws crawled halfway up my pants leg, trying to get at it. I scooped the smelly mush into his bowl and set it on the floor. Mr. Paws ate like he hadn't been fed in a month.

Red joined me in the kitchen. "How are you feeling?" she asked.

Good question, I thought. "Bad," I said. "Shocked. Horrified. Take your choice."

"Anything new since you called?"

"No. I'm going to call the detective in charge tomorrow morning and ask for an update."

"Sounds like a plan," she said. "You look beat."

"I am."

"Let's go to bed."

"Ok, but no hanky-panky. I'm too tired."

She rolled her eyes.

We got into bed. I asked how her party had gone.

"Pretty well," she said.

"What's the name of that show you all watch?"

"'Knots Landing,'" she said.

"And who's that actor? Ted Knight?"

"Ted *Shackleford*," she said. "Ted Knight played Ted Baxter on Mary Tyler Moore."

"Not the same fella, then."

"As if you didn't know," she said. "And by the way, we don't just watch 'Knots Landing' to make goo-goo eyes at Ted Shackleford. It's actually a pretty good show, which you might discover if you ever gave it a chance."

"You're probably right," I said.

I have to admit, sometimes I'll draw a line around something, whether it's a TV show or a sport or some kind of artsy thing, like it's just for one sex or the other. Maybe things used to be like that, but not as much anymore. The world's changing every day.

On the other hand, Red definitely has a crush on that "Knots Landing" fella. I reckon the odds she'll ever meet him are about the same as me ever meeting Sophia Loren, so neither of us had anything to worry about.

"Oh well," I said, as I closed my eyes. I was glad to be home and feeling a little better than when I'd walked in the door.

That feeling had a shelf life of slightly more than seven hours.

***

I woke up bright and early the next morning, thinking about the few typed pages of John's that I'd found, and wondering if there was more.

The sky outside our bedroom window was just turning from dark to light. I got up to go to the bathroom, and a floorboard creaked as I got back in bed. Karen bolted upright. "What was that?" she said, still half asleep. "Just me going to the bathroom," I said. She lay back down and, in an instant, had fallen back asleep. I looked at our bedside alarm clock. It said 5:33.

An hour later, she'd woken up on her own. I'd never gotten back to sleep.

"Why're you up so early?" she asked.

"I can't stop thinking about what John might've done with those notes."

"Maybe I was wrong," she said with a yawn. "Maybe there weren't any."

"No, you were right," I said. "I'd bet Mr. Paws' life on it." Hearing his name mentioned, the cat jumped on the bed, walked the length of my body, perched on my chest and stuck his face an inch from mine.

Meow! he barked.

Karen translated in fake cat-speak: *"Don't you go using my name in vain, buddy!"* I picked him up and dropped him on the floor and said, "Sorry, Mr. Paws."

Karen got out of bed and started to put on her uniform. "Did you ask that detective? What was his name? Blanchard?"

"He said all they found were the same pages I'd made copies of."

"You believe him?"

"I don't know why he'd lie."

"Could they have the other stuff without realizing it?"

"Possibly," I said, "but they'd have to be pretty dumb to miss it."

"Maybe they're dumb."

"Maybe they are, although this isn't John Joe Heckscher we're dealing with here," I said, citing an Oklahoma Bureau of Investigation agent I'd had cause to deal with several times over the years.

"Does that mean he's smarter or dumber?"

"Than John Joe?" I said. "I meant he's probably smarter, but John Joe's not dumb, really."

"He's just ambitious and only sees what he wants to see."

"Exactly."

I got out of bed and joined Red in getting dressed. She and Joel had been doing all the work while I'd been in Norman, so I told her to relax. "I'll go in first this morning," I said; we generally take turns going in early. "That would be good," she said. "I've got a ton of laundry to do."

I got to the station too early to get hold of Blanchard, so I waited until 10:00 to call. He answered the phone himself.

"Detective Blanchard," I said. "This is Emmett Hardy from yesterday."

"How're you doing," he said.

"I'm fine, I was just wondering if there's been any new developments since we last spoke."

"You mean since 4:30 yesterday?" he said sarcastically. "Nope, nothing new."

I chuckled. "Yeh, I reckon it hasn't been very long, has it? I also wanted to ask if you're absolutely sure there wasn't anything from John's classroom that looked like notes for that book we've been writing."

"Why do you keep *asking* that?" he said. "I appreciate y'all were working together on this thing, but you act more concerned about the book than the fact your friend was murdered."

"Nah, it's not that, it's just that he—we—put in so much work on that book, I'd hate it if I couldn't finish it for him."

"Could this book or notes or whatever be something the killer might've been after?"

"Maybe," I said. "I honestly don't know." That much was true. I didn't know, I only suspected, but I felt like I needed to be honest, so I added: "I think they might've been."

A few seconds of roaring silence later, he responded with, "I think you and I need to have another face-to-face."

That's not what I wanted to hear.

"Ok," I said. "I'll be there later this afternoon."

I found Red at her desk. She asked if I'd spoken to Blanchard. I said I had. "Judging by the look on your face," she replied, "I'm guessing he was no help."

"*Worse* than no help," I said.

"What does that mean?" she said.

"He guessed why I wanted the notes."

"What do you mean, 'he guessed why you wanted the notes?'"

"He asked me if I thought the notes might be what the killer was looking for. I couldn't lie. I had to say yes."

She nodded thoughtfully. "You did the right thing."

"I know I did. So why does it feel so wrong?"

She made a face. "Because he's another cop, meaning he's your sworn enemy."

"Oh, come on, that's not true."

"Any progress on his end?"

"Not yet. Or so he said."

"You believe him?"

"I think so," I said. "Hard to say."

"Is it possible he's actually found the book or the notes or whatever, but doesn't want to tell you because he considers you a suspect?"

"I'll ask him next time I see him."

"When will that be?" she asked.

I looked at my watch. "In a couple of hours. I've got to drive back to Norman. He told me we need to meet again, face to face."

***

In recent days I had consistently underestimated my need for folding money, relying instead on my credit card. This time, before I left for Norman, I stopped at Wes Harmon's Sinclair to cash a check. "You're lucky I didn't make a deposit yesterday," he said, handing over a wad of bills.

Low temperatures and overcast skies on the drive to Norman made the passing scenery look like the beginning of "The Wizard of Oz" when Dorothy's still in Kansas, before she gets bonked on the head and wakes up in the Land of Technicolor.

I was sitting across from Blanchard by 2:30. "That book you're writing is all about that girl who killed Burton Murray back in '76."

"That's right," I said.

"Tell me why you think your friend's killer might've been looking for this book."

"Right before he died, John told me he'd heard a story about Carrie Fitzjarrald, the girl who shot Murray, being raped and tortured by her uncle." I hesitated, then added, "Her *rich* uncle."

"And you believe this gal's rich uncle might've found out and killed John Smith to keep it from getting out, is that it?"

"I'm only saying it's a possibility."

"I don't suppose you'd know where we could find this 'rich uncle,' then?"

If I did, I'd have found him by now, I thought. "No, I don't."

"What's his name?"

"His real name might be Fitzjarrald," I said, and spelled it out. "It's also possible he changed it. In fact, I think that's likely the case."

"Why is that?"

"John hinted the guy was some kind of big shot. Apparently, he looked high and low for other Fitzjarralds who spell their name in that peculiar way, but he couldn't find any."

Blanchard clasped his hands behind his head and leaned against the wall behind his desk. The loose skin around his neck bunched under his collar, making him look like either Sidney Greenstreet or a walrus; I couldn't decide which. Smugly, he said, "We're working another angle that doesn't have a bit to do with this Carrie person, or Burt Murray, or any other crimes except for the use of illicit drugs by the deceased."

"Now hold on a dang minute," I said. "John Smith wasn't into drugs at all. He drank too much and might have been an alcoholic, but he didn't do drugs."

Blanchard's smile showed off a set of choppers that didn't deserve to be shown off. "Well, apparently the girl did. The autopsy found heroin and cocaine in her system."

I wasn't surprised, given what Destiny had told me. "What do you think that means?" I asked, not being sarcastic, because I really wanted to know.

"In my opinion, it means these murders were likely the result of a drug deal gone bad."

He could be right. I had no way of knowing.

"Are there any other signs of drug involvement?"

"Not presently," he said. "But we're looking into it."

***

I left Blanchard's office irritate over having driven all the way from Burr to Norman to no good end. When I asked him why he'd insisted I come, Blanchar said: "I just wanted to see your reaction when I told you about the drug angle." I felt like punching him.

I mean, the least he could do was front me the money for gas.

I stopped by Mary's for lunch before driving back. Once again, Mary was behind the counter, happily lording it over her customers. The jukebox was playing "Luckenbach, Texas," to which she added her high-pitched squawk. A dozen or so patrons joined in, none of them with voices better than mine, which is to say, no more musical than a tomcat in the heat of passion. Mary smiled down at me as I took a seat at the counter.

"I see you picked up your change last night," she said. "That was you, wasn't it?"

"'Good-looking fella who can't sing?' I assume that was me. Thank you."

"You're more than welcome, hon'," she said, then asked what made me bolt out of there in such a hurry. I explained that I'd known the folks who'd been murdered. "That's horrible," she said. "You doin' alright?"

"I'm fine," I said. "We weren't close, but they were good people."

"I'm sorry you have to go through that," she said. Brightening a tiny bit, she said, "What can I get you?"

"Burger and fries," I said. "Unless I can have hash browns instead."

With a kind smile, she said, "You can have Mary's hash browns anytime, sugar." She called my order back to the kitchen and set a Diet Rite in front of me without my having to ask.

Stranded at a diner counter without anything to read, I people-watched until my food came.

In a booth behind me was a young couple with two noisy toddlers, a boy and a girl. Each had a doll: the boy, a talking GI Joe; the girl, a talking Barbie. Both dolls were naked. The kids took turns pulling the strings in the back of the dolls' necks, trying to get them to have a conversation. Nothing the dolls said matched up. GI Joe said, "Cover me, I'll get that machine gun!" Barbie would answer, "Would you like to be a model?" Finally, after several tries, Barbie said, "My name's Barbie, what's yours?" and GI Joe replied, "GI Joe, US Army, reporting for duty." You've never seen two happier kids.

My attention was then drawn to a booth on the far side of the diner next to the restrooms. An older fella was accompanied by a much younger gal. The woman's face was turned away, but I could see the man was Cha Cha Mulvaney. He looked quite a bit older than on the billboards and TV commercials. Before this, the only time I'd seen him in the flesh was when I was a kid and his high school wrestling team came to town. Back then, Cha Cha was already about as famous as a youngster his age can be. Pretty near every man, woman, and child in Burr turned up at the Burr High School gym that night to watch him make mincemeat of the poor kid going against him. Cha Cha pinned his over-matched opponent in less than three seconds, which was then, and maybe still is, the shortest high school wrestling match on record.

Looking at him now—old and paunchy, with cauliflower ears and a bright-red nose crisscrossed by spiderweb veins—it was hard to believe he'd once been one of the greatest amateur wrestlers this state has produced.

Mary noticed me looking at him. She leaned close and, in a confidential tone, said, "I see you noticed our celebrity."

"Cha Cha's a regular, is he?"

"He comes around a lot," she said, "usually with a pretty girl on his arm. We keep that booth empty in case he shows up."

In due course, the caffeine in the Diet Rite assaulted my bladder. The path to the restroom led past Cha Cha's booth and allowed me to get a closer look at his dinner companion: it was Destiny, the gal who told me about Chastity's less-than-honorable treatment of John. Minus her makeup and dressed in a loose-fitting University of Oklahoma sweatshirt and a pair of baggy jeans, she looked a lot different from the last time I saw her. Our eyes met, and I thought I detected a hint of recognition. As I closed the bathroom door behind me, I heard Cha Cha ask her, "Who's that guy?" but I didn't hear the answer.

I finished doing my business and returned to my seat at the counter. Mary was there waiting. "What's his story?" I asked.

She leaned close and put her hand in front of her face, as if she didn't want anybody reading her lips. "You probably know he's running for governor, right?"

"I've heard," I said. "I also see him up on those billboards plugging that law against strip joints. Now I see him in here with a stripper. What's that about?" I belatedly realized I'd all but admitted going to a strip club. I must've blushed, because she said, "Hon, you don't have to be embarrassed. Heck, I did my share of exotic dancing back in the day!"

Somehow, I could believe that.

"Seriously, though," I said. "What's he doing dating strippers, then trying to take their jobs away?"

"Well, if you ask *him*, he's not dating those girls but trying to save their souls. But I get what you're sayin'. I guess that's just Okie politics for you: strange bedfellows and all that. I've heard people say the state question is just something Cha Cha and his people came up with to get him on TV, to help him get elected governor."

"You mean the whole thing was Cha Cha's idea?"

"Woah!" she said. "I wouldn't go *that* far. Cha Cha ain't exactly the leader of the pack in the brains department. He's got some powerful, smart people behind him, though. One of them probably thought it up."

A customer drew her attention away for a moment. "The funny thing about that State Question deal," she said, turning back to me, "is that it doesn't really outlaw strip clubs. It just makes it illegal to serve alcohol where folks are taking off their clothes in public."

"What's the point in that?" I asked.

"Hon'," she said expansively, "I'm just a poor working gal. Them kinds of things are *way* over my head."

The chime rang, and through the door came the truck driver in the Peterbilt hat. "You're going to have to excuse me, handsome," she said to me, practically giggling. "I've got to tend to that hunka-hunka burnin' love over there." She called out, "Hey, good lookin', whatcha got cookin'?"

The fella grinned. "I've got me a hot rod Ford and a two-dollar bill!" he said. "What'll that buy?"

It was enough to steal Mary away.

Cha Cha and Destiny got up and walked over to the cashier. On her way out, Destiny gave me another impersonal smile. I watched out the front window as they drove off in a black Cadillac Fleetwood.

***

All this running back and forth to Norman was wearing me out. I drove more than two hours to get there, spent half an hour with

Blanchard, then 45 minutes eating lunch, and it was time to turn around and go home.

I got back to the station around five. Cindy was at the front desk, but Red and Joel were nowhere to be found. I asked Cindy where they were. "Joel is on patrol. Last time I checked, Ms. Hardy was in your office," she said. "Something in the mail got her all excited."

I walked back. Karen sat in my chair, smiling.

"What are you so happy about?" I asked.

"This," she said, handing me a cardboard-bound notebook. The cover was a splotchy black-and-white pattern. In the upper right-hand corner was a strip of adhesive tape bearing the initials "C.F."

"Is that what I think it is?"

She handed me a slip of paper. "It came with this."

I opened the notebook. My excitement died a quick death. Inside was page after page of chicken scratches. I thumbed through it, but couldn't make out a single word.

"What is this?" I asked.

"Read the note."

"Dear Emmett," it said. *"This notebook contains everything I've learned so far about Carrie and her family. Sorry for it being in shorthand. Old habit. After parting company tonight, I realized this would be safer in your hands. Yours, John Smith."*

"Where'd it come from?" I asked.

"The postman brought it a few minutes ago."

"Do you still have the envelope?" She handed it over. It was postmarked Norman, OK, March 15th, 1979, the morning John and Chastity were killed.

Karen said, "John must've dropped this in the mail right after you left them that night."

I remembered something John said in the Henny Penny's parking lot: If we couldn't get together the next day, he'd mail it. I must've convinced him that I intended to go home, and he decided to do it that night.

For the first time since this had all started, I felt optimistic. Nobody had found John's notes because he'd already mailed them. To us. He obviously didn't feel comfortable holding on to the notebook, apparently for good reason, since a few hours after dropping it in the mail, he and his fiancée were dead.

But the killer hadn't found the notebook, and now we had it. Hopefully something in it would help us find the son of a bitch.

CHAPTER TEN

Karen can read shorthand a little bit, but she's nowhere near being fluent. I don't read it at all, of course, and neither do Cindy or Joel, so it fell on her shoulders.

Quitting time came and went. We locked up and headed for home. I whipped up a box of Kraft Macaroni and Cheese, and we sat down to eat.

"This looks like a case for Nancy Drew," I said, wolfing down my half of the gloppy orange mess.

"Did Nancy Drew know shorthand?" she asked.

"Don't remember," I said, "but you do."

Scoffing, she held her finger and thumb a sixteenth of an inch apart. "This much. *Maybe.*"

"That's more than me."

"Don't you think we should take it to an expert?"

I didn't like the idea of some civilian reading through it. "I'd rather keep it in the family."

"You could hand it over to that detective in Norman. Or the OSBI."

"Nope."

"So I guess that leaves me."

"Yup. If you wouldn't mind."

She sighed. "I'll give it a try, but it might take a while."

"I'm not worried."

"That makes one of us."

She switched off the kitchen light. "Alright," she said with a sigh. "But not tonight."

"Why, you got plans for the evening?"

"I've got plans to *sleep,* is what I've got plans to do. I've been up since five o'clock."

"Oh, ok, ok," I said. "Tomorrow's fine.

***

We drove to work together the next day. It was my turn to go in early, but Red wanted to get started cracking John's puzzle.

I let her work in my office so that she'd have some peace and quiet. Joel wasn't scheduled to come in until noon, so whatever calls that came in would be my responsibility.

Bernard Cousins, the Tilghman County sheriff's deputy who patrols Burr and its environs during the overnight hours, stopped by at 7:00 am, as usual. He filled me in on what happened during his shift, which was basically a whole lot of nothing. I treated him to breakfast at McDonald's. Bernard had known John a little bit, so I told him where things stood on his killing, until he got so sleepy he couldn't keep his eyes open. I sent him home, then went back to the station. Karen was at the front desk, bent over John's notebook.

"I think I found something," she said. Using magnifying glass, and a ruler to keep her place, she peered closely at the page. "If I'm reading this right," she said, "it looks like Carrie's mother was named Zelda, and she had an uncle named Bazil—spelled with a 'z'."

"Is he rich?"

"Doesn't say."

"I'm impressed you figured that out so quick"

"So am I," she said. "This place is a waste of my talent. I should be working for the FBI."

"Any idea where to find these people?'

"Not specifically, but it does say where the family comes from."

"Where?"

"Flat-Nose, Texas."

"You don't say?" The last time I saw him, John hinted Carrie was from around here, but Flat-Nose? I wouldn't have imagined that.

"I do say. If John got it right, Carrie grew up right over the Texas border in Longabaugh County."

***

To hear me talk, you might think Tilghman County is home to mostly cows, sheep, and prairie dogs. That is not strictly correct. While I see scores of cows and sheep every day of my life, in all the years I've lived here I've never seen a prairie dog.

It is true that there was a time when we were Oklahoma's most sparsely populated county, but it's also true that, thanks mostly to the oil boom in the early part of this decade, the county's population has surpassed 8,000 actual human beings. I know that doesn't sound like much, but compared to Longabaugh County, we're practically stacked on top of each other, gasping for air.

According the 1970 U. S. Census of Population Report—a bound copy of which I keep on a bookshelf in my office, alongside a paperback version of *The Grapes of Wrath* signed by the author, and a 1952 *Farmer's Almanac* that neither I nor my predecessor as police chief ever got around to throwing away—Longabaugh County, Texas, used to be home to 1,237 people (I doubt that number is any bigger today; in fact, it's probably shrunk). It's located in the Texas panhandle, directly across the border from Tilghman County, and boasts a population density of one-and-a-half persons for every one of its 800 square miles.

Legend says the county was named after Harry Longabaugh— better known as the Sundance Kid, of Butch Cassidy & the Sundance Kid fame. Local historians dispute this, despite the fact that almost every town in the county is named for various members of Cassidy's Wild Bunch: Elzy (Lay), Flat-Nose (Curry), Bullion (for Laura Bullion, a female member of the gang), and Carver (for William "News" Carver, so nicknamed because he loved seeing his name in newspaper articles about the gang's exploits).

Also, the county seat is named Cassidy, so I'll let you be the judge.

I'd heard of Flat-Nose, but had never been there. Like a lot of my fellow Tilghman County residents, I'd hardly ever stepped foot in Longabaugh County, despite the fact it's directly adjacent to Tilghman County. Sometimes we treat the border separating Oklahoma and Texas like a brick wall instead the imaginary line it really is. Which is not to say that Texas is off-limits to Oklahomans, and vice versa, although maybe that should be the case.

Texans and Oklahomans don't like each other

Once, when I was in my teens, a high school football player from Temple City raped a young woman from Cassidy and left her for dead on the Texas side of the border. A gang of white Texans hunted down the rapist. They scalped him, cut out his tongue, cut off his head, ran it up the flagpole in front of the Tilghman County courthouse, then crossed back into Texas without being captured. Everyone knew the identities of the perpetrators—even today, I could probably recite the list—but the State of Texas refused to extradite them.

The rapist was dead, so no one was ever convicted of either offense—although, for some reason, a gang of angry whites from our side of the border lynched a Mexican vaquero with no connection to either crime.

Once Red told me the Fitzjarrald family came from Flat-Nose, my immediate impulse was to jump in my truck and cross over into Texas—that is, until I realized that at best I only had a general idea where Flat-Nose was.

Kate Hennessey, the librarian at the Burr Public Library, has helped me numerous times over the years, so I drive to the library to see if she could help. She listened to my request, then dug around and until she unearthed an old Texaco roadmap for the Texas panhandle.

I asked if I could borrow it, she let me, although she made sure I knew that they don't normally lend reference materials. Kate's a stickler with just about everyone except me. Red thinks it's a crush, but I know for a fact she's wrong, because Kate's seeing Joel on the sly. They're keeping it under wraps for now, since he's black and she's white, and the entire town would go crazy if they knew.

I radioed the station to let them know where I was going, then stopped at home and changed into civvies. After studying the map for a few minutes, I felt I had a good idea where to go. I headed out.

There wasn't a "Welcome to Texas" sign when I crossed the border. The road I used was too puny. I didn't know which state I was in until the road signs changed shape.

It had been years since I'd last been in Longabaugh County. It was always sparsely populated, but it seemed even more deserted than I remembered. I drove for miles without seeing anything man-made, aside from a few pumpjacks and shotgun shacks; most of the pumpjacks were rusted tight, and the shacks seemed permanently uninhabited. On every side the land was dirt, rocks, and brush. Unfarmable, by the looks of it.

I left the state highway where the map told me to, just outside of Elzy. As soon as I did, it started raining. Longabaugh County's roads were just a layer of gypsum bulldozed into red clay, so when they got wet, they turned slicker than snot. I drive for miles without exceeding 15 mph.

Eventually, I crossed a set of railroad tracks and xame upon a metal sign riddled with bullet holes, The words were almost too faint to read.

It said, "Flat-Nose, Texas, Pop. 12."

I swiveled my head for a look around, and decided that number was a little high.

There weren't any people around. Except for a rusty water tower, there were only a few abandoned man-made structures.

The first to catch my eye was a two-story red brick building with a sculpture of an eagle over the entrance. Below the eagle were the initials F.O.E., which I knew stood for "Fraternal Order of Eagles." Every window was broken, so the interior had been exposed to the elements for who knows how long. The rain had eased up, so I got out of my truck and peeked in. I saw what looked to be a broken-down stage, flanked by a long bar, with rusty beer taps and shelves of broken whisky bottles. Those Eagles must really like to drink.

A few yards away was a small, square structure made of rough-hewn bricks and corrugated metal. I've crisscrossed Oklahoma enough times to recognize it as an old-fashioned jail, the kind where anyone curious enough could go by and peek at the local miscreants.

Across the street and catty-corner to the jail was an abandoned Skelly gas station—the old kind, built out of bricks and mortar, with a narrow driveway running between the building and the pair of rusted pumps. Next door to it was a small, abandoned wood building with a sign that said, "General Store."

That was it for downtown Flat-Nose.

I got back in my truck and drove the side streets. They were in decent enough shape, but strangely enough, there weren't any houses, just empty lots. Some had a concrete foundation where a house used to be, but there weren't any now. I wondered if maybe a chemical spill at the nearby railroad crossing had caused a mass evacuation. I reckon I probably would've heard about it if there had been, but you never know.

In any case, it was eerie as hell.

I consulted the map again, looking for a dot on it big enough to denote the presence of human beings. Unfortunately, all the dots were the same size as the one for Flat-Nose. I barely knew which way was up, never mind north or south, so I just picked a direction and started driving, hoping I might eventually run into someone who answered to the name Fitzjarrald.

After a few minutes I came upon a small country store about a mile from downtown Flat-Nose. In front was a pair of gas pumps. The building itself was constructed of pre-fabricated metal. It looked brand new. There was a pole for a sign, but no sign. Instead, a piece of cardboard on the front door read, "Pop's Gas and Go."

I needed gas, so I pulled up to the pump and waited for someone to come out and fill my tank. I soon realized this was one of those self-serve places that I am philosophically opposed to. Ordinarily, I'd have taken my business elsewhere, but my gauge was sitting on E. I reckoned I'd have to swallow my pride and pump it myself.

I grabbed the nozzle, before noticing a handwritten sign taped to the pump: "Pay First, Pump Later." I went inside.

The interior smelled like fresh paint and burnt coffee. Unpacked boxes were stacked everywhere. Behind the counter was an old fella who looked like he'd eaten fried cactus for breakfast.

"Are you Pop?" I asked.

"No, I ain't Pop, goddammit."

"Sorry," I said. "I figured that since the name of the place was Pop's—"

"—and I'm so old," he sneered, "you reckoned I must be Pop. Well, I ain't."

"Excuse me, my mistake."

The mass of wrinkles on his caved-in face, and the white film over his eyes told me he had to be at least 80. Why wouldn't I think he was Pop?

"Well, what the hell do you want?" he snapped. "Gas?"

As patient as I tend to be with the elderly, this fella had me wanting to walk out and never come back, which I might've done, if I wasn't so low on gas and hadn't needed help—any help at all—in finding me a Fitzjarrald.

For all I knew, this fella could've been one, himself.

"Yes," I said. "I'd like some gas."

"How much?"

"I'd like to fill it up."

"Leave me a twenty and I'll give you change."

"It's not going to take 20 dollars' worth."

"Well, if it don't," he said, his voice rising in pitch and volume, "I'll give you your goddam *change!*"

I handed him a twenty and went out to fill my tank.

I finished, and went back and told the old fella, "Eight-sixty's worth."

"I know how much it took!" he scowled, then slammed my change on the counter so hard it rattled.

I pocketed it. "By the way," I said, "would you know of anyone around here named Fitzjarrald?"

I didn't really expect an answer, but I reckoned it couldn't hurt to ask.

To my surprise, the old fella said, "There's Sheilah Fitzjarrald."

Sheilah Fitzjarrald. Carrie Fitzjarrald. Had to be the same family. My heart beat a little faster.

"I don't suppose you'd know where I could find her?"

"I do, but it'll cost you 20 dollars."

I took out my wallet and started to take out one of the twenties I'd gotten from Wes Harmon the day before.

"No, goddammit!" the old fella shouted. "I don't want your goddam money, but she sure as hell will!" I just stared, not knowing what he was talking about. Obviously angry that I didn't understand his meaning, he leaned across the counter and spat: "She's a whore! Works out of that dang ol' whorehouse trailer over by the state line!"

I suddenly remembered the last time I'd been to Longabaugh County.

Back in '65, Bernard Cousins were on patrol, and I stumbled across the body of a dead black girl. After some investigation, we discovered she was a prostitute working out of what I now assumed was Pop Johnson's "whorehouse trailer." Parked very near if not always directly *on* the Oklahoma/Texas border, it once catered mostly to truckers driving the east-and-west route between Amarillo and Oklahoma City. Another one of the prostitutes working there helped us solve the case.

I had not been back since.

"I'm surprised that place is still in business," I said.

Meanwhile, the old fella had turned his back. He seemed to be putting something in his mouth.

Suddenly, he turned around and grinned, showing me a set of glossy-white fake choppers. "Hell yes, it's still in business!" he lisped, grinning like a demon, his cataract-clouded eyes bugging out of his head. "I go there on weekends to wet my wick. Put in these here teeth and them gals don't even know the difference!"

When I didn't respond, he leaned across the counter again and sprayed coffee-colored saliva in my face. "You think I can't?" he hollered. "You think I'm too old to get my wick wet? I'll tell you one thing, it'll be a cold day in hell when Pop Johnson can't get his wick wet!"

"But you said you weren't Pop," I muttered.

Sputtering with rage, the old fella pulled out a tin of Copenhagen and licked out the contents down to the last speck, causing him to gag, which I took as my signal to leave.

"Thanks for your help," I said. I could still hear him retch while I walked to my truck. The last thing I heard him yell was: "Go to hell!"

I think he was talking to me.

CHAPTER ELEVEN

I'd always thought of the trailer as Yvette's, the young woman who helped us on the case. She wasn't the boss or the madam, just someone slightly older who the younger girls working there looked up to.

It wasn't hers, though. In fact, it never had a name that I know of. People just called it what Pops did, or a rough approximation thereof: "the whorehouse trailer over by the state line."

Maybe folks reckoned if they didn't have a name for it, they could pretend it wasn't there.

But it *was* there, and everyone knew it. Prior to the aforementioned case, I had no dealings with it. It wasn't on my patch, so policing it was a county matter. It was parked in the parking lot of a diner located very near the state line on what at one time was a heavily traveled highway.

When I say "very near" the state line, I mean it went back and forth. The diner itself and part of the parking lot were officially located in Oklahoma; the rest of the parking lot extended into Texas. The trailer often moved from one side of the border to the other, depending on which state's law enforcement had its hand out.

I first visited it while investigating a murder. One of my officers and I found the body of a young black woman with her throat cut on the railroad tracks just outside Burr. At the time, Burr hadn't had a murder on the books since long before I became chief. The Oklahoma State Bureau of Investigation took charge, but in the end, my people and I did most of the heavy lifting.

The victim was a prostitute. Her name was Cheryl. We tracked down her place of employment to the whorehouse on the state line. She met the guy who killed her through her work. Fell in love with him, in fact. His daddy was rich. I guess he told her pretty stories about how he was going to take her away from all this, but instead cut her throat in a fit of jealousy. How he expected her to be faithful, given the business she was in, I never could figure out.

Yvette had tried looking after Cheryl, but there wasn't much she could've done. I kept in touch with her for a while after we'd sent the killer to jail, but it'd been years since I'd seen either her, or her place of business.

Now that I think of it, maybe the reason I was so affected by Carrie's situation is because she seemed so similar to Cheryl. Carrie wasn't a prostitute, and she wasn't murdered, but they were about the same age when they died. Both suffered abuse: Cheryl, at the hands of her "fiancée;" Carrie, by the whole world, but specifically by who*ever* it was—maybe a male relative, an uncle, if Chastity's information could be trusted—who raped and mutilated her.

I'd never driven to the brothel from the Texas side of the state line, always from Oklahoma, so finding it turned into an adventure. I knew the Oklahoma name of the highway it was on, but the road turns into something else once you cross into Texas. It took me a while, but I eventually found it. Part of me expected that Pop Johnson had been hallucinating, and that it had gone the way of the Flat-Nose chapter of The Fraternal Order of Eagles.

But no, there it was, as big as life: now painted a sickly shade of pink instead of the sickly shade of green it used to be.

That wasn't the only change. The last time I'd been there, it was parked in the diner's parking lot on the Texas side of the border. Now the diner had been abandoned. The trailer was parked next to it, on the Oklahoma side. It was no longer mobile. The wheels had been removed and it was mounted on cinderblocks.

I parked and got out of my truck. I noticed someone pulling aside a curtain and peeking out a window, then heard a loud girlish squeal. The door burst open. A woman in a light blue terrycloth bathrobe hurtled down the steps, threw herself into my arms, and kissed me full on the lips.

"Emmett Hardy, is that you?" the woman said.

I had to smile. "Hey, Yvette."

She backed away and looked me over. "You haven't changed a bit."

"Neither have you," I said, which wasn't any truer than when she said it to me. She did look good, though. "I didn't expect you'd still be here."

"Sure, I'm here!" she said. "I'm the boss. Little ol' Yvette's a small business owner!"

"Well, good for you," I said, without really meaning it. I'd always liked Yvette and would've liked to believe she'd gotten out of the sex-for-money biz. Hopefully, being the boss meant she was able to pick her spots, so to speak. To be honest, if I'd really thought she'd still be there, I'd have sent Joel.

Not that I have anything against Yvette. It's just that she never tried to hide her affection for me. That got me in trouble with Karen. Yvette had always made it clear she'd be happy to share her job-related expertise with me. Needless to say, I never took her up on it. I told Karen about it the first time it happened, back when we were working that case I mentioned. We weren't married at the time, weren't even dating, in fact. We were still more like buddies. I thought she'd think it was funny. She pretended to that first time but stopped being amused when it kept happening. I eventually quit telling her whenever I had to talk to Yvette.

Am I overexplaining? Maybe I am.

I will just add: It didn't help that Karen and Yvette share a good number of physical characteristics in common.

"Does this mean you've finally come to your senses and realized little ol' Yvette's the girl for you?" she said in a baby-doll voice.

I tried to peel her off without being too obvious about it. "I reckon you didn't hear the news," I said. "I'm happily married now."

With a lascivious wink, she said, "So are most of my customers." Hooking her arm through mine, she said, "Come inside. Let's catch up."

As far as I can remember, I'd only been in that trailer once, although I still had a pretty fair recollection of what it looked like. Yvette had spruced it up. Back then, the only decorations were a few Playboy centerfolds taped to the walls. Now, there were framed art prints of ballet dancers and old-timey ladies doing the can-can. The ratty furniture I remembered had been replaced by red velvet couches and chairs. Strands of Christmas tree lights used to line the hall leading to the bedrooms. They'd been replaced by electric candles with tiny flame-shaped bulbs.

The place still looked like what it was, but of a higher quality.

Yvette had changed, too. She didn't slather on the make-up as heavily as she once did, although it was still early in the day. The lines on her face and the flecks of gray in her reddish-brown hair didn't make her look old, but gave her a worldly, sophisticated look—more Sophia Loren and less Jayne Mansfield. Her wardrobe had changed, too. She used to emphasize her physical assets by putting them more or less on full display, wearing the tiniest shorts and the most revealing tops. Now, as I could see when she casually let that terrycloth robe fall open, her look was a little more modest and refined. Her hairstyle was different, too; she wore it looser, letting it hang just below her shoulders. She and Karen still resembled one another; Yvette's job just required that she show a little bit more skin.

She sat down in an easy chair across from me and crossed her legs, exposing the top of one black stocking attached to a garter belt. I sat across from her on the couch and tried not to notice.

"So who'd you marry?" she asked. "Not that red-haired dispatcher y'all used to have?"

"She's the one," I said.

"I should've known," she said, pretending to pout. "She never liked me anyway."

"So how have you been?" I asked.

She lit a cigarette, a Virginia Slims, the same brand Destiny and Chastity smoked. "Surviving. Barely."

"I would've thought you'd moved on."

She shook her head emphatically. "Well, I didn't. Like I said, I'm my own boss. I could never go back to working for someone else."

I knew that "someone else" meant "pimp." I'd always thought Yvette was tough enough not to need one.

"So now that you're the boss, does that mean you've retired from active duty?"

"Not completely," she said. "I still cater to a few select gentlemen. By appointment only." Licking her lips, she leaned forward, rested her elbow on her knee and her chin in her hand. "In fact, I've got an opening this afternoon, if you're interested."

"You're a hard gal to turn down," I said, trying to laugh it off, "but I just came here looking for somebody."

She'd obviously expected me to say that. "Somebody besides me, you mean."

"Don't get me wrong," I said. "It's great to see you, but ... yeh."

She sat up straight, in the process covering the semi-exposed leg. "Who're you looking for?"

"A girl by the name of Sheilah Fitzjarrald."

"Why are you looking for her? Is she in trouble?"

"You know her?"

She ground out her cigarette. "You answer my question, I'll answer yours."

"Fair enough," I said. "She's not in any trouble, at least that I know of. I'm looking for a male member of her family, and I thought she might be able to help."

"I've never heard of Sheilah Fitzjarrald, but I do have a girl working for me named *Zelda* Fitzgerald."

"You sure that's her real name? Zelda?"

She smirked. "It probably isn't. A lot of my girls use fake names."

"Could her real name be Sheilah?"

"I suppose."

"Any idea how she spells her last name?"

"I don't ask to see their birth certificates."

"Any chance you could introduce her to me?"

"Only if you promise me she's not in trouble."

I held up my right hand. "I swear."

"Ok," she said. "Come back tonight."

"I will." I stood to go.

"What?" she exclaimed, surprised. "You just got here!"

"If my wife finds out I've been here at all, I'm in big trouble."

"She still doesn't like you talking to me, I guess."

"Well," I said, "you haven't come up in conversation for a while, so I can't say for sure, but I'd just as soon not find out."

"Oh well," she said, "I've got a customer coming anyway."

Hooking her arm through mine once again, she walked out the door. "Who told you Zelda works for me, anyway?"

"Some nasty old buzzard who runs a store over by Flat-Nose. I told him I was looking for members of the Fitzjarrald family. He mentioned this Sheilah, said she works here."

"What's this guy look like?"

I wanted to say, *an animated corpse,* but settled for, "Like Don Knotts, only not as good looking, and about 30 year older. And he wears false teeth, although maybe not all the time."

She grinned and nodded. "Yeh, I know that guy. He comes in once a month or so."

I got into my truck.

"What time should I be here?" I asked through the open window.

"I don't expect any drive-ups until it starts getting dark," she said. "Around 7:00 should be fine."

"So, how is it, being a businesswoman?"

"Tough," she said, leaning up against the door. "Not many truckers come through anymore, not since they opened up I-40. That's why I got this place so cheap." She looked off into the distance. "Probably not the greatest decision I ever made," she said, as if weighing the consequences, "although it's still better than working on Lincoln Boulevard." Lincoln Boulevard is OKC's red-light district.

"Why'd you take the wheels off the trailer?" I asked. "Now it's got to stay in Oklahoma."

She made a disgusted face. "Oh, the Texas cops started getting greedy, so when the diner closed, I had it hauled over here and mounted on blocks. Okie cops are nicer, and they don't charge as much." She pulled the robe tight around her—there was a chill in the air—and looked up and down the road in both directions. "You know, I've got a special customer due any minute."

"Then I should get out of your hair."

Her smile was too sad to look at. "Are you doing ok?" I asked.

"I guess so," she said with a shrug. "Heck, I don't know." Her eyes started to water.

"Maybe you should find another line of work."

She wiped away a tear. "I don't know what else I'd do."

"Wait tables," I said. "Work at McDonald's. There's got to be something."

"I don't know," she said. "I'm too old to start over."

If anything, she was too old to be doing what she was doing, but I kept that thought to myself.

Suddenly, I heard the sound of a car engine. A bronze Cadillac wheeled into the parking lot. "That's him," she said. "I've got to get inside." She leaned through the open window and gave me an awkward hug. Like always when Yvette shows me affection, I pulled away a little bit.

She frowned. "When are you going to learn I don't bite?"

With an embarrassed grin, I said, "Maybe I don't trust myself."

She smirked. "Well, it was good to see you."

"I'll be back tonight."

"You'd better be."

"I will," I said, knowing I probably shouldn't. As I learned a long time ago, the best way to avoid temptation is to stay clear of it.

Driving away, I watched in my rearview mirror as Yvette greeted her client. The way she treated him didn't seem a whole lot different from the way she treated me.

CHAPTER TWELVE

I spent the drive back to Burr trying not to think about how sad it was to see Yvette stuck in the same old rut.

I preferred to focus on what to do next. I wondered what it meant that Carrie was from Flat-Nose, especially as it related to her having killed Burt Murray. We knew Leon Qualls traveled from Norman to Burr with the idea of seeing his rich grandfather. We always assumed Carrie had simply followed him, but could she have also come to visit family? Flat-Nose was pretty close to Burr.

Red was still sitting at my desk when I got back to the station, poring over John's notebook. "Any new discoveries?" I asked.

She looked up at me and seemed to do a double take. "It looks like John mapped out Carrie's family tree," she said, looking at me strangely. "According to this, her mother was named Zelda Fitzjarrald."

"What about her father?"

"He hadn't figured that out yet."

"If Carrie had the same last name as her mother, that probably means her mother never married the father."

"Agreed," said Karen. "Zelda also had two brothers. Bazil and Hazil."

"No sisters?"

"Not according to what John wrote," she said, still eyeing me in a peculiar way. "Why do you ask?"

"Because I got a lead on someone named Zelda Fitzjarrald, although I suspect her first name might be Sheilah." I told her about my encounter with Pops Johnson, and how he steered me to the trailer house brothel.

"I'm surprised that thing's still around."

"It is still around, and you'll never guess who's running it."

"Your old girlfriend?"

"If you mean Yvette, that's right."

"Oh, ok," she said, like all of a sudden she understood something she hadn't before.

"What does that mean, 'Oh, ok?'"

She waved the question aside. "Nothing," she said. "So this Sheilah works for Yvette?"

"Right."

She tapped on the table with a pencil. "You think this Sheilah could be Carrie's cousin?"

"Her cousin, her mother ... I don't know how they're related," I said. "I just reckon they are. Hopefully I'll find out when I talk to her tonight."

"You're going back out there?"

"Don't worry," I said. "I'll take Joel with me."

"I'm not worried," she said. "She doesn't have anything I haven't got."

There was an awkward pause. She turned her attention back to the notebook

I said, "It was sad to see Yvette still doing what she does."

"As long as she's not doing it with you, I don't care one way or the other."

"Oh, come on. You've got to feel bad for her."

"I guess."

"At least she's gone up in the world."

"Ha!" she erupted. "Because she owns the place? Her parents must be so proud!"

She glanced up at me, then looked away.

I reckoned now would be a good time to drop the subject. "Ok then, I'll leave you to it."

Before I got to the door, she said, "How's she look?"

"Yvette? Like she used to. A little older."

"Gray hair?"

"A few. She told me she's mostly retired." Knowing how she used to feel when the subject of Yvette came up, I said, "Listen, you've got about as much to worry about with her as I do with that fella on Knot's Landing."

"Maybe," she said, "but Ted Shackleford's not leaving lipstick marks on my face."

She tapped her cheek. I rubbed mine. My hand came away red.

"Why didn't you say something?"

"I wanted to see if you'd confess," she said. "You did, so you're off the hook." She got back to her deciphering. I'm pretty sure that if she had a victory cigar handy, she'd have lit one up.

***

I collared Joel in the outer office. "Feel like earning some overtime?" I said.

"You're paying overtime now?" he said.

"No, but I do have something I need your help with." I told him about my pending trip to Yvette's trailer.

"You think this Zelda woman is related to Carrie?"

"That's what I aim to find out."

"Sure, I'll go," he said. "But I'd better clear it with the boss first."

"I already told Mrs. Hardy."

"Not her," he said. "Kate."

Since I didn't want any of our vehicles—including my truck—to be seen parked in front of the brother, we took Joel's blue and white

Chevy Silverado. The library was closed for the day, so we drove by Kate's house. I stayed in the car while Joel went in to secure her approval. Kate was fine with it; she always likes to lend a hand to our investigations.

I'd never ridden in Joel's Silverado. "Nice truck," I said.

"Gets me where I want to go."

"A bicycle will get you want to go, and it won't cost four thousand dollars."

"True," he said, "but you can't listen to Charlie Parker on a bicycle." He reached into a box next to him and pulled out a cassette tape. "*Bird with Strings*," he said as he plugged it into the truck's tape player. It's not my favorite Charlie Parker record, but it's better than anything we could've dialed up on the car radio. The sound quality was even better than my home stereo.

Part of the reason I brought Joel along was in case I ran into trouble; I probably wouldn't, but you never know: a nervous customer thinking he might be arrested could panic and do something rash. Mainly, though, I brought him to act as a buffer between me and the girls working there. Joel's flat-out the handsomest man I've ever met and therefore more likely to attract their attention.

There was a single semi parked outside when we arrived. "In the old days," I said to Joel, "there'd be trucks lined up half a mile down the highway with fellas waiting to get in." That was a little bit of an exaggeration, but it still surprised me to see just one lonely White-Freightliner instead of the three or four big rigs that in the old days always seemed to be waiting for service.

The porch light glowed red. I knocked. A young woman with black hair wearing a slinky red satin robe opened the door a crack. "May I help you, officer?" she said.

"Don't worry, young lady," I said. "My name is Emmett, and I'm here to speak with Yvette. She's expecting us."

The gal yelled, "Yvette, there's a cop here to see you! Says his name is Emmett!"

A voice called out, "Let him in!"

The girl opened the door wider. I guess she hadn't seen Joel standing behind me; when he followed me in, she said, "And who is this?" in a tone you might use if someone unexpectedly gave you a brand-new Rolls-Royce.

"This is my friend Joel," I said.

The black-haired girl and a scantily clad young blond I hadn't noticed said in unison: "Hel-lo Joel!"

The black-haired girl invited us to take a seat, then walked down the hall to the back of the trailer. Sitting cross from us, the barely dressed blond pretended to read a copy of *People* magazine while sneaking looks at Joel. Gals used to look at me like that.

Yvette appeared after about a minute. Instead of what I thought of as her work clothes, Yvette was wearing a dress with an African-looking pattern. It reached all the way to the floor, hiding her shape.

"Who's this?" she asked, smiling at Joel. I introduced him, and she introduced the two other girls. The black-haired girl called herself Baby, and the blond, Crystal. All of them—even Yvette, maybe even *especially* Yvette—were obviously enraptured by Joel.

Just then, a disheveled-looking gentleman in a flannel shirt and a Miller High-Life cap stumbled into the room. He stopped cold when he saw Joel and me in our uniforms.

"Don't worry, Henry," said Yvette. "These gentlemen are friends of ours."

"Pleased to know you," he grumbled as he bolted out the door. Crystal and Baby giggled.

"Joel," I said, "how 'bout you entertain these nice ladies while Yvette and I go in the back room and have a talk."

"Sure, chief, no problem."

Yvette led me to a small, dimly lit bedroom. A full-sized four-poster bed took up almost all the floor space. The spread was made of quilted white satin. Matching pillows were lined up along the headboard. The wallpaper was pink with a pattern of fuzzy red hearts. On the bedstand, a lava lamp glowed, the goo inside dancing like a ballerina.

We sat side-by-side on the bed. "I couldn't help but notice that neither of those gals out there is named Zelda," I said.

She looked pained. "I think I might've messed up, Emmett."

"Uh oh."

"After you left this afternoon, I called Zelda and told her you were here looking for her."

"What did she say?"

"She was just quiet for a second, then said she was glad I called because she was sick and wouldn't be in."

I can't honestly say I was surprised.

"Do you think she'll be here tomorrow?"

"I don't know," Yvette said with a shrug. "Sometimes girls disappear, and I never see them again."

"Right," I said. "I don't suppose you knew where she lives?"

"I think Temple City, but I'm not sure."

"So you don't have her address."

"No," she said, seeming about ready to cry. "But I do have her phone number." She produced a pen but had nothing to write on. "Give me your hand," she said and wrote down a number with a Temple City exchange. "Emmett, I'm so sorry," she said once more. "Maybe she really was sick. Maybe she'll be in tomorrow."

Back in the living room, the blond was talking a mile a minute about something. Joel smiled and nodded, but I could tell he was just trying to be polite. He stood up when he saw me. The two girls on the couch made little sounds of disappointment, like they didn't want us to go.

More likely, they didn't want Joel to go.

"Don't worry," said Yvette. "They'll be back tomorrow. Won't you, Chief Hardy?"

"Sure."

Yvette cupped my face in her hands and gave my head a little shake. "You swear?" she said.

"I swear."

She kissed me on the cheek.

We showed ourselves out.

In the truck, I asked Joel if that kiss of Yvette's had left any traces.

"You mean lipstick?" he said, peering closely at my face. "Nah, nothing."

After a few minutes of not saying much, Joel came out with, "That Yvette looks a lot like Mrs. Hardy."

"Huh," I replied. "I never noticed."

***

Speaking of Mrs. Hardy, Red wasn't in a great mood when I got home. I started to tell her about our visit and how Yvette had accidentally scared Zelda/Sheilah away, but she pretended to be too busy with housework to sit and listen. I followed her from room to room, asking her what I'd done wrong, even though I knew darn well what this was about. Eventually she went to bed, leaving me alone in the living room.

The next morning at breakfast she acted as if nothing had happened, which was fine with me. Later in the morning, I called the number Yvette had written on my hand. Nobody answered. I tried several more times as they day progressed. No luck. That night I went back to Yvette's without Joel. Yvette still hadn't heard from the girl *she* called Zelda, but who *I* thought of as Sheilah.

I repeated the process the next day with the same results. At the trailer that evening, Yvette seemed less glad to see me. She told me she'd already given up on Zelda and hired a replacement. The new girl called herself Terry, and she looked awful young. I checked her ID. If she was below the age of consent, I would've stepped in, but her driver's license said her name was indeed Terry and that she was 21. Still young, but old enough to make her own decisions. I chose not to intervene.

Yvette escorted me to my truck. "It's been great to see you, Emmett," she said in a way that implied our reunion had run its course. I told her it was good to see her, as well, and asked her to give me a call if Zelda showed up. "She won't, but if she does, I'll call. Ok, then. See you later." Without so much as a peck on the cheek, she turned and went back inside.

I drove away feeling a little sad.

CHAPTER THIRTEEN

Red didn't make tons of progress on John's notes the next morning. Instead, she spent several hours filling out paperwork that we are required by the State of Oklahoma to submit if we want to keep our doors open. After lunch, however, she found a lot.

"It looks like the father of the Fitzjarrald clan was named Harald," she began. "Harald married a woman named Mamie Elendar. They had at least three kids—two sons, Hazil and Bazil, and a daughter, Zelda. Hazil was the oldest, and Zelda was the youngest. The name Sheilah Fitzjarrald pops up, too, but John's not sure of her relationship to Harald and Mamie. Could be their daughter, could be their granddaughter."

"Ok, let me get this straight. The Fitzjarrald paterfamilias—"

"Wait," she said. "What in heck does that mean?"

"It means the male head of the family."

"Where'd you hear that?"

"A book I'm reading about English history," I said. "Now, do you mind?"

"No, go ahead."

"The male head of the family is Harald Fitzjarrald. Harald married Mamie Elendar, and they had three kids: two sons, Hazil and Bazil, and a daughter, Zelda. Am I right so far?"

She nodded. "Please continue."

"There's also a family member named Sheilah, but we don't know where she fits in, only that her last name is Fitzjarrald, so she must be related somehow."

"You got it," she said.

"So are any of them still alive?"

"Don't know about Mamie, but Harald's long gone, apparently. Looks he was a real piece of work."

"What do you mean?"

"John suspected he was sleeping with his daughter Zelda and whoever this Sheilah was."

The thought almost made me lose my lunch, and I hadn't even had it yet.

"How does Carrie fit into this?" I asked.

"John doesn't seem to know exactly," she said, thumbing through the pages. "If I were to guess, I'd say she was Zelda's daughter, which would make her Mamie and Harald's granddaughter."

I considered how that might tie-in with John's and Chastity's murders. Being exposed as someone who has sex with his daughter would be enough to ruin a man's reputation—if he were still alive and had a reputation to lose. Neither was true of Harald Fitzjarrald.

Red said, almost apologetically, "To be honest, Emmett, I'm not sure this the most promising line of inquiry."

"What do you mean?"

"I mean that supposing John and his fiancée were killed to keep them quiet about an attack on Carrie seems kind of far-fetched," she said. "For one thing, Carrie's dead, and even if she were alive, she wasn't exactly the kind of person who people take seriously. Let's say John did put it in a book or a newspaper or magazine article; the attacker could just deny it. It's not as if Carrie would be around to support the story."

I confessed to having the same thought. "But I'm not going to give up on it just yet. I can't shake the feeling that there's some connection between this family and what happened to John and Chastity."

As for the brothers, Red had deciphered about a third of the notebook and hadn't found anything in it about them becoming rich, or famous, or powerful. She did discover one important thing, however: Bazil Fitzjarrald lived Eureka Springs, Arkansas.

"Bazil's the middle kid, right?" I said.

"Right. Hazil was the oldest, Zelda the youngest."

"It might be a good idea to talk to him," I said, meaning Bazil. "I don't suppose you've had time to call around and try to locate any of the other Fitzjarralds."

"As a matter of fact, I have. I contacted the highway patrol to see if any of them had been arrested, the Department of Motor Vehicles to see if any of them had a car registered in their name, the Department of Education to see if any of them had attended a school in the state, plus pretty much every other state agency that keeps track of people. None of them had a dang thing that would help."

"What about Texas?" I asked.

"The State of Texas says we have to go through proper channels.."

"What are the proper channels?"

"When I figure it out, I'll let you know." She paused, then added, "You know, Emmett, it might not be a bad idea to tell that Detective Blanchard what we've figured out."

"Nah, that's not something I'm inclined to do."

"I knew you'd say that," she said, "so listen: I've got a friend on the Eureka Springs police force. I called her and asked if she'd ever heard of Bazil Fitzjarrald. She hadn't heard of him, but she did manage to dig up a phone number and an address."

"Did you try calling him?"

"I was waiting for you to get here."

We dialed. The number had been disconnected. That could either mean he'd moved, or perhaps neglected to pay his phone bill. Either way, it was doubtful I'd find him at that address.

But it was more likely I'd find him *there* than I would sitting around *here*.

"I'm going to Eureka Springs."

Red groaned. "Come on, Emmett. What if he's moved? How're you going to find him then?"

"I'll deal with that if or when it happens."

Red grudgingly assured me that she and Joel could handle things in my absence. Seeing that we had plenty of daylight left, I figured I might as well get underway. But first I had a few things to do.

I drove my truck to Wes Harmon's Sinclair, hoping he could replace that balky universal joint. My Ford F-150 had been on its last legs almost since I drove it off the showroom floor. The Ford dealer in Alva I bought it from had since gone out of business, which served him right for selling me a lemon. I was ready to trade it in, but for what, I wasn't sure. My daddy had always been a Ford man, and he passed that down to me, but I really liked Joel's Chevy Silverado. Another acquaintance of mine recently bought a Dodge D200 pickup with a 318 V8 and a four-speed transmission. I could live with that, as well.

Anything beat throwing good money after bad by trying to keep my Ford on the road.

Fortunately, Wes was able to fit me in. He'd had the u-joint in stock for weeks and was just waiting for me to bring it in. The leaky radiator was also a problem, but getting it fixed involved removing it and sending it to a radiator place. That would take a day or two, and I was in a hurry.

Wes said he had a can of stuff that supposedly plugs radiator holes. "It should keep it from leaking for a while," he added, "but I wouldn't advise you to drive it all the way to Arkansas."

Blessed as I am with an under-abundance of good sense, I told him to pour it in and I'd take my chances.

He said he'd pray for me.

As for what to do if—or when—I confronted Bazil Fitzjarrald, I'd have plenty of time to cook up a plan on the drive there. Seeing that I had no idea what kind of fella he was, I tucked my trusty .38 into my boot, just in case. It'd come in handy before, and probably would again.

If Bazil Fitzjarrald had a hand in killing John and Chastity, he was likely capable of anything.

***

The drive was long, hard, and dull. I stopped three times—twice to get gas, and once at a McDonald's to get something to eat. I tried to listen to a tape Joel had recently loaned me, an album by a jazz musician by the name of Jackie McLean, but Mr. McLean's reed squeaked like a castrated mouse so much, it set my teeth on edge. I had to turn it off.

Instead of listening, I spent time trying to formulate a plan for what I'd do when I met Bazil Fitzjarrald. I wouldn't be in a position to arrest him, of course, so if it turned out he was who I was looking for, I'd have to get someone else to do it, which probably meant waiting until I could contact Detective Blanchard, who would hopefully set things in motion. That was jumping the gun, I knew, but I dearly wanted to nab someone for John's and Chastity's murders.

I reckoned I'd get Bazil's attention by telling him I had news of his sister, which wasn't altogether a lie; I was pretty sure this Sheilah gal was his sister. He was related to Carrie somehow, too, so maybe I'd bring her up, as well, and judge his reaction.

Other than that, I reckoned committing myself to a specific plan of action would be counterproductive. I needed to be flexible and ready for anything.

Of course, John and Chastity and the way they died weighed on my mind. I could relate to that a little bit. There've been a few times in my life, both as a Marine and as a cop, when I thought I was done for, but somehow I'd always managed to escape. They hadn't been so lucky.

Thinking along those lines brought to mind Stafford and the folks he killed. Guys like him are different from the sort of outlaws we used to have. Back in the day, Oklahoma bad guys like Bill Doolin and the

Dalton gang were mainly in the business of robbing banks. They killed sometimes, but their victims were mostly cops or people standing in between them and the money they were after. Not even the worst Okie gangsters of the 1930s, Ford Bradshaw, Aussie Elliott, and Pretty Boy Floyd among them, murdered kids, or lay in wait to attack good Samaritans.

What in hell is going on? Has simple human decency gone the way of the honest politician? Kindness is what led John to help Carrie when she didn't have any place to go. It's what led him to search for her family after she died, so they'd know she'd passed. It was concern for a fellow human being that inspired him to expose her abuser, maybe at the cost of his own life.

I'm not sure if a hankering for justice is the same as kindness. If it is, then John had both.

***

I reached Eureka Springs well after midnight, thinking that both Karen and Wes had probably been right: I should've waited.

People talk about how hilly San Francisco is. I've never been there, but I reckon Eureka Springs could give it a run for its money. The state highway leading into town was fairly flat, but as I negotiated the side streets, I felt like I was driving on a rollercoaster. For one thing, most of the streets are narrow, barely wide enough for a Volkswagen, never mind a full-sized pickup. And not only do those skinny byways constantly go up, up, up, and down, down, down, they're as squiggly as a snake. Every turn is a hairpin turn; every intersection is blind. Darkness made things even worse. The sky was overcast, so there was no moon to light the way. I almost broke my neck several times, trying to see around the next curve or over the next hill.

Given that I didn't know my way around Eureka Springs any better than I would the insides of a computer, the address I had for Bazil Fitzjarrald wasn't worth much. I briefly considered seeking help from the local police before thinking better of it. Instead, I stopped at a convenience store and asked the clerk for directions. He thought the address looked familiar, but he couldn't pin it down. He did give me a map, though; it was one of those tourist maps meant to highlight local attractions. It wasn't even drawn to scale, but I reckoned it was better than nothing. I borrowed a pen and circled where I thought Bazil's house should be, thanked the gentleman behind the counter, and commenced searching.

I immediately turned onto a street that the map said would get me nearer to where I wanted to go. Unfortunately, driving up it was like trying to climb a mountain in a go-kart. I could smell engine coolant by the time I got to the top. Steam was rising from under my hood. The temperature light glowed red.

I should've listened to Wes.

I pulled over and shut off the engine. I reckoned that if I could make it back to that convenience store, I could fill the radiator or maybe even find a place that sold engine coolant. I let the engine cool for a few minutes, then started it back up. I only managed to drive another couple of minutes before it got too hot to drive. I stopped and repeated the process a few times, but unfortunately was never able to find my way out of the spider's web of cross streets. Before long, the engine refused to start. Maybe the engine block was cracked, or the cylinder heads were warped. Whatever the cause, my truck had finally gone belly up. If I were going to find Bazil Fitzjarrald's house, I'd have to walk to get there.

The only thing I took from the truck was the map and my flashlight—or flashclub, as I call it. About fifteen years ago, I had a machinist contrive me a combination billy-club/flashlight. In recent years, mass-marketed versions have hit the stores, but as far as I know, we invented it. I generally leave it in one of our patrol cars, but a few days earlier, I'd retrieved it and shoved it under the seat of my pickup. Anyway, thank goodness I had it on me. I needed it to read the map.

Luckily, I was closer than I'd realized; the Fitzjarrald house was only a couple of hundred yards from where my truck had broken down.

My heart sank when I saw it up close. It had burned to the ground. A few charcoaled beams supported a partially intact roof, but what shingles that remained were charred and warped, and the exposed interior showed no signs of life. Wherever Bazil was, it wasn't here.

As I started to walk back to where I'd come from, I saw something I hadn't noticed before. The house had been built on the side of a hill. The part that burned was just the top floor of a three-story building. Underneath, two more levels appeared to be undamaged.

In fact, the bottom floor looked almost lived in.

There was a light shining in the window.

I gripped my flashclub a little tighter.

CHAPTER FOURTEEN

A wooden staircase snaked down the side of the building. It led to a door on the first floor, next to the window with the light. The first few steps were pretty well-burned. Using my flashclub to light the way, I stepped over them as best I could. Descending the rest of the way wasn't too difficult. Everything was fine until I stumbled on the bottom step, which caused me to bang against the wall of the house.

The light in the window extinguished as surely as water tossed onto a campfire.

I'd squandered my element of surprise, so I went ahead and knocked. There was no response. I called out: "Bazil Fitzjarrald, are you in there?" Seconds later, a raspy voice said: "Who is it?"

"Mr. Fitzjarrald, my name is Emmett Hardy. I have some information about your sister."

There was a long pause. "It's open," the voice said.

I opened the door and instinctively felt around for a light switch. I found one, but when I jiggled it, nothing happened. Fortunately, I could see well enough using my flashclub.

The room was small and narrow. At one point had been a kitchen. Now it was nothing more than a garbage heap. The walls were marked by soot and water stains. The floor was knee-deep in debris. Just to come inside, I had to wade through, among other things, empty soda cans, cereal boxes, and several glass orange juice bottles with furry beards of green mold. The room smelled of smoke, sour milk, human feces, and urine. On the stove were a couple of large plastic garbage bags. At one point, they'd been full, but there were large gaping holes in each, as if someone had lit the stove, thereby melting the bags and letting their loads of rotten eggs, dirty paper towels, and blackened banana peels add to the pile of refuse on the floor.

I heard a rustling sound. I aimed my flashclub to see where it was coming from, and saw the rear end of a rat sticking out of an empty Alpo can.

I am not unused to rank odors—Burr used to have its own meat processing plant, after all—but I swear to God, I've never been in a worse-smelling place.

So far, the rat had been the only sign of life.

I called out, "Mr. Fitzjarrald." From behind, a voice said: "Here." I turned to see where it came from.

Cowering on the floor was an elderly, obese man, with vivid red sores across his face. Where there weren't sores, the skin was as white as those albino fish that live their lives in underground caves. His hair was long but sparse. It fell in wisps across his face and seemed to grow only from a patch at the very top of his head. His chin had a scraggly growth of beard. Except for a filthy orange sport coat, he was nude—his shriveled privates on full display, his legs misshapen by knots of varicose veins. Breathing obviously required great effort. Every rise and fall of his chest produced a wet gurgle. On the floor beside him was an unlit candle jammed into the mouth of a Coke bottle and a book of matches. In one hand, he held one of those little toy puzzles that have tiles with letters on them that you move around to form words.

My first thought was: *If Carrie was assaulted by her rich uncle, it sure as hell wasn't this guy.*

I briefly shined the light in his face; he feebly tried to wave it away. "Don't," he whimpered. I aimed the light away, grateful to not have to look at the poor bastard.

Hands trembling, he struck a match and relit the candle, then reached over his head and set it on the windowsill.

"Are you Bazil Fitzjarrald?" I asked.

After a pause, he answered, "Yes."

"I wanted to talk to you about your sister."

"Zelda?"

"No, not Zelda. Carrie."

He coughed. "Carrie's dead."

"I'm aware of that," I said. "She's buried in a prison cemetery in Oklahoma. I'm looking for a family member to claim her body."

He stared at me without comprehension.

"Did you hear me, Bazil? I'm looking for a family member to claim Carrie's body."

He opened his mouth, then his face stiffened. For a second, I was afraid he'd died on me. "Bazil? You alright?"

"Ask Zelda," he said hoarsely.

I wondered if Zelda was the young woman I'd scared away from Yvette's.

"I'd like to, but I don't know where to find her."

His open mouth produced a bloody spit bubble, but no words.

Again, I asked if he knew where I could find Zelda.

He shook his head slightly, and, in an almost inaudible voice, said: "Try the Red Dog."

The only Red Dog I knew of was a strip club in Oklahoma City.

"You mean the Red Dog Saloon, Bazil?"

He nodded. "Or another one of them titty bars," he said, his voice little more than a metallic whisper. He closed his eyes and swallowed hard, then added: "She's a slut, just like her mama."

"You mean Mamie, right?"

He shook his head and wheezed, "No. *Zelda.*"

If I'd ever had a grasp on the Fitzjarrald family tree, by now I'd lost it entirely. I had originally thought the man I'd be speaking to would be the younger of two brothers, and that they had a sister named Zelda. Now Bazil seemed to be saying Zelda was his mother, and that she danced in strip clubs. Bazil had to be 80, meaning his mother would be in the neighborhood of 100, which I think most of us would agree, is a little old for that line of work.

Was the Zelda he was talking about the gal who worked for Yvette, or was she Hazil and Bazil's sister? She couldn't be both.

Clearly, Bazil was in no condition to set me straight. I hadn't exactly expected him to be ready to go 12 rounds with Muhammad Ali, but I hadn't thought he'd be in such terrible shape. Clearly, he suffered from a serious disease. He needed to be in a hospital or nursing home, not wallowing in filth on the bottom floor of a burned-out house.

I asked about his brother Hazil.

"Dead," he replied.

"When?"

"Years ago."

The rat abandoned the Alpo can, and now dug into an open bag of Fritos. Crunch, crunch, crunch. The foul odors and the sound of the rat brazenly chomping away was almost enough to make me upchuck the Big Mac I'd had for supper.

Obviously, this poor SOB couldn't have killed John and Chastity. I doubt he could raise his foot high enough to crush a bug. That said, the cop in me felt obligated to pin him down on the subject.

"I don't reckon you've been to Norman recently?"

He stared but said nothing. I asked again, a little louder.

"You don't have to shout," he croaked. "No, I ain't been to Norman."

"Ever heard of a man named John Smith?"

"Nuh-uh."

"I'm asking because he and his girlfriend were murdered a few days ago. Would you know anything about that?"

He stared into space, slack-jawed. "No," he said.

I wanted to get out of there, but at the same time, I felt bad for the poor SOB.

"How long have you been sick?"

"A long time," he said.

"Do you have anyone around to help you?"

"No."

"What's wrong with you, Bazil?"

"Syphilis," he said. "I should be dead." He smiled, revealing a few broken, black teeth, and added, "I'm still kicking, though."

As if that was something to celebrate.

I'd had enough.

I left him where I'd found him and hiked the 100 yards or so to my truck, where I bedded down until daybreak.

***

I was awakened by a rooster's *cock-a-doodle-doo*.

After rubbing the sleep out of my eyes, I recognized where I was and realized I was in a bad way. My truck was shot. I could've hunted down a mechanic and had him put a new radiator in my truck, but that would probably mean hanging around Eureka Springs for another day or two or three, and I needed to get home.

Thinking about my truck, I was sick and tired of dealing with it. The danged thing spent more time in the shop than it did on the road. On the spot, I made the executive decision to trade it for something else. *Anything* else. I didn't care what it looked like, as long as it was affordable and dependable—something I could drive back to Burr without the driveshaft falling out in the middle of the highway, or the engine spontaneously combusting.

First, however, I needed to eat. I consulted the little tourist map I'd procured the night before and noticed a little Mexican restaurant near downtown. I found it after a semi-lengthy search. I had myself an order of huevos rancheros. It was delicious, despite looking a little like the Denco Darlin' John had tried to push on me.

I tried to ask the guy who ran the place if he knew of any car dealerships in town, but his English wasn't too good, and my Spanish is non-existent, so we kind of talked around each other.

I walked around for a while looking for a phone booth. I wanted to call for a taxi, but before I could find a phone, one pulled up beside me.

"Need a lift, fella?"

"Y'all got any car dealerships in town?"

He considered it. "Not that sell new cars," he said. "There's a couple that sell used cars."

"Alright then, take me to one of them."

I got in. He drove up and down a few hills until we hit a highway. He slowed and stopped in front of a garage with a couple of dozen cars parked in front. The sign said Mort's Motors. "How about here?" he said.

"What kind of fella is Mort?" I asked.

"God-fearing," he replied in a snap, like he was ready for that very question.

"I reckon that's a good quality for a used car dealer to have," I said.

While we settled up, a fella in a pair of grease-stained coveralls and a lit cigarette hanging from his mouth emerged from the garage.

"Hey, Sonny," the driver hollered.

"How's it hanging, Bud?"

The driver yelled, "Knee high, brother!" and drove away.

"Mort around?" I asked.

"Nah, Mort's sick. I'm runnin' things today."

"Are you as God-fearing as he is?"

Sonny looked at me with suspicion. "I have accepted Jesus Christ as my personal Lord and Savior, if that's what you mean."

"That's just what I wanted to hear," I said.

I told him about my situation, specifically that I wanted to trade my non-running Ford pickup for something that ran, and that I didn't care what I got in return as long as it would get me back to Burr, Oklahoma, in one piece.

"You say you want to trade in a Ford F-150, and you don't care what you get back?" he said.

"Understand, now, it doesn't run. But yeh, I'll take anything in an even-up trade, as long as you can guarantee it'll get me home."

He squinted through the smoke from his cigarette. "Ok then," he said. "I reckon I should look at it first."

"Bring a tow truck, because it's not going anywhere on its own."

We found it without any trouble. Looking at it for the first time, Sonny said: "That's a pretty good-looking truck."

"Looks can deceive."

I was in no mood to deceive. The truck was a piece of junk, as he would discover soon enough. If I could trade it even-up for some ugly car that would, at a minimum, get me home, I reckoned I'd be coming out ahead. Sonny hooked it up, and we towed it back.

I trailed behind him as he strolled through the lot, trying to decide which junker he could afford to trade—or more likely, which junker he could trade without angering his boss, the presently ill but God-fearing Mort. He lingered over a little brown number that looked more like a golf cart than a car.

"Basically, all I can give you is this little gal," he said. "It don't look like much, but mechanically it's in perfect condition."

The car was a 1972 Honda Civic. To say it didn't look like much was an understatement. The hatchback was partly crumpled and held shut by a piece of clothesline. There was a sheet of cardboard where the driver's side back window should've been. I tried to open the passenger door, but nothing happened. "That door don't open from the outside," said Sonny.

"That's ok," I said. "I won't be picking up any hitchhikers."

I asked him about the spots of rust surrounding the wheel wells. He told me he'd bought it off a guy from Galveston and that the salt air had done a number on it. "Still runs nice, though," he added.

"Will it get me back to Oklahoma?"

"Whereabouts in Oklahoma are you from?"

"Place called Burr, a little town in the western part of the state, almost in Texas."

He chewed a greasy thumbnail. "I reckon it will," he said. "Just keep it under fifty. Want to test drive it?"

I almost said, "No need, I trust ya," but I've done that too many times over the years and always regretted it.

I drove it around town and found it pretty spry for such a little car. It went up and down those hilly Eureka Springs streets without a problem. The brakes were good and the transmission didn't clunk. I took it back and told him I'd take it. We signed over each other's titles, and that was that.

I hadn't gotten far before I started thinking I'd made a mistake. I'm no Wilt Chamberlain, but that car wasn't built to be driven by even a normal-sized man. It rattled so much and in so many places, I couldn't begin to guess all the things that were wrong with it.

On the other hand, while my ex-pickup looked better, in its current condition it only ran downhill.

I resolved to accept my situation gracefully.

After driving around a while, I finally found a non-self-serve gas station. The gas gauge said it was almost empty, but it cost less than five dollars to fill up. I've heard those little Hondas will run forever on a tank of gas. If that were true, at least I'd save myself some money.

Now that I had a car, I could leave at any time, but there were still a couple of things I wanted to know about Bazil Fitzjarrald.

CHAPTER FIFTEEN

So much about this didn't make sense. For instance, Bazil's age: I'd expected to find a man in his 50s. The Bazil I talked to was 80 if he was a day. The part about Hazil being alive as recently as four or five years ago didn't surprise me as much; Bazil didn't strike me as a compulsive truth-teller. It was also possible that the fella who introduced himself to Lulu Baker could've been masquerading as Hazil.

And how about that red-hatted limo driver? Who was that? Another Fitzjarrald, perhaps?

***

The gutted top floor of Bazil's looked even worse by the light of day. I crept down the stairs and tried to get him to talk to me again. He wouldn't, so I climbed back up to street level and walked over to the next-door neighbor's. In the backyard was a slender woman with long gray hair tied into a ponytail, pushing a green Lawn Boy. She saw me approach and shut it off.

"How are you doing on this beautiful spring day?" I said.

"It's not spring yet," she said, wiping her face with the back of one glove-covered hand. "It's getting there, though."

I offered my hand. We shook. "Emmett Hardy," I said.

"Lulu Baker," she said. "What can I do for you?"

"I'm looking for information on a person who lives across the street."

"Bazil?" she said. "He's probably on the first floor. I think that's where he's been living since the fire."

"I met him last night. He wasn't in any condition to talk, so I thought I'd ask his neighbors about him."

"He almost never is," she scoffed. "In condition to talk, I mean."

"I'm wondering if you could tell me how long he's been living here?"

She thought on it. "Oh, a long time. Since 1953 or '54, I'd say."

"He seems to be having some serious health problems," I said. "Would you know anything about that?"

"Nothing specific, although I've heard people say he has the VD."

"You notice if he ever has visitors?"

"His brother came around way back when Bazil first moved in, then again about four or five years ago," she said. "I'm pretty sure he owns the house."

"What makes you say that?"

She scrunched he face like she was trying to remember. "One day this fella in a suit and tie comes knocking on my door, tells me that he just bought the house across the street for his brother to live in. He said his brother had some health issues, and asked if I could go over there once in a while and check on him. I said I'd do it for free, but he insisted on paying. Every month for years I got a check for $100, right up until three or four years ago, then they stopped coming."

According to John, Bazil had one brother. Last night, Bazil told me his brother was dead.

"Are you sure this fella was Mr. Fitzjarrald's brother?"

"He *claimed* he was his brother. I'll never forget his name. 'Hazil' he called himself." She giggled. "I'd never heard of a man called Hazil."

Maybe John was wrong. Or maybe Bazil was lying.

"You say the last time you saw this fella was four or five years ago?"

"That's right, about the time the checks stopped coming."

"During those years when he was paying you, did he ever call to check up on Bazil?"

"He never called me. He might've called Bazil, but not me."

"You remember anything else about him?"

"Just that he looked rich."

"What makes you say that?"

"Well, for one thing, he showed up in a limousine he couldn't be bothered to drive himself. Does that sound like he's rich to you? Because it sure does to me."

"So he had a driver?"

She nodded. "Yeh. Some man in a red cowboy hat. Looked about the same age as Bazil, as a matter of fact."

"Anything else?"

She shrugged. "Not really, just that he took me over and introduced me to Bazil, said he was his brother. They must've been step-brothers, though, because Bazil looked old enough to be his father. And he was sick. Very sick."

"He was already sick when you first met him?"

"He didn't have those sores all over his face, but you could tell there was something wrong with him. Not just in his body, but also in the head." She counted off his infirmities. "He was hugely overweight, but couldn't keep down his food, which I thought was really strange. He didn't have an ounce of shame; practically every time I went over there, he was naked, or almost." She put a forefinger to her lips, trying to think of something else. "Oh," she said, "and he farted a lot."

I raised my hands, asking for mercy. "I have kind of a weak stomach."

She smiled. "Sorry about that."

"So what about his brother? You remember what he looked like?"

"Different from Bazil," she said. "A *lot* different, and not just because he was younger. The brother was respectable-looking, with a suit and tie. About your size. Brown hair. Brown eyes."

"But you say he was younger."

"The first time I'd say he was in his twenties. The last time he was older, of course, but still looked youthful." She paused, then added: "And rich."

I reckoned John could have gotten that part wrong, maybe gotten their names mixed up. But that still didn't explain Bazil being so old.

"What can you tell me about the fire?" I said.

"I guess it started in his living room," she said. "Fortunately, the firemen put it out before it spread."

"Did they ever say what caused it?"

"They said Bazil was burning candles because his electricity had been shut off. One of them got too close to a pile of oily rags and set them on fire." She added, "I was the one who called the fire department."

"You probably saved his life," I said, thinking that, given his condition, she probably hadn't done him too much of a favor. "When's the last time you saw him?"

"The night of the fire, over a month ago. I was looking out my front window and saw the flames. I went into the kitchen and called the fire department, then ran outside. Bazil was lying in the weeds in front of his house, crying like a baby. I sat on the ground next to him and held his hand. We prayed until the ambulance came."

"I'm sure that was a great comfort to him."

"I hope so."

"What's Bazil like?"

"Hard to say, really. We didn't talk much. I'd go over there pretty much every day to make sure he was ok. Of course, with that disease he has, he never was doing great, but in the beginning it wasn't too bad. It got worse, though. A lot worse. Fortunately, it was about the time—" She caught herself. "I don't mean *fortunately*, but it was about that time the checks stopped coming."

"So you stopped going over to look in on him."

"Well," she said, crossing her arms like she was fending off an attack, "it's not like I'm a nurse or a doctor or anything like that. He needed more help than I could give. That's the main reason I stopped going over there, not because I stopped getting paid. Plus, if you've been inside that house, you know what a mess it is. How bad it smells." She waved her hand in front of her nose, as if to blow away the stench she remembered.

"About those checks, do you remember the name of the account they were drawn from?"

"It was a company: Hide and Seek? Start and Stop? Something like that."

Neither rang a bell.

"Does anyone else ever go in and out of there?" I asked. "Like maybe a doctor?"

"Hmmm. I know Bazil gets his groceries delivered, although I don't know what he does with his garbage. He never puts it on the curb to be picked up."

I knew, but I kept the information to myself.

"But no doctors?"

She shrugged. "Maybe. I don't know. I'm not one of those nosy neighbors."

***

I asked Lulu Baker if any of Bazil's other neighbors would know anything more about him. She laughed and said, "I seriously doubt it. They all cross the street when they walk by his house."

I then folded myself into the Honda and drove in search of a pay phone. I found one at the convenience store I'd been to the night before. I called the station collect. Cindy accepted the charges and handed the phone over to Karen.

"You in Eureka Springs?" she said.

"I'm sorry I didn't call, but I had a heck of a night."

"Are you ok?"

"I'm fine," I said. "Yes, I'm in Eureka Springs, and yes, I found Bazil. I'll tell you about it when I get home. I just wanted to let you know I got here and that everything's ok."

"So, how did it go? "

"Bazil's not our guy."

"What do you mean? He's Carrie's kin, isn't he?"

"Yes, but he didn't kill John and Chastity. He's sick, almost at death's door. No way could he have made that trip to Norman, never mind killing two people. He can't even stand up. I'll tell you all about it when I get home, but believe me, he had nothing to do with killing John and Chastity. Anything new there?"

"Your girlfriend from the brothel called. That Zelda person you're looking for called and told her she's working in Norman at someplace called Henny Penny's."

How and why did she end up there? I wondered.

"Oh, and one other thing: John found Harald Fitzjarrald's grave."

"Did he say where?"

"Flat-Nose. Apparently, its marked by a homemade wooden marker."

"I don't suppose you or Joel could drive there and take a look, could you?"

"What? Go on a wild goose chase and let the town fend for itself? I'm thinking that might not be something I want to do, especially since I don't have the slightest idea where it is."

"Fair enough," I said. "Listen, I'm going to stop in Norman and try to find Zelda or Sheilah or whatever she's calling herself this week. I might be home tonight, but if I'm not, I'll check into that motel I stayed at before, the Sooner Arms."

"Sounds good. Call and let me know if you're not going to be home."

"Will do," I said, and we ended the call.

The day was young, yet it had already taken a toll. Wearily, I wondered what could've happened to Bazil that made him turn out this way. The man was almost literally a leper, alone and confused, yet at some point in his life, he must've had someone who cared about him.

That's what I'd thought about Carrie three years ago, when John and I first vowed to find her people.

Everybody loves somebody, sometime.

CHAPTER SIXTEEN

I didn't feel excessively cheery on the drive home. I stopped at a gas station just barely on the Oklahoma side of the border, bought a warm Tab that I didn't want, and sat on the hood of my little Honda to consider the situation.

I'd driven to Arkansas hoping Bazil might shed some light on John and Chastity's deaths; I thought he might've even done it himself and hoped that maybe I could wrangle an acknowledgment of that fact. Bazil's diminished physical condition disabused me of that notion.

Bazil was supposed to be the younger of the two Fitzjarrald brothers, yet his neighbor, who was the only person I'd encountered who actually met both, said Bazil was much older. Obviously, Bazil didn't have any reputation to lose, but based on Lulu Baker's description, the other brother she described—Hazil, presumably—looked like he might. Looked at in that way, it seemed possible that Hazil could've killed John and Chastity.

Maybe my theory wasn't so cockamamie after all.

On the other hand, what evidence did I even have that Hazil was even alive, never mind that he might've killed John and Chastity?

I had none.

Bazil could've been lying—indeed, after speaking with Lulu Baker, I was of a mind to think he was—but if Hazil was alive, where was he?

I was now beginning to understand I might never know who did what to whom. Maybe I didn't deserve to know. For three years, I sat on my butt, without raising a finger to do something I'd sworn to do. Meanwhile, John had enough time to write a book about it.

At this point, I figured the best I could hope for was to meet this Sheilah or Zelda and convince her to work with me, as Carrie's next of kin, to have her exhumed from Peckerwood Hill and reinterred in a decent cemetery. That had been the original plan all along.

John had handed the ball off to me. It was my duty to carry it the rest of the way.

***

I was surprised at how nice my new/old Honda drove. Other than being a symphony of rattles, it was kind of fun to drive. The salesman said to keep it under 50, which wasn't a problem. I doubt it could've gone much faster than that, anyway. By the time a got to Norman in the late afternoon, I'd decided to stay overnight, go to Henny Penny's and meet Sheilah.

I checked into the Sooner Arms again. The same old gentleman who checked me in previously, did this time, as well. I took another stab at making small talk, but he was too busy watching *The Andy Griffith Show*. He swiped my credit card without a word and handed me the key to the same room I stayed in the last time.

Good to be back, old-timer.

After getting situated, I walked down the street to Mary's Diner. She talked me into ordering the blue plate special: roast turkey with gravy, cranberry sauce, and mashed potatoes. It was fine, but I've never been all that fond of standard diner food, and you can't get much more standard than turkey and gravy. I should've ordered a hamburger.

I walked back to the motel and called Karen and explained the situation.

"You're going to bankrupt us with all these fancy motels," she said.

"10 dollars a night don't buy fancy."

"Ok, Mr. Moneybags," she said. "Good luck finding that woman."

We said our goodbyes, and I left for Henny Penny's.

This time it cost much less to get in. I flashed my membership card and paid five dollars. The doorman stamped my hand, and I was in. I was glad I'd eaten at Mary's; all that was left of the buffet was a shriveled fried pickle and a few fossilized French fries.

A dancer wearing an extremely abbreviated version of a dress Vivien Leigh might've worn in *Gone With the Wind* greeted me when I went in. I interrupted her spiel to tell her I was looking for Zelda.

"I am quite sho' that we most certainly *do not* have a dansuh heah by that name," she drawled. Evidently, the Scarlett O'Hara get-up was part of her persona.

"How about a Sheilah?"

"I'm sorry, no Sheilahs, eithuh."

"Destiny?"

"Oh, I know Destiny!" she said. "Want me to go get her?"

"Yes, please."

While I stood waiting, Joe, the bouncer who before who'd given me such a hard time, glared at me. "Is there a problem?" I asked. He pointed at his head, and I realized I was still wearing my fedora. I removed it and held it in front of me. He turned his attention elsewhere.

Destiny arrived shortly. Considering that I've already breached the bounds of good taste several times in this account, I will refrain from describing her attire.

"Oh hey, it's the cowboy," she said, smiling half-heartedly.

"Yeh, the guy with all the questions. I promise, it'll just take a minute."

She nodded at my hat. "Why aren't you wearing it?"

I inclined my head toward the bouncer. "Someone suggested I take it off."

"Ah," she said. "That means he doesn't like you."

She put her arm through mine and escorted me to a table, then immediately lit a cigarette. The casual self-assuredness she'd shown the first time we'd met was gone, replaced by a deep sadness.

"How are you doing?" I asked.

"We buried Chastity today," she said, her voice flat and emotionless. "She didn't have any family, so we took up a collection. Mike arranged the service."

"Mike?"

"Mike Fike, the manager."

"Oh, right, that young fella in the pink suit."

"He's older than he looks," she said. "The acne makes him look sixteen."

For a moment I thought back to that first night, and how John scuffled with Fike after slapping Chastity on the rear-end. Could that have made Fike angry enough to kill them both?

Unlikely, especially since he and John laughed it off immediately. What did that mean? Maybe something, maybe nothing.

"Have you heard anything about a funeral for John?"

Destiny said, "All I know is that his parents claimed his body and took it back to wherever he was from."

As far as I could remember, in all the time I'd known him, he'd never mentioned his family.

Another reason to feel sad.

Destiny looked at her watch, a tiny little thing with an elaborate gold band. "No offense, partner," she said, "but we're going to have to keep this short. I've got to make some money tonight."

"That's fine," I said. "I was told you have a new dancer named Sheilah. I'd like to talk to her, and thought you could help."

"We always have a lot of new dancers, but no Sheilahs. Not now, at least."

"She might be calling herself Zelda."

"Ah," she said. "A girl name Zelda just started the other night. You want me to find her?"

"I would appreciate that."

A couple of minutes later she returned with another woman. "Zelda," she said, "this is Emmett. He came especially to see you." Destiny then gave me a little wave, put on a brave face, and went off in search of someone who's not as much in love with his wife as I am.

With a practiced smile, Zelda said, "Hi, Emmett. Would you like to buy me a drink?"

Almost before I could answer, a waitress swooped in and took our order: a rum and Coke for Zelda, a Tab—excuse me, a *Diet Rite*—for me.

Zelda looked at me like she was trying to remember if or when we'd met. I looked at her like I was trying to decide who she reminded me of, because she definitely reminded me of some woman in my past.

"Have you seen me dance before?" she asked. "Or do I know you from somewhere else?"

Right away I knew this woman was at least 40 years too young to be Bazil Fitzjarrald's sister. I couldn't detect a resemblance, either, although to be fair, Bazil was so decayed in appearance as to barely look human.

On the other hand, if I used my imagination, I thought I could see an alikeness between Zelda and Carrie. I'd only seen Carrie that one time, but I remembered she was cute in a puppyish way. This woman was too, absent Carrie's disfigurements.

She overdid it with the makeup, and I didn't have to guess why; behind her forced smile, she looked worn out. Deducting a few years for the physical and emotional demands of her profession (or professions), I guessed she was probably in her late 30s, which seems to me pretty old for a woman in her line of work.

"I don't believe we've ever met," I said. "I think I might be familiar with some of your kin, though. Is your last name Fitzjarrald?"

Her smile faltered. "Uh, we dancers aren't allowed to give our last names."

"Of the Flat-Nose Fitzjarralds?"

Her smile disappeared entirely. "Why are you asking me that?" she asked nervously. "Are you from Flat-Nose?"

"Nah," I said, "I'm from Burr, Oklahoma. But it's close by."

Suddenly, a wall went up between us. "I knew it," she said, slapping the table. "You're that cop who was looking for me at Yvette's." She got up to leave.

"Please don't go," I said. "I wanted to ask you about Carrie."

She froze. "What about her?"

Bingo.

"Maybe we should talk about this someplace else."

"Do you have a car?"

"Right outside."

"Drive it around to the back door. I'll be out in five minutes."

I tossed a ten on the table for the drinks, went outside and drove the Honda around to the back door. Zelda was waiting. She'd put on a flannel robe that covered her from her chin to the tops of her feet. I had to open the passenger side door from the inside so she could get in.

Before she'd even pulled the door shut, she snapped, "How did you know Carrie?"

"I didn't." I started to tell the story about being there when she shot Burt Murray, but Zelda cut me off before I got too deep into it. "I know about all that," she said. "Is that all?"

I then described John's and my own efforts to find Carrie's next of kin so that they could claim her body and get her out of that prison cemetery. I also expressed my suspicion that John's good intentions had gotten him killed, then explained why: Some fella told Chastity about that he'd witnessed an assault on Carrie a few years ago; Chastity told John, and John was about to tell me, but before he could, both he and Chastity were killed. "All he told me was that the attacker was Carrie's rich uncle, who I'm thinking could be this Hazil Fitzjarrald fella. The problem is, I can't track him down."

I studied her face for a response, but there was none.

She started to say, "You don't know—" then stopped, shook her head, and said, "Never mind."

"Never mind, what?"

She hesitated, then said, "You don't know anything about my family."

"That's why I wanted to talk to you."

Her only response was to shake her head.

I kept after her. "Your real name is Sheilah, isn't it?"

She shrugged. "So what? Lots of girls dance under fake names."

"Why'd Zelda?"

She looked at me like I was an idiot. "My last *name!*" she said. "Haven't you ever heard of Zelda Fitzgerald?"

"Can't say that I have."

"Have you ever heard of F. Scott Fitzgerald?"

"Oh yeh, I've heard of him. *The Great Gatsby*, and all that."

"Zelda was his *wife*," she said. "Back then, she was almost as famous as he was. My grandmother loved *The Great Gatsby*. It was the only book she read, over and over. That's why she named my mother Zelda."

"So your mom was Hazil and Bazil's sister," I said. "That makes them—"

She cut me off. "I'm not going to talk about my family. The only reason I'm here at all because you had something to tell me about Carrie. If all you've got is what you've already told me, I think we're done."

She started to get out. Before she could, I said, "Did you know my friend John was writing a book about her?"

That stopped her. "Why bother?" she scoffed.

"Well, for one thing," I said, a little irritated by having to explain to one of Carrie's family members that she'd led a tragic life, "he wanted to find a family member who would have her body exhumed and reburied in a proper graveyard."

"It's a little late for that, isn't it?"

"Better late than never."

"Alright, if you say so," she said. "Let me know how it turns out. Are we done?"

To keep her from leaving, I shot questions at her, rapid fire. "How are you related to Carrie?"

"She was my little sister," she said, "Now can I go?"

"So Carrie was your mother's other daughter?"

"Right."

"How is your mother, by the way?"

"Dead."

"I'm sorry."

"Don't be," she said. "Is that it? Because I've got to get back to work."

"Why'd you run off when Yvette told her I was looking for you?"

"You don't think me being a hooker and you being a cop is enough of a reason?"

"I reckon that's fair," I said, although I strongly suspected there was more to it. "You know," I continued, "I just got back from Eureka Springs."

"No kidding?"

"Have you ever been?"

"Never have."

"So you've never visited your Uncle Bazil?"

"Uncle Bazil?" she said with a smirk. "No, I haven't. I'm guessing that's why you went."

"That's exactly why."

"How was he?" she said.

"Not good," I said. "He's very sick."

"Is he going to die?"

"He's got an advanced case of syphilis."

"Figures," she said. "Did he say anything interesting?"

"Not much, except it seems like he doesn't have too high an opinion of the women in your family."

She smiled bitterly. "Yeh, well, I kind of don't blame him for that."

"Why?"

"No reason."

"No, really. Why?"

"Nothing."

"I thought you'd be interested in news from your uncle."

She only shook her head.

"I talked to his neighbor," I said, trying to goad her into saying something relevant. "She said Bazil's brother bought the house for him. That would be your Uncle Hazil, right?"

Carefully, she said: "Hazil was his brother."

"What struck me is that the neighbor said Hazil was a lot younger than Bazil, which is strange, because as I understand it, Hazil is the older one."

"What do you want me to say?" she asked. "Hazil died years ago."

"How'd he die?"

"I don't know. It was before my time."

"Your mother never told you?"

She paused, like she was trying to keep her story straight. "She died before Hazil did."

"So you were around when Hazil died, you just don't remember it."

"I was little, ok?" she said. "My mom died, Hazil died, and nobody ever told me how or why." Abruptly, she opened the car door and got out. I held the door open before she could slam it.

"Hey, I'm sorry if I upset you," I said. "I was wondering if it would be possible for you to help me get your sister moved out of the prison cemetery?"

She answered with a flat, "No," and leaned back into the car. "Listen, Emmett. Carrie was like my sister, but we came from one of the all-time messed-up families." She used a harsher term than *messed up,* but I got the drift. "She's better off where she is."

It physically hurt me to hear her say that.

"Hold on a second," I called out, but it was too late. She muttered something I didn't understand, slammed the door in anger, and went back to work.

CHAPTER SEVENTEEN

I stopped at a place called Taco Mayo on my way back to the Sooner Arms, had me an enchilada, and thought about what—if anything—I'd learned from my conversation with Sheilah. The place was lit up so bright, it almost made my head hurt, but that was ok, because the whole Carrie thing was having the same effect.

Obviously, Bazil couldn't have killed John and Chastity, nor could he have raped and tortured Carrie. For one thing, Chastity's customer said the attack he witnessed happened four years ago. Also, according to his neighbor, Bazil had been in Eureka Springs and sick as a dog that whole time—plus, he was obviously poor as a church mouse. If it was true that Carrie had been assaulted by a rich uncle, this wasn't him.

It followed that unless John was all turned around, her assailant had to be Hazil.

The trouble was that, according to his brother (and now his niece) Hazil was dead.

As for Sheilah, I didn't necessarily believe her claim that Hazil had died, or, for that matter, much of anything else she said. Not only did she seem to be making things up on the fly, but I was also willing to bet that the tough-girl attitude she put up was just a front.

The complexities of it all (the younger brother being much older than the older brother; Hazil or a man purporting to be him buying his seriously ill brother a house in a town hundreds of miles from home, then stranding him there) didn't add up.

Was Hazil dead or alive? Was he alive five years ago, but dead now? Did John make mistakes in his research? Was Sheilah flat-out lying?

Thinking about it made my head hurt.

I left Taco Mayo and headed back to the Sooner Arms. All this crap was going through my head, when suddenly I flashed on the last thing Sheilah said.

"Carrie was like my sister."

Earlier she claimed Carrie *was* her sister. As she left, she said Carrie was *like* her sister.

What did that mean? If they weren't sisters, what were they?

I pulled a u-turn in the middle of Lindsey Street and headed back to Henny Penny's. I found Destiny and asked if she'd seen Zelda. Zelda had gone home. I asked her if she had Zelda's phone number or if she knew where she lived. She did not.

I left in a bad mood.

I'd suspected all along that the fella who attacked Carrie was the same person who killed John and Chastity. At that moment my prime suspect was Hazil Fitzjarrald. John had been unable to track down anybody by that name. Red had called every official agency in the state, and she couldn't find him either. Hazil Fitzjarrald was a ghost.

Playing the devil's advocate for a minute, I considered that maybe it wasn't Hazil. Hell, it could've been Sheilah; she ran when Yvette told her I was looking for her, and she didn't seem to have much of a warm spot in her heart for her sister or cousin or whatever their relationship was.

Crazy to think about, but not something easily dismissed.

Back to the motel, I called Red and described my conversation with Sheilah.

"She sounds like she doesn't know which way is up," she said, then switched gears.

"Joel and I drove to Flat-Nose today."

"Why?"

"We were looking for Harald Fitzjarrald's grave."

"You said you weren't going to do that."

"Yeh, well, we did."

"Did you find it?"

"Yup."

"What about Hazil's?"

"Nope."

"What were the dates on Harald's gravestone?"

"It wasn't a stone, just a wood slab," she said, "and there weren't any dates. It just had 'Here lies Harald Fitzjarrald, beloved father,' carved into it."

This was getting me nowhere.

"Red, help me here," I said. "If Hazil's dead, who set Bazil up in Eureka Springs?"

"I think the obvious explanation is that Hazil isn't dead, and that Bazil and Zelda are lying."

"Why do you say that?"

"Because Hazil's the one who raped and tortured Carrie, and probably killed John and Chastity."

"So you think I might be right? That they were killed because Hazil found out Chastity knew about his assault on Carrie, and he didn't want it to get out?"

"I'm not sure I'd go that far," she said. "You may be right, but something tells me it would take something more than an allegation about a dead girl to inspire someone to kill like that."

I couldn't disagree. The conversation wound down. We said our goodnights and ended the call.

***

I drove all the way to Burr the next morning, only to have to turn around and drive right back to Norman. While I was on the road home, Detective Blanchard called the station and told Red that they'd arrested a suspect in John and Chastity's murder. I called him back when I got back to Burr.

"I understand you've made an arrest," I said.

"Yup. Fella named Fletcher Fluke. Deals drugs out of a back room at Henny Penny's. That name ring a bell?"

"Can't say that it does," I said. "How'd you get him?"

"Someone phoned in a tip last night. Said the guy who killed the teacher, and the stripper was asleep in a back room at Henny Penny's. We went and arrested the son of a bitch. Even found the gun he used. I reckon it's about as open and shot a case as I've ever had."

"He had the gun on him?"

"Yup. Stuffed into a jacket pocket. We did a ballistic test on it this morning. Perfect match with the slugs that killed your friends. Fella's got a date with the electric chair."

Oklahoma's official method of execution these days is lethal injection, but I didn't bother to correct him.

"You mind if I talk to this guy?" I asked.

"If you want to drive all the way back here, then have at it."

"Where is he, in your lockup?"

"He is now, but we expect to move him to the Cleveland County jail this afternoon. Try here first, and if he's not here, try the county."

I stopped at home before I left and changed into a fresh set of clothes. Knowing it was possible and even likely that I'd end up staying in Norman overnight, I packed a few other things in a small canvas bag, stuffed my little .38 into my boot, and headed out.

***

I asked the uniformed officer manning the front desk for Detective Blanchard. The fella picked up a phone and told him I was there. "He'll be right with you," he said.

Blanchard appeared shortly, his lower lip bulging with a load of snuff big enough to choke a hippopotamus.

"Is he still here?" I asked.

"He is" he said. "Come on back."

He led me to his cubicle. We sat.

"I guess this means there's no connection to the Burt Murray case or John's book," I said.

"None whatsoever," he said. "The girl Chastity was the target. Her real name was Thelma Jean Parham. The autopsy showed heroin in her system. She had railroad tracks on her arms and neck."

"On her neck?" I asked incredulously.

"I know," he said. "The world is getting sicker every day. Anyway, Fluke was her dealer. We have a witness who heard him threaten Thelma Jean's life over some money she owed him." He paused and spit tobacco juice into a cup. "She wouldn't pay, so he made an example of her."

"You're sure about this?"

"Like I said, Fluke had the gun in his pocket and his fingerprints were all over it."

"What kind was it?"

"Ruger MK I, .22 caliber."

I knew the gun. It was originally made for target shooting, not killing. Shoot someone in the head with it, though, and they'll die. Mob hit men like .22s because they're clean and quiet. The slug doesn't make a mess because it almost never exits the skull. With a suppressor attached, it makes about as much noise as a pop gun.

"I assume he denies it," I said.

"Sure he does. So would I if I were him. He admits to selling her the drugs and threatening her over some money she owed him, but maintains he didn't kill her."

"Does he have an alibi?"

"He told us some fairy story about how he's being framed by his boss and his boss's boss. Bunch of horseshit if you ask me."

"Wait," I said. "How's that supposed to have worked?"

"I know," he said, shaking his head. "It's crazy. Something about a conspiracy to ship drugs up from Mexico."

"And you don't think there's anything to it."

"Nah, it's a pile of horseshit," he said, spitting in the cup again. "Thelma Jean owed Fluke money. She wouldn't pay, so he killed her. John Smith didn't have nothin' to do with it. He was just unlucky."

On its face, his solution seemed a little too cut-and-dried, but I wasn't about to argue. Not at this point, anyway.

I stood, anxious to get started. "So can I talk to him?"

He rose up out of his chair. "I reckon that's why you're here," he said, "although I don't see what good it's going to do."

I said, "It might set my mind at ease."

"Alright then," he said. "Let's do it."

I followed him down a couple of hallways. We stopped outside a heavy metal door. An officer sitting at a desk told us we'd need to check our firearms. Both Blanchard and I turned over our guns. From there, another officer, a big fella with a crew cut named Mead, led us down yet another long corridor to a second large, metal-reinforced door. Mead unlocked it and we followed him past a row of tiny six-by-eight-foot jail cells.

We stopped at the last one.

On the cell's bed sat a pale, skinny young man in his 20s. He wore a black T-shirt and a pair of khakis. His arms hung slack at his sides. Angry red sores covered much of his left arm. He didn't seem to notice we were there. He just stared at the floor and muttered under his breath.

Blanchard barked, "What's that you're sayin' there, Fletcher?"

"Nothin'," the kid said in a dull voice.

Blanchard seemed to find that funny. Chuckling, he said, "Fletcher, this here is Emmett Hardy. He's the police chief over in Burr. He was friends with the fella you killed and wants to ask you about why you did it."

"I didn't do it," said the kid, like he'd given up hope of anybody believing him.

"Oh right," said Blanchard sarcastically, "that's why your fingerprints were all over the murder weapon." He turned to me and said, "He's all yours, Chief Hardy. Officer Mead will be here if ol' Fletcher pulls a knife out of his butt or something like that."

I asked Mead if it would be ok to talk to the kid from inside the cell. Mead called out to Blanchard, who by now was heading back where we'd come from, and asked the same question.

"Sure," said Blanchard, "if he can stand the smell."

Mead unlocked the cell door, and I went inside. It did indeed stink.

I offered my hand. The kid flinched at first, then realized I was just being polite. We shook. His grip was weak, his palm cold and clammy. "Emmett Hardy," I said. He didn't say anything, just stared hard at the floor.

The cell was your usual 6' x 8'. There was a toilet against the back wall. Kitty-corner from that was a sink. Both were filthy. On the floor, there was a clogged drain with a puddle of dark liquid forming around it. Unless I wanted to sit on the toilet, there was no place for me to sit. I have an aversion to contracting social diseases, so I decided to stand.

All I could really see of Fluke was the top of his head. His shaggy brownish-blond hair was greasy and parted on the side. He wore a T-shirt with a picture of a naked man with angel wings. Underneath it read: *Led Zeppelin, United States of America, 1977.* They'd taken away his belt, so his already oversized khaki trousers gapped and sagged around his waist.

"Detective Blanchard tells me it was you who killed John Smith and Chastity."

He looked up at me for the first time. He was in better shape than Bazil Fitzjarrald, but not by a whole hell of a lot. His cheeks were hollow, his skin pale with blotches of red. He wore glasses with thick yellow lenses. They made his eyes the size of raisins. His mustache was as long and shaggy as a walrus's, and his nose ran like a waterfall. Every few seconds, he'd hawk up some phlegm and spit it onto that drain in the floor.

"I didn't kill no one," he said as he lifted the neck of his t-shirt and wiped his nose. "I admit, I did sell junk to Chastity. I even admit I threatened to hurt her if she didn't pay me what she owed me. But I wouldn't have done it, not in a million years. Chas was my friend." He paused, then added, chant-like: "I didn't kill her. I didn't kill her."

"How'd that murder weapon wind up in your pocket, then?"

"Someone must've planted it on me while I was asleep."

"Who would do a thing like that?"

"Mike Fike."

"Henny Penny's manager?"

"Yeh, that guy. Always wears a pink suit." He wiped his nose with his shirt again. "He acts like a clown, but cross him and he'll freaking kill you."

"Why would he have picked you as the one to frame?"

"Because I know some things."

"What sort of things?"

"That he and his boss are smuggling drugs. And that's just part of it."

Smuggling drugs is a pretty big deal all by itself, I thought, but if there was more, I wanted to know. "What else?"

"They killed Chastity and her boyfriend," he said, more confident now. "I don't know if it was Fike or someone else, but he was involved, I'll bet you anything. Heck, I've never shot a gun in my life. They must've planted it on me when I was asleep, then called the cops."

Mead, who'd been muttering throughout Fluke's explanation, suddenly erupted in laughter.

Fluke yelled, "It's not funny!"

"Oh yeh? I think it's hilarious," said Mead with a contemptuous grin. "You've got some kind of imagination, punk. I'll give you that."

Ignoring Mead, I asked Fluke, "Do you have any evidence of drug dealing?"

"No," he said, his voice downcast. "It's just something Chastity told me."

"What about the murders?"

"No."

I can almost always smell a load of crap when it's put in front of me, but I wasn't getting that here. Something about Fluke's passion had me inching over to his side.

"You say you were asleep when you were arrested?"

"Yeh."

"And you were arrested at Henny Penny's?"

"Yeh, in the back room."

"Is that where you always sleep?"

"Yeh, most of the time."

"You don't have a place to live?"

He shook his head. "Nah."

"Does this Fike fella and his boss know you sell drugs out of the club?"

"Hell, yes!" he said. "Who do you think sells me the stuff?"

"What kind of drugs are we talking about?"

"Smack, mainly. Some pot, but heroin's where the money is. Once they're hooked, they keep coming back."

"How does it work, your setup with Fike?"

"Fike sells it to me for a certain amount, then I mark it up and sell it to the dancers. Fike double dips: I pay him for the drugs, then I have to kick back a percentage of what I sell."

"Why doesn't Fike just sell it to the dancers himself?"

"He calls it 'plausible deniability.' I guess that means if someone accuses him of selling it, he can point to me and say, 'It wasn't me, it was him.'"

"I don't get it, though. What's in it for you?" His eyelids had begun drooping and I sensed he was fading out on me. I snapped my fingers in front of his face. When that didn't work, I slapped lightly him on the cheek. That did the trick. "Fletcher," I said. "What's in it for you?"

His eyes opened a little wider. "What else?" he mumbled. "Money and drugs."

What else, indeed?

Every cop who's ever made an arrest knows a strip club can serve as a front for all manner of illegal activity, including, and even especially, the sale of drugs. That he was so ready to shoot down Fluke's story bugged me.

"Where do the drugs come from?" I asked.

"Mexico," he said, now a little more alert. "Fike's boss owns a used car lot, Stop and Go Motors, out by the interstate."

Where had I heard that name before?

"He gets most of his cars from Mexico," continued Fluke. "I guess he goes down there, buys a truckload, stuffs them full of heroin and pot and cocaine, then drives the truck back to Oklahoma, takes out the drugs, and sells everything. The cars *and* the drugs."

"How do they get it past customs?"

"Chastity said they have a guy at the border who's in on the deal."

"Chastity told you this?"

"Some weirdo who liked to watch her dance works for Fike's boss. He told her all about it."

"You haven't told me the name of Fike's boss."

His eyebrows came together to form a vee in the middle of his forehead. "You don't know?" he said.

"I don't."

"Scott Sayre," he said, like that's a name I'd naturally be familiar with. It meant nothing to me.

"Does this guy own Henny Penny's, too?"

"Heck, I don't know," he said. "Probably. I know he owns Stop and Go Motors. He also runs one of the state political parties, I forget which one."

That's when it hit me; "Stop and Go" was very similar to the name on the account that Hazil Fitzjarrald used to pay the woman in Eureka Springs to take care of Bazil. "Start and Stop," I think she said. Not identical, but close.

As for which party Sayre ran, it had to be the Republicans. I was personally acquainted with the head of the state Democratic party, and his name wasn't Scott Sayre.

"You're saying this Sayre fella who runs the state Republican Party, also owns Henny Penny's, a car dealership, and smuggles drugs on the side?" A big shot politician owning a car dealership made sense. Owning a strip club did not, however, nor did running a drug smuggling operation.

Giving voice to it all made Fluke's claims sound ridiculous, and for an instant I felt myself becoming skeptical.

Then I thought of Burt Murray and the stunts he pulled over the decades: bribing judges; poisoning old men so he could get his hands on their oil leases; killing anyone who got in the way of his ambitions. I'm sure that if Burt had the know-how, smuggling drugs was something he would've done.

"Listen, man, I ain't lyin'," Fluke pressed. "I always knew Fike was bringing in the drugs, since he sold them to me. But it makes total sense that Sayre's behind the whole thing."

"Because that's what Chastity said."

"Right."

Other than being kind of sexy in the way a college cheerleader gone bad can be sexy, Chastity hadn't impressed me much. Then again, I didn't really know her. Fluke did. In fact, it sounded like he knew her better than John did.

"And you believed her?" I said.

"Chastity was a blabbermouth, and a whore, and she didn't pay her debts. But one thing about Chas: She didn't lie."

That was like saying: *Sure, the Son of Sam killed all those young women, but he owned up to it.* But Fluke obviously meant it.

"Alright, Fletcher," said Mead, sliding the key into the lock. "You've had your fun. This fella's got better things to do than listen to you make shit up."

The thing is, I wasn't finished. "That's alright, Officer Mead," I said. "I'm finding it all pretty interesting."

Mead said, "I think we need to shut this down right now." Pointedly, he held open the door so I could leave. I walked out and he slammed the door shut.

I asked Fluke if he'd spoken with a lawyer.

"They say they'll get me one after I get to the county jail."

That's not the way it's supposed to go.

"Did you ask for one before Blanchard questioned you?"

"I did. He said *'Mañana'*. Exact words. Or word."

"Don't talk to anyone else until you get one."

At that, Mead grabbed me by the upper arm and tried to pull me away. I shook myself loose. "Don't be grabbing me, son," I said, as menacingly as I felt. I started down the hall. Mead rushed up behind me.

"Whose side are you on anyway?" he asked.

"Justice," I snapped. "How 'bout you?"

"Justice?" he scoffed. "You're kidding, right?"

CHAPTER EIGHTEEN

Mead led me back to where I'd left my gun. I reclaimed it, then followed him through the maze of hallways back to Blanchard's desk. He whispered something into the detective's ear then walked away. Blanchard frowned and peered at me over his glasses.

"Is that true?" he said.

"Is what true?"

"That you buy Fluke's load of crap?"

"I wouldn't say I believe him 100%," I said, "but if it were my case, I'd look into it."

He took a tin of Skoal from his shirt pocket and jammed a wad of it into his mouth.

"But it's not your case," he said, "it's mine, and I say Fluke is full of shit." He shook his head. "Slandering Mr. Sayre like that, I swear to Jesus. Anyone'll tell you, there ain't a kinder, more God-fearing man in the state of Oklahoma than Scott Sayre. Did you know he gives more money to charity than any man in the state?"

"I didn't." Until a few minutes ago, I'd never heard of the man.

"Who do you think put up the money to build that new football dormitory on the OU campus?"

"I'm guessing you're going to tell me he did."

He nodded so hard, he dislodged his glasses. "Damn straight," he said, as he returned them to their proper place.

Clearly, Detective Blanchard and I had different ideas about what constitutes Christian charity.

I said, "So you think Fluke is just making all this up?"

"I don't *think* it. I *know* it. Scott Sayre is about as much of a drug kingpin as I am."

"What about Fike, the fella who runs Henny Penny's?"

"That's another reason Fluke is full of shit," he said with a frown. "Mike Fike doesn't run Henny Penny's. Cha Cha Mulvaney does. Cha Cha owns it, in fact. Fike runs Mr. Sayre's car lot, Stop and Go Motors." He paused and in a softer voice said, "Fike's another kettle of fish. We've had some run-ins with him, but since he's gone to work for Mr. Sayre, he's been a model citizen. I reckon you could say he's been Mr. Sayre's pet project these last few years."

I couldn't get past the idea that Cha Cha Mulvaney owned Henny Penny's. "You're saying Cha Cha Mulvaney, the poster boy for the law to outlaw strip clubs, actually owns one?"

With a pitying look, Blanchard said, "Where've you been, boy! Everybody knows. Cha Cha's going to close Henny Penny's, buy up all the surrounding land and turn it all into a big church and theme park, just like that place in South Carolina."

I vaguely recalled a report on the news a few months back about a TV evangelist who built a Las Vegas-style resort for born-again Christians.

"Why does he keep it open?" I asked. "You'd think if he were really against strip clubs, he'd shut it down."

"Hell, boy, he just bought the place! He'll shut it down soon enough."

"Who'd he buy it from?"

"Well, uh, uh," he stuttered, "I don't reckon I can recall it, but if you really want to know, you can look it up somewhere. City Hall, maybe."

"What makes you think this whole state question thing isn't just an act to get himself elected governor?" I asked.

Blanchard gasped. I might as well have disparaged Robert E. Lee in the company of Jefferson Davis.

"Only someone who hasn't accepted Jesus Christ as his personal Lord and savior would ask such a goddam stupid question," he sputtered. "Cha Cha has a checkered past, I'll give you that. After that scandal in college when he got stripped of his medals and kicked off the wrestling team, he went straight downhill, boozing and whoring and the like. But the Lord forgives. Mr. Scott Sayre knows that, which is why he took Cha Cha under his wing and helped him find Jesus, same as he did with Mike Fike."

His outrage was so exaggerated, it seemed like a put-on.

"So Cha Cha's atoning for past sins," I said. "Is that what you're saying?"

"Damn straight!" he said again, this time slapping his open palm on his desk. "And guess who's loaning him the money to do it? Mr. Scott Sayre, that's who!"

Because Scott Sayre walks on water, I thought but did not say.

"About Fletcher Fluke's arrest," I said, having had enough talk about religion, "You say someone called in a tip?"

"That's right."

"Was it man or woman?"

"Woman."

"Any idea who?"

"Nah. That's why we call them 'anonymous tips.'"

I ignored his patronizing tone. "What exactly did the caller say?"

"That the fella who killed that dancer was asleep in the back room at Henny Penny's and that he still had the gun on him he used, and that we should get there quick and arrest him."

I wondered if the tipster had been Destiny or perhaps Sheilah Fitzjarrald.

"Alright then," I said, having already gotten more out of my visit than I'd bargained for, "thank you for letting me meet this fella."

My thanks were sincere. After what I'd just heard, I was close to being convinced I was on the trail of something. What, I wasn't sure.

But something.

***

The more I thought about it, the more Fluke's story rang true.

For one thing, it fit my original theory: John and Chastity were killed to keep one or the other of them quiet. Originally, I'd believed John had been the target; the person who assaulted Carrie had something to lose and didn't want the story to get out. If Fluke's story was true, however, Chastity—or Thelma Jean Parham, as Blanchard called her—was actually who the killer wanted to silence. Not over some attack on Carrie, either, but to keep Chastity from revealing what she knew about Mike Fike's and his boss Scott Sayre's drug smuggling operation.

The thing is, you can't put the toothpaste back into the tube after it's all been squirted out. By the time Chastity had been killed, she'd already told Fluke about the smuggling scheme, and probably John, as well. And she might've told others. Sayre and Fike would want to make sure the news didn't spread further, either by killing the messengers or by making sure they knew their time on earth had an expiration date if they didn't keep their mouths shut.

Fortunately for Sayre and Fike, the detective didn't believe him, or at least didn't want to believe him. By the looks of things, Blanchard didn't intend to even look into Fluke's allegations. I supposed it was possible he thought the story too fantastical to be true, but whatever his reasoning, the fact that he dismissed Fluke's tale out of hand bothered me. Could it be that he already knew about the smuggling and decided not to do anything about it? Was he being paid to look the other way? I hated to think such a thing about one of my colleagues, but over the years, I had a front-row seat to the many crimes of ex-Tilghman County Sheriff Burt Murray and his cronies, so I know things like that occasionally happen.

I'll tell you one thing: If Blanchard *was* a party to the scheme, I wouldn't give two cents for Fluke's life while he was in jail. And now that Fluke had told me, there could but a target on my back, as well.

But I'm a big boy, and I carry a gun.

I could think of one person in particular who Chastity might also have told, and I was pretty sure she didn't carry a gun.

Her roommate. I needed to talk to Destiny.

***

Yogi Berra calls it "*Déjà vu* all over again." That describes how I felt when I checked back into the Sooner Arms, like I was reliving the same thing over and over. The same elderly gentleman as before checked me into the same room, and we both pretended we'd never met.

I unpacked the few things I'd brought with me, then called Karen and told her about my conversation with Fluke. She agreed with me that there might be something to his story. I told her Blanchard didn't put any stock in Fluke's allegations.

She said, "Sounds to me like Detective Blanchard is either stupid or crooked."

I couldn't disagree.

"You think somebody might be after you, now that you know about this drug smuggling operation?"

"That occurred to me, but honestly, I don't even know if there *is* a drug smuggling operation. All I have is the word of a drug addict with a murder rap hanging over his head, and that's just hearsay. I'd be more concerned about other people Chastity might've told."

"Any ideas about who that might be?"

"Her roommate, for one. I'll try to talk to her tonight."

"Are you telling me you're making another trip to that nudie bar?"

"That's the only way I know to get in touch with her."

"Then I guess that means you're staying overnight in Norman again."

"The Sooner Arms, like before."

She sighed. "Alright, but dang it, get this thing over with and come home. Mr. Paws misses you."

"It's nice to hear that *some*one does."

"I wouldn't say some*one*, exactly. Mr. Paws is a cat."

***

A police car came up on by bumper on the drive to Henny Penny's. It gave me a jolt, but he turned off onto a side street, so I could breathe.

Recent events had left me wondering who my friends were.

I arrived there a few minutes after 7:00. I was again met by a pretty young thing who treated me like I was Paul Newman's twin brother. I'll say one thing about Henny Penny's: They had separating a man from his money via flattery down to an absolute science.

I asked the gal if she could find Destiny for me. While she went looking, I caught sight of Sheilah greeting a man who came in after me, who, thanks to his prominent teeth and bald head, bore more than a passing resemblance to a naked mole rat.

"*Hello,* sweetheart," she said to the fella, like she'd just laid eyes on the man of her dreams. The fella's homely face lit up like a Christmas tree.

She saw me and her smile vanished.

"What are you doing here?" she asked.

"I'm here to see Destiny," I said, "but it's good to see you as well, Sheilah."

Turning back to the mole rat, she reapplied her grin. "But you can call me *Zelda,*" she told him in a loud voice, because everything is loud at Henny Penny's. She walked away arm-in-arm with her new boyfriend.

Destiny appeared shortly, once again, undressed to kill.

"Back so soon?" she said with a sardonic smile. "Must be my magnetic personality."

"I need some financial advice," I said.

"Then let's step into my office." She led me to a booth near the back where we could hopefully hear each other over the noise. I thought about the girls Fluke had sold drugs to and wondered if she was one of them. I snuck a look at her arms. No needle marks, which I was glad to see.

We slid into a booth. A waitress swooped in and took our drink orders. We made some small talk.

"What's your real name?" I asked.

"Destiny," she said.

"No, I mean your real name."

"Destiny is my real name."

"Really?"

"Really."

"I don't believe you."

"Then don't," she said with a shrug.

The waitress served our drinks. She sipped her bourbon and Coke. I gulped down my Diet Rite.

"They arrested someone for Chasity's murder. Guy named Fluke."

"I know," she said. "I was here last night when it happened."

"You're not the one who called in the tip, are you?"

She blew a raspberry. "Are you kidding?"

I was glad to hear that.

"What do you know about Fluke?"

"He sells drugs out of the back room. Sleeps there, too."

"Did Cha Cha know he was selling drugs?"

She looked puzzled. "Why would Cha Cha care?"

"Because he owns this place."

She gave me the same pitying look Blanchard gave me earlier. "Cha Cha doesn't own Henny Penny's. Scott Sayre does. Cha Cha's his flunky."

"That's not what Detective Blanchard says."

She rolled her eyes. "I'm sure your detective buys into the fiction that Sayre's a saint who would never sully himself by owning a strip club. Trust me, Sayre owns Henny Penny's. Cha Cha's just the front man."

"What about Mike Fike?"

"What about him? He's the manager. Cha Cha couldn't run a lemonade stand."

Interesting. "I heard a rumor about Chastity and John that I wanted to run by you. Actually, it's more like I wanted to warn you."

The gently amused grin she'd been wearing faded. "Warn me? About what?"

I told her Fletcher Fluke's story.

When I finished, she pulled a pack of Virginia Slims out of her short silk robe and lit one up. "Sounds about right," she said. "I've always suspected something along those lines."

"You mean this Scott Sayre guy really is smuggling drugs?"

She looked around as if to make sure we weren't being spied upon. "Listen, Cowboy, I've got to be careful. You should be, too."

I moved closer so as not to be overheard. "But you believe Fluke's story is true?"

She took a puff and said, "It squares with what Chastity told me."

"Listen," I said, "if Chastity was killed because of what she knew, whoever killed her might come after you, too."

She chuckled. "I'm sure Chastity didn't tell only me. That child couldn't keep her mouth shut about anything. I'm sure she told *everyone*."

"Meaning all the dancers?"

"Meaning everyone."

"I guess there's safety in numbers," I said.

"Let's hope so."

I asked, "Any idea who called in that tip?"

"Zelda," she said. "Obviously."

"Why 'obviously?' Did you see her do it?"

"No, but it had to be her. If Mike or Sayre tell her to do something, she does it." She ground out her cigarette. "She and Sayre are an item, by the way."

"No kidding?"

"That's what I hear. I haven't talked to her about it. Heck, we've barely spoken five words to each other, but Sayre's been hanging around ever since she started, putting his hands all over her. She's the one girl Fike never touches, which tells me he knows he'd better not if he knows what's good for him." She took a sip of her drink. "Why are you so interested in her?"

"We know some of the same people," I said, not wanting to get into the real reason, which I feared was now too convoluted to explain in the full-length book John had planned, never mind in 100 words or less. "Anyway," I said, winding things up, "I wanted to tell you Fluke's story so you could take precautions."

"Like what?" she said wryly. "Wear a bullet-proof vest?" She gulped down the last of her drink. "I should go." She started to ease out of the booth.

"A couple more things," I said. "The other day when I saw you at Mary's with Cha Cha—"

"Oh, that!" she said, sitting back down. "The girls all take turns going to lunch with Cha Cha, but I have to get up early for class, so he takes me to breakfast. He's actually very sweet. Not too bright, but sweet."

"What's he up to these days?" I asked. "Besides shutting this place down and opening his own religious theme park, that is."

"You mean that State Question he's shilling for?"

I nodded.

"Don't take that too seriously. That's part of some grand scheme to get him elected to the Senate. It was probably Sayre's idea. It's funny," she said with a slight smile, "If you read the fine print, it only outlaws nudity where alcohol is being served. Places like this will just start charging five bucks for a Coke."

"What about turning Henny Penny's into a religious theme park?"

She smirked. "Never going to happen. As soon as Cha Cha gets elected, he'll pretend to sell it back to Sayre, and Henny Penny's will continue serving the same pool of degenerates it always has. They'll just have to get drunk in the parking lot before they come in."

"You think Cha Cha has anything to do with this smuggling thing?" I said. "Assuming it's true?"

"I've never heard him mention it, but of course he wouldn't. But if Sayre is running something like that, I'd be more surprised if Cha Cha *wasn't* involved." She lit another cigarette then tossed the pack and book of matches on the table. "Basically Cha Cha does whatever Scott Sayre tells him to do."

"That's interesting," I said.

"What?" said Destiny, putting a hand to her ear.

"That's *interesting*!"

She shook her head like she still couldn't understand. "Listen, I've got to go. It's time for my feature."

I took out my wallet and slipped her a ten. "For your time," I said.

She folded the bill and stuffed it into her bra. "Thanks," she said. "Nice seeing you again, cowboy."

I didn't leave the club, not right away. But I didn't watch her dance. I reckoned it would be unseemly, especially now that I knew her real name.

CHAPTER NINETEEN

Learning Sheilah was dating Scott Sayre shed new light on things. Destiny had made it sound like he hung out at Henny Penny's regularly, but up until then, our paths had not crossed—not that I was aware of, at least. If I could wangle an introduction through Sheilah, it might give me insight into whether he could've engineered John and Chastity's deaths.

I spotted her coming out of the "Dancers Only" door dressed in civilian clothes: jeans, black Converse All-Stars, and a black and white rabbit fur jacket. I tossed a five on the table, hoping it would be enough, and followed her out to the parking lot.

I caught up to her as she stood next to an orange Trans Am, digging through her purse for the keys.

"Hey," I said, a little bit out of breath. "Could I talk to you for a minute?"

She turned around and saw it was me. Her shoulders slumped. "Do I have to?" she groaned.

"I'd really appreciate it."

She sighed and popped the lock. "Get in."

She'd already removed her makeup, and the lights in the parking lot gave her face a yellow glow, but she was still cute as a button. Once again, she reminded me of somebody, but I couldn't pin down who.

It was kind of chilly, so she started the engine and turned on the heater. At first it blew cold air, so she blew into her gloved hands then tucked them under her armpits. "What now?" she said.

"Destiny tells me that you're friends with Scott Sayre."

"So?" she said, blowing on her hands again.

"It's just that I've been wanting to meet him, and I thought maybe you could introduce me."

"I can't really do that."

"Why not?"

"Well, for one thing, I don't really know you."

I smiled. "Oh, sure you do. We're practically best friends!"

She grinned a little. "I don't know, Scott's really busy—"

"What if I said it has to do with Carrie?"

Apparently, that was the wrong thing to say. "Yeh, right," she said brusquely. "Listen, I've got to go." She reached across and reopened the door for me. "Y'all take care," she said, and practically shoved me out.

My car was parked nearby. Sheilah was stuck in a long line of cars exiting the parking lot. I got the Honda started and fell in behind her, a few cars back. She was half a block ahead of me before I got out of the lot. The Trans Am would've left me in the dust if she hadn't gotten stuck at a traffic light.

Without a clear notion of why, I followed her, always at a safe distance. After a while, she turned onto a side street in a residential neighborhood. Unable to hide in traffic any longer, I cut my headlights and inched along—far enough away, I hoped, to make it hard for her to see me, but not so far that I couldn't see her.

She pulled into the driveway of a large two-story house next to another car—a dark blue Caddy or a Lincoln; it was hard to tell from a distance. I pulled over to the curb at the end of the street; it gave me a clear view of the house. Sheilah went to the front door and rang the bell. A man answered. I only got a quick look, but I recognized him instantly. His face was plastered on billboards all over the state.

Cha Cha Mulvaney.

I drove to the end of the street and turned around. On my way past the house, I noted the name on the mailbox.

Scott Sayre.

I wrote down the address.

I had a feeling I might be back.

***

Evidently, Destiny was right. Sheilah was involved with Scott Sayre. Of course, it was Cha Cha who answered the door, so it was possible she was seeing him, but Destiny didn't make Cha Cha sound like much of a ladies' man.

I sat there for a while and watched the house, but after an hour when no one went in or out, I headed back to the motel.

On the way, I considered what I knew ... or, at least, what I *thought* I knew.

An admitted drug dealer is heard threatening the life of a woman who later turns up dead. He insists he didn't kill her, but fingers a respected local businessman, who also happens to be the leader of the state's Republican Party.

The detective in charge of the investigation says there isn't anything to investigate. He caught the admitted drug dealer in possession of the murder weapon. End of story.

Furthermore, the detective describes the respected local businessman in terms that would make a saint blush.

The only thing the two men's accounts had in common?

Chastity was the primary target.

Who—and what—should I believe?

I'll say this: While it might seem natural to take the word of a pillar of the community over that of a druggie's, I know from experience that some of those so-called respectable fellas are as dirty as a bowling alley toilet seat. The difference between them and someone like Fletcher Fluke is, when someone dies as a result of *their* crimes, they're hard to nail; fellas like that usually manage to put a few layers between themselves and the person who actually does the killing.

It's called plausible deniability. It's something the best politicians are very good at.

So far, I'd only heard Fluke's side of the story. He'd been pretty convincing, but drug addicts get a lot of practice at lying. I couldn't be sure he was telling the truth until I heard what the other fella had to say.

The other fella, in this case, being Scott Sayre.

***

Before leaving the motel the next morning, I reserved my room for another night. I didn't know for sure that I'd need it, but I expected I would, and I didn't want to go through the hassle of doing everything all over again the next day.

I ate breakfast at Mary's. The newspaper had an article about State Question 339. Like everything else I'd read on the subject, it neglected to mention that it didn't really outlaw strip clubs, but instead just made it illegal to serve alcohol in a room full of naked women.

I reckoned I'd just have to take Destiny's word on that.

I'd already decided to visit Stop and Go Motors. If I couldn't get Sheilah to introduce me to Scott Sayre, I'd just drop in and introduce myself.

I kind of remembered seeing the sign when I'd driven into town. On it were the words Stop and Go in bold red letters, flanking a large cartoon traffic signal: red on top, yellow in the middle, green on the bottom. The green light had a dollar sign in the center, and was the only one lit—shining like a beacon, an invitation to those without transportation to join the 20th century.

The lot sat off by itself, about 100 yards west of an access road that merges onto I-35: a large building featuring a glassed-in showroom with a repair shop attached, and a paved lot where lots of cars waiting to be bought. Its closest neighbors was a shopping mall about a quarter mile away and whatever rodents that lived in the undeveloped grassland surrounding it.

I parked the Honda near the door to the repair shop and got out of the car. Before I'd taken two steps, a burly fella in blue coveralls, long stringy hair, and a five o'clock shadow that looked like it had been smeared on with used motor oil, stood in my way. A large crescent wrench hung from a loop on his hip. He stroked it like he would a woman's breast.

I recognized him immediately; it was Joe, the bouncer from Henny Penny's. Evidently, the two establishments had more in common than just Scott Sayre.

"You got an appointment?" he said.

He didn't seem to recognize me. I expect he strong-arms a lot of fellas.

"Why would I need an appointment?"

He nodded toward the Honda. "To get that pile of shit worked on."

I gave him the fake-friendly smile I once reserved exclusively for highway patrolmen who stopped me when I was driving under the influence. "No sir, I'm just here to talk to Scott," I said, implying that Mr. Sayre and I were good buddies.

It didn't cut any ice with Joe.

"I don't give a damn who you're here to see," he said, "that piece of shit is blocking my driveway."

First it was a "pile of shit," then it was a "piece of shit."

Make up your mind.

Knowing that it's never wise to tussle with a guy who looks like he opens beer bottles with his eye sockets, I moved my car before I went inside the showroom.

Most of the cars there would've looked real nice in my driveway.

All except one: a boxy little metal-flake blue number that looked like a slightly oversized Soap Box Derby car. I was shocked to see that it was a Ford Mustang. I'd lusted over Mustangs since they first hit the streets, ten or fifteen years ago. This one was different, and not in a good way. It looked like a sports car designed by a committee of people who'd never actually seen a sports car.

I was willing to bet it was also the kind of automobile an eager beaver car salesman would be in a hurry to sell. I chose it to be the one I'd pretend to be interested in.

It worked like a charm.

"Ah, I see you have your eye on the Mustang," a way-too-friendly voice called out from behind my back. I turned and saw a young fella in a plaid three-piece suit come near. His dark hair was sprayed stiff enough to withstand an attack by flying monkeys, and the light reflected off his smile could've melted an iceberg. He looked like the kind of used car salesman they make jokes about.

"The name's Tom Musgrave," he said.

"Emmett Hardy," I said, and we shook hands.

Gazing lovingly at the Mustang, he added, "Sweet little thing, ain't it?"

I thought it looked like something a little kid might peddle around his daddy's driveway. "It doesn't look like the Mustangs I remember," I said.

"Oh, but this is a beautiful new *breed* of Mustang!" he enthused. "Sports car design! One of the most efficient aerodynamic styles of any car built in America!"

"Wasn't the Mustang always a sports car?" I asked.

"And it still is," he said, still beaming. "But this one is *new*. Better mileage, more comfortable. Better handling! Modified MacPherson Strut Suspension!"

I didn't know or care what a modified MacPherson Strut Suspension was, nor did I have any idea why mentioning it got this plaid-suited glad-hander so excited. I needed to be nice to him, though, if I wanted to finagle an introduction to his boss.

"To be honest, I'm really more of a pickup fella,' I said. "Actually, I was just wondering if Mr. Sayre is around."

"Oh, well, you know," he said, "we've got lots of trucks on the lot if you want to take a look—"

"Maybe later," I said. "Right now I just need to talk to Mr. Sayre."

"Well, he's not here today, I'm afraid."

"Any idea where I might find him?"

"Hmmm," he said, scratching his head, before remembering his hair had been lacquered into something resembling a football helmet. He tried to pat the displaced hairs back in place. "Mr. Sayre's in Mexico on a business trip," he said. "He should be back tomorrow, though. Are you a friend of his?"

"I am," I lied. "Haven't seen ol' Scott in a month of Sundays and thought I'd surprise him. What's he up to these days?'

"I really don't know," he said, forgetting to smile. "He's not around all that much. He's got other business interests that need tending to."

Like drug-smuggling, I thought.

"What's he doing in Mexico?" I asked, as if I didn't know.

"Buying cars. That's where a lot of our stock comes from."

Fletcher Fluke got that much right, which I thought was a good sign.

"Why's he buy 'em down there?" I asked.

"I'm pretty new here, so there are some things I'm not all that clear on," he said doubtfully. "He just gets better deals on 'em, I guess."

I guess he suddenly remembered that he was on the clock. With a hastily reconstituted smile, he blurted: "And we pass along the savings to our customers!"

I was starting to feel like I was in TV commercial.

"Are you telling me a man as important as Scott Sayre goes down to Mexico and brings those cars back all by himself?"

He shook his head. "No," he said, "Mr. Fike goes with him."

"I don't believe I recall Scott mentioning a Mr. Fike."

"Mr. Fike's my boss. He's Stop and Go's sales manager."

"I see. So when do you think they'll be back?"

"Tonight after midnight," he said. "Mr. Fike has a special crew that unloads and preps them. By the time I get here tomorrow, I expect they'll be on the lot, ready to sell."

I thanked him for his time and said I'd be back tomorrow to see my old buddy Scott.

"Maybe we'll have something in the new batch you'll be interested in."

I smiled back, trying to match the wattage of his grin. "I wouldn't be surprised if you did."

CHAPTER TWENTY

I spent the rest of the morning trying to think of a plan to discover if Fletcher Fluke's story about Scott Sayre being a drug smuggler was true.

My plan—half-baked as it might have been—was to stake out Stop and Go that night and wait for the load of cars to arrive. That's assuming the young salesman was right, and they were in fact being delivered. I'd find a vantage point near where I could see what was going on, and watch for signs drugs were being removed.

It seemed simple enough, before it hit me that I couldn't be sure I'd get close enough to see what I wanted to see. I stopped at an Army surplus store, figuring a pair of night-vision binoculars would do the trick. The fella who sold them said they were based on the scopes the US Army used in Vietnam. He guaranteed they'd work.

I reckoned I'd find out.

***

Lunch that day was kind of interesting.

I went back to Mary's. Once I find a place I like, I stick with it.

I got there around 11:00. The little bell rang over my head when I walked in. For once, the jukebox was silent. The place was nearly empty, except for the fella in the Peterbilt cap who'd told me about

John and Chastity being shot. He sat at the counter where he'd sat before, drinking coffee and gabbing with Mary, while she and Blanche, the skinny waitress, darted around getting the place ready for the lunch rush. Mary gave me a friendly smile but was too busy to flirt.

This time I got a booth. Blanche gave me a quick smile and a menu, then filled my coffee cup before I could tell her not to. I ordered a western omelet with a side of hash browns.

The place started to fill up. Folks entered in groups of twos and threes, giving the bell over the door a good workout. Of course, someone cranked up the jukebox, which meant it was showtime for Mary.

Her first song was "Roll in My Sweet Baby's Arms," the Flatt & Scruggs version. Oh my, how those country boys could play. Mary's voiceover version was bawdier, with lots of innuendo. I was starting to get the feeling she only owned the joint so she'd have a place to perform.

Before long, every booth on the place was occupied except for the one where Cha Cha and Destiny sat the last time I'd been there. I needed to use the restroom, so I had to walk past the table. I saw that someone had folded an index card in half and made a small sign: "Reserved for Future Oklahoma Governor Cha Cha Mulvaney."

I returned to my table around the same time that Cha Cha walked in, accompanied by my favorite short-haired exotic dancer.

Cha Cha had on a big red cowboy hat, a cranberry-colored polyester leisure suit with a yellow western-style shirt underneath, and a bolo tie with a silver clasp shaped like an armadillo. Destiny was dressed much the same as when I'd last seen her in Cha Cha's company: blue jeans, sneakers, and a gray sweatshirt bearing the University of Oklahoma logo. They settled into Cha Cha's personal booth.

Destiny sat facing me, but all I could see of Cha Cha was his back. She saw me, but pretended not to. They looked to be making small talk for a few minutes, then someone called out to Cha Cha, and he went over to yak.

With Cha Cha distracted, I got her attention. I crooked a finger, inviting her to join me. She gave me a small, quick shake of her head. Cha Cha—who by now had finished talking to the well-wisher— looked in my direction to see who she was shaking her head at. He swiveled back to Destiny; they exchanged a few words, then he turned back to me, and with a friendly smile, waved me over.

It would've been rude not to go.

"Hey there, Destiny," I said. "Who's your friend?"

Cha Cha held out his hand. "Cha Cha Mulvaney," he said.

"Emmett Hardy," I said. "I'm chief of police in Burr, a little town over in the western part of the state."

"Burr?" said Cha Cha, his jaw working on a wad of gum. "Ain't that the town where Burt Murray was killed?"

"It is," I said solemnly. "That was a terrible day."

He nodded in recognition. "Yeh, I heard about you," he said. "You're the one who let a little retarded girl beat you on the draw."

That comment hit hard, and I mean *hard,* but I wasn't there to fight. As calmly as I could manage, I said, "I'd like to have done better, that's for sure."

"Ah, hell," he said, "we all make mistakes. Care to join us?"

Destiny's eyes said *go away.* But I don't take orders from anyone's eyes. Except for maybe Karen's, once in a while.

"Don't mind if I do."

I scooted in next to Destiny.

We engaged in some small talk. He asked me how I knew Destiny. She told him I was a fan, her voice thick with sarcasm, which went all the way over Cha Cha's head.

"Oh, so you like the way she dances?" he said. "Well, you'd best get your fill while you can. Before long, that place is going to be a church."

"I heard tell about that," I said. "What's that all about?"

"I bought the place a while back, with the idea of making it a church, like the one Jim and Tammy Fay Bakker built in South Carolina: a big place with lots of fun ways for folks to worship."

Like maybe Bumper Cars for Jesus and Noah's Ark-a-pa-looza? I thought, but did not say. I mentally set my B.S. detector on "high," trying to determine whether he was serious or not, but I guess the machine was on the blink. I had no idea.

He then leaned across the table until his face was less than a foot from mine. His breath smelled like Juicy Fruit gum. "Chief Hardy, have you accepted Jesus Christ as your personal Lord and Savior?"

"These days, I mostly pray God will help me lose a few extra pounds."

"Oh, I'm with you there, friend," he said, patting his oversized belly. "I'm just glad I don't have to make weight anymore."

I peeked sideways at Destiny. Her face was as red as a tomato.

"How about you two?" I said. "How do y'all know each other?"

Destiny rolled her eyes without actually rolling her eyes. Cha Cha didn't appear to notice.

"Met when I bought Henny Penny's," he said. "I've been tryin' to get her to marry me, ever since. But she's a hard one to convince."

"Really?" I said, looking wide-eyed at Destiny. "I'd think you'd jump all over the chance to marry the best college wrestler this state ever saw. You know, Mr. Mulvaney—"

"Call me Cha Cha, Emmett."

"You know, Cha Cha, I saw you wrestle in Burr when your high school team wrestled ours. Pretty near the whole town came out just to see you. I was kind of young at the time, but I remember you pinned that poor Burr kid in about ten seconds."

"Four seconds," he corrected me. "It's still a record for fastest pin."

Destiny sighed long and loud, puffing her cheeks out in the process.

I didn't let it stop me. "Is it true Scott Sayre's trying to get you to run for governor?"

"Mr. Sayre has helped me immensely in my work for the Lord. As for runnin' for governor, we'll see what the good Lord has to say."

He sounded like he'd locked himself in the bathroom and practiced saying those lines over and over.

"I don't hear much about Scott Sayre up where I live," I said. "I've been hearing a lot about him since I've been in Norman, though. Sounds like my kind of fella. I'd like to meet him sometime."

"Well, heck," chortled Cha Cha, "I'm sure he'd be proud to meet you. You know, he's the state's number one backer of law enforcement."

That's exactly what the Dallas cops said to me about Jack Ruby all those years ago. Hopefully, owning strip clubs was the only thing they had in common.

Cha Cha reached into his shirt pocket and pulled out a business card. "Here ya go," he said, handing it over. "That there's my home telephone number. I'm actually staying at Mr. Sayre's for the time being, so if you give me a call, maybe we can get him on the line, too, and set something up."

"That's right kind of you, Mr. Mulvaney," I said.

"My friends call me Cha Cha."

"Alright, then, Cha Cha."

"Now, if you'll excuse me," he said, "I've got to use the toilet." He got up and went into the men's room.

"What are you doing?" Destiny said the second the men's room door closed.

"Why does he reserve the booth right next to the restroom?" I asked in a half-whisper.

"Because he has to pee every five minutes!" she hissed. "He's almost 70, for godsake."

"So he wants you to marry him?" I said teasingly.

She shivered like a cold wind had blown across the room. "He keeps asking," she said, "and I keep saying no."

"Maybe you should stop letting him take you to lunch."

"You don't understand," she said. "He helps me in a lot of ways."

I didn't much care to hear about them

"I'd like to have your phone number," I said, "in case I need your help."

"Help for what?"

"Finding out who killed Chastity."

She looked torn. "Alright," she finally said. "Give me something to write on."

I handed her Cha Cha's card. She pulled a pen out of her purse and scribbled down a number. "Don't tell *him*," she said, nodding at the men's room door. "He's very protective. If he thinks you're after something, he's liable to lash out." She paused. "Trust me. You don't want that."

***

Destiny and Cha Cha finished eating and made their exit. I lingered over my burger and enjoyed Mary's spirited versions of "Coal Miner's Daughter" and "D-I-V-O-R-C-E."

Afterwards, I drove around a little bit, before going back to the hotel to kill time before my stake-out. If that salesman had his facts straight, the truck delivering the Mexican cars wouldn't arrive until late. I didn't want to chance missing it, but I also didn't want to get there too early. Stop and Go closed at 8:00, but at that hour, employees would still be hanging around, and anyway, it would be dusk.

I settled on 9:30. By then it would be as dark as it was going to get.

Some car dealerships have night watchmen, some don't. If Stop and Go did, I'd need to park my car some distance away, walk to the lot and find a hiding place. I didn't know one way or the other, so when I got there, I got out and pretended to look over some late-model pickups. No one came out to shoo me away, and nowhere did I see a vehicle that looked like it belonged to a private security company, so I figured the coast was clear.

I drove slowly around the lot, trying to ascertain where someone might park to unload a car carrier full of cars stuffed to the gills with illegal drugs. They wouldn't unload it in the open; they'd do it someplace where they couldn't be seen from the road.

At the rear of the building, I came upon a narrow driveway between the building and a ten-foot-tall Cyclone fence. I drove through and found that it led to a large tarmac, about a hundred yards long and about fifty yards wide. On one side, slightly recessed into the building, were three overhead garage doors. A sign over the middle one said, "Body Shop." The other three sides were enclosed by the tarp-covered fence, shielding the area from view on all sides.

This had to be the place.

At the far end, catty-corner to the building, were several older-model cars that Scott Sayre probably considered too junky to sell. My brown Honda fit right in. I backed into a space between an old Chevy Corvair station wagon without a windshield, and a Ford Galaxie that looked like it had lost a demolition derby. Facing the driveway from my front seat, I should be able to see the car carrier as it drove in.

I settled down to wait. I'd brought a paperback to read, but there wasn't enough light, and firing up my flashclub might attract undue attention, so I leaned back in my seat to think. Pretty soon, I was asleep.

I was awakened by a low-pitched rumble. I opened my eyes to see a dozen men on Harley-Davidson motorcycles drive onto the tarmac. I looked at my watch. It was after 1:00. I'd been asleep for almost three hours.

The men parked their bikes along the side of the building. I peeked over the dashboard with my night vision binoculars. Other than making it seem like I was peering through a dish of lime Jell-O, they worked well.

The bikers were all dressed the same: jeans, t-shirt, leather jacket, and motorcycle boots. On the back of their jackets, there was a picture of the Devil holding a gun to his own head; above it were the words "Satan's Executioners." Underneath that, it said: "O-KKK-lahoma City."

Stupid, sure, but bikers aren't known for the size of their brains.

They immediately started kicking up a racket, shouting and laughing, and drinking enough beer to give an elephant the DT's. One fella started his machine and gunned the engine. A much bigger guy went over and slapped him upside the head. The gunner meekly shut off his engine.

Minutes later, a dark-colored Lincoln turned the corner. A pair of men got out. One was overweight and wore a fedora similar to mine.

Detective Blanchard.

The other was slim, red-haired, and had a face that looked like it had been shaved with a cheese grater.

Even in the dark, Mike Fike's pink suit stood out.

Right away, Fike began jumping around and screaming at the bikers. Most of them were so big, they probably could've ripped him to pieces, but Fike seemed to have them spooked; sometimes acting like a lunatic will do that. Finally, the guy who'd whacked the fella in the head a few minutes earlier pulled Fike aside. They had a few words and Fike seemed to cool down.

The middle garage door started to raise. Lights flickered on inside the body shop. Floodlights lit the tarmac. A semi tractor with a car carrier in tow entered through the narrow driveway; there was just enough room between the building and the fence for it to make it through. The truck swerved to its right and backed up, close to the open garage door. It carried eight vehicles—five on top, three on the bottom. Two were pickups: a red-and-white late-model Ford F-100 and a dark blue Dodge Ram.

The semi stopped and the driver got down from the cab. He had a few words with Fike, then got to work untying something here and unlatching something there, before getting into each vehicle and driving it very slowly off the carrier. He did this eight times; every time one rolled off, a biker took over and backed it into the body shop. At a certain point, every vehicle except the semi was inside, including Fike and Blanchard's Lincoln. The truck left the same way it had come in, the overhead door closed, and the floodlights went dark.

Crouching in the dark, behind the wheel of the Honda, I realized I'd miscalculated. I'd been wrong to think I could observe from where I was. I had to get closer.

Fortunately, next to the overhead door was a regular door with a glass window. Someone had tried to cover it up, but some light leaked around the edges. If I got right up next to it, I might be able to see inside.

I waited a few minutes and watched through my night vision glasses, to make sure the coast was clear. When I was satisfied it was, I got out and trotted to the door.

My stomach felt like I'd swallowed a live rattlesnake. Any minute those floodlights could be switched back on, and my goose would've been thoroughly cooked.

Sure enough, whoever had taped the brown butcher paper over the window in the door had left a gap of at least a half-inch along the bottom.

I bent over and peered inside. I watched as one of the bikers removed the interior panel from the passenger's side door on one of the pickups. Once it was off, he reached inside the door and pulled out an oblong white brick wrapped in plastic. He pulled out another, then another, then another. I didn't have to be told what I was looking at.

I'm sorry I ever doubted you, Fletcher Fluke.

Already, I'd seen enough to sic the Feds or the OSBI on Scott Sayre. I slowly backed away from the window, but before I could, a beefy hand gripped my shoulder, turned me around, and shoved me against the wall. A man was pointing a gun at my face. I didn't recognize him, but I knew who he was.

"Excuse me," he said with a grin. "Don't believe we've met." The whiteness of his teeth almost lit up the night. "I'm Scott Sayre. Pardon me if I don't shake your hand."

CHAPTER TWENTY ONE

"Emmett Hardy, am I right?"

"Guilty as charged."

"Correct me if I'm wrong," he said, "but aren't you a police chief in one of those little towns where men marry their cousins and everybody's sister is their aunt?"

I took a deep breath and counted to three. "The name of the town is Burr," I replied.

He turned me back around, pushed my face to the wall, and frisked me.

He did not check my boot.

"Ok, Mr. Police Chief of Burr," he said waggling the barrel of the gun, "how about you and I go inside and talk over a few things."

I've always said, you should never go anyplace with someone who's holding a gun on you; he's probably just looking for a more secluded place to put a bullet in your skull.

Sadly, sometimes you have no choice.

Gun to my back, he walked me around the corner of the building and through a glass door. We walked through a couple of empty hallways until we came to a glass door with his name written on it in gold leaf. We entered some kind of outer office. He guided me through it to another door, and through that into what was obviously his inner sanctum.

"Sit," he said, pointing to an attractive upholstered chair. I sat. It looked comfortable and it was. Sayre removed his fleece-lined denim jacket, hung it on a coat rack, then sat behind his desk across from me.

For the first time, I got a good look at him.

He wasn't especially tall, five-nine or thereabouts, but you could tell by the way he filled out his red-plaid Western-style shirt that he was built like a brick outhouse. His hair was orange like an orangutan's, but unlike an orangutan's, the roots were gray. His face was handsome and smooth for a man his age, which I took to be a few years younger than me. His blue jeans were sharply pressed and fancier than the regular Wranglers or Levi's that most fellas wear.

He sat down behind his desk, laid down his gun, and punched a button on his phone. "Phil," he said, "have Joe bring a drop cloth to my office." He paused. "Send Blanchard, too."

I figured Joe must be the guy who'd insulted my car when he thought I'd brought it in to get fixed. That same Joe was also the bouncer at Henny Penny's. On my first visit, John had urged me to stay away from him; Destiny had more or less echoed that warning. He gave off an air of barely suppressed violence and seemed like a good guy to stay away from.

It didn't take a fortune teller to see into my immediate future: a desperate politician trying to save his career, his hired goon, a crooked cop, plus a drop cloth, equals Emmett being shot, wrapped up in plastic and dumped in the nearest large body of water.

He wedged the phone between his shoulder and his ear, picked up the gun and twirled it on his index finger like a gunfighter in a cheap western. With his free hand, he punched in another number.

Swiveling his chair from side to side, he said, "Hi, sweetheart. Just wanted you to know we're back." I leaned back and crossed my left leg over my right knee. The hem of my jeans rode up enough so I could see the top of my .38 from the corner of my eye. As he said goodbye to whoever he was talking to, his chair swung away from me slightly.

I snatched my gun from the holster and pointed it at him. He tried to counter my move with his gun, but it fell out of his hand onto the desk.

He raised his hands. "Ok, Wyatt Earp," he said. "Better make your getaway. The cavalry will be here in a minute."

Then I'd better get out of there in less than a minute.

I backed up against the door. I heard voices in the distance. With one hand, I reached for the doorknob. With the other, I held the gun on Sayre.

"I'm going to keep my eye on that outside door when I leave," I told him. "Stick your head out, it's going to get blown off." I meant it. He grinned confidently. "You'd best take your own advice," he said. "It's your head that's going to get blown off, not mine." I backed out of his office and made my way to the hall. There was no one in sight. The voices were still far away.

The red exit signs led in the opposite direction from where the voices came from, so I followed the signs. There were no windows down the hallway, just a bunch of offices with their doors closed. I got to the end. What I thought was another hallway was actually a fire exit. I could open it and risk setting off an alarm, or cower in place and hope that whoever those voices belonged to wouldn't come looking.

Opening the door triggered a siren. I'd come out of the side of the building next to the service area, near where, earlier in the day, I'd encountered Joe the Bouncer fondling his giant crescent wrench.

Twenty or so yards in front of me was a long row of cars with prices written in white shoe polish across their windshields. I ran toward the first car, a Buick coupe. There was a blast and a *thunk* as a bullet pierced the passenger-side door. I ducked behind the car and peeked over the hood, expecting to see Sayre. But it was Blanchard. He kept firing randomly. Bullets pinged everywhere, some close, some far away, as if he didn't have a clue on where I was; I found that somewhat comforting.

I wondered why the bikers didn't join the fray; I guess they didn't hear. Maybe the body shop was soundproofed, or maybe what they were doing was so loud, it drowned out the noise Blanchard was making.

I continued zig-zagging through the rows of cars, doing my best to keep low and remain unobserved. Somehow, I managed to reach the last car in the last row next to the access road. A grassy slope led down to the highway, 100 or so yards in the distance. I heard sirens and in the distance saw a couple of police cars driving in the direction of Stop and Go. I stuck the .38 back in my boot and clambered down until I reached the shoulder of the southbound lanes of I-35. Even in the middle of the night, trying to cross an interstate highway on foot is a tricky proposition, but somehow I managed it. I walked for a while until I reached a street with lots of fast-food restaurants and convenience stores. Most were closed, but I finally found a 7-11 that was still open. I asked the clerk—a young kid with long hair wearing an orange smock with little 7-11 logos all over it—if he knew any taxi services that ran this late. "No," he said, eyeing my grass-stained shirt and pants suspiciously, "but I've got the Yellow Pages." I looked up "Taxi Services" and called the first one. A few minutes later, a cab was pulling into the 7-11's parking lot. I told him to take me to the Sooner Arms. Within a few minutes, I was in bed.

***

But sleep didn't come. I lay there with my eyes wide open, trying to remember if I'd told Detective Blanchard where I was staying while I was in town. The first officer I talked to didn't ask, so I didn't tell. Did Blanchard? I didn't think he did, but I wasn't sure. If he did, I would've told him, in which case I could probably expect him and Sayre's bikers at my door any minute.

Meanwhile, I had plenty to think about.

Fluke's tale appeared to be true. Scott Sayre was smuggling drugs, aided and abetted by Mike Fike, Detective Blanchard, and a motorcycle gang unashamed of advertising it's fondness for the Ku Klux Klan.

Blanchard was had just been pretending to disbelieve Fluke, when actually he was part of the conspiracy. He could even have killed John and Chastity. What better way to cover up the crime than assume authority over the investigation?

Whoever did the actual shooting, however, I had little doubt that the man behind it was Scott Sayre. Chastity hadn't been killed by a member of Carrie's family, but by someone who didn't want Sayre's drug-running scheme exposed.

By daybreak, when no one had come to the door of my motel room and arrested me, I decided the best course of action would be to get the hell out of Dodge. Detective Blanchard and Sayre's thugs would no doubt be on the lookout for me. I could even end up in jail on trumped-up charges, same as Fletcher Fluke. Or, after failing to eliminate me the night before, Sayre might've sent some of those bikers out to finish the job.

In any case, my continued presence in Norman was not in my best interest.

Unfortunately, I didn't have a car. I'd been forced to leave the Honda parked behind Stop and Go Motors when I made my escape. I could go try to get it back or leave it and find another mode of transportation, but I'd have to be a total fool to show my face again at Stop and Go. Maybe when this was all over, I'd go back and get the Honda, but for now, the best thing to do was rent a car.

I checked out of the motel and took a taxi to the nearest car rental place. The only vehicle available was a Chevy Vega. I knew by reputation that the Vega wasn't much of a car, but it was better than thumbing a ride. I told the rental agent that I'd bring it back in a week, then headed for home.

I needed to talk to the only person in the world whose opinion I trust on issues of life and death. It's my good luck that she sleeps next to me.

CHAPTER TWENTY TWO

Red was rocking back and forth on the porch glider when I pulled up to the house.

"Why do you keep coming home with these itty-bitty cars?" she asked.

I sat down next to her and explained what had happened. She reacted the way she always does when I get in some sort of scrap: outwardly calm but obviously concerned.

When I'd finished, she took a deep breath and blew air out of her cheeks. "That's more or less the situation you suspected, isn't it?"

"More or less," I agreed, "except for the crooked cop. I didn't expect that."

"Sure you did," she said. "You agreed when I said that fella had to either be stupid or on the take."

"I guess I was leaning more toward stupid."

"The two aren't mutually exclusive."

"Sad but true," I said.

We rocked a little bit. I knew she'd offer advice when she was ready.

Finally she said, "So what's the plan?"

"Don't have one yet," I said. "I was hoping you might have some ideas."

"First, let me ask if, by some miracle, you intend to wash your hands of this whole business and come home to do the work the town of Burr pays you for?"

"Nope."

"I didn't think so," she said. "Ok, this is what I think. I think you should go to the OSBI."

The OSBI is the Oklahoma State Bureau of Investigation, our homegrown version of the FBI. I'd also been thinking along those lines, albeit with some reservations.

"I reckon I could," I said, "but if I do, I'll have to deal with you-know-who."

The "you-know-who" in question was Agent John Joe Heckscher, who I'd often dealt with in the past. I don't like him, and I suspect he doesn't like me, but he's the only connection I had left in the bureau. He'd been recently promoted, yet was still working part-time in the field. Last I heard, his beat was still Tilghman County.

"I don't see that you have any choice," she said.

"I could go to the district attorney and tell him what's going on."

"That would be taking a *huge* chance."

She was right. Scott Sayre is such a big deal in Norman, it'd take balls of iron to go after him. There aren't many prosecutors in this state who can be so described.

"Ok," I said reluctantly. "I'll drive to Oklahoma City and see Heckscher."

She gave me a little punch in the shoulder. "Come on, now, it won't be that bad. John Joe's a human sloth, but at least he's honest. He's so ambitious, I'm sure he'll jump all over this."

Sure he will, I thought, as long as he can get someone else to do the work.

***

I first met Agent John Joe Heckscher of the Oklahoma State Bureau of Investigation back in '65. We were both working a murder case, the same one I mentioned earlier, involving the young black prostitute. Heckscher was a slippery SOB then, and he's only got slipperier over the years. I went a long time without having to deal with him, until a couple of years ago when the Murray assassination took place in my backyard. Heckscher led the OSBI investigation into Murray's killing of Carrie's boyfriend, as well as Murray's and his cronies' scheme to murder old farmers for their mineral rights.

Heckscher didn't come anywhere near to putting all the pieces together—my people did that—but he did manage to hog all the credit. As an investigator, Heckscher's only actual skill is fooling folks into believing he's working hard. I reckon if you're as bone idle as he is, it's a valuable skill to have. It's gotten him all the way to the top, or near it, anyway. He'd been promoted to Chief Assistant Director of the Department. One more step up the ladder and he'd be running the whole shebang.

If I were his boss, I'd hire a food taster.

Heckscher's also a racist and a bully. Given that the victim in '65 was black, he made it clear at the outset that he wasn't too interested in solving the case. Thankfully, at the time, he was just a second banana. His boss, the fella in charge of the investigation, was a real pro, and we were able to secure arrests and convictions.

On the positive side, Heckscher's naked ambition has made him fairly incorruptible, if you discount his reluctance to work on cases where the victim is a minority. That's hard to do, I admit, but I thought maybe I could trust him on this case, given that the principals were white.

I hate to have to think like that, but that's the way things are in the south, and make no mistake: Oklahoma is part of The South.

My drive to Oklahoma City wasn't pleasant. I'd already developed something like a hatred toward that little Vega, with its little hamster-wheel engine, clunky transmission, and front-end shimmy whenever I drove it faster than 45 mph. There's nothing more frustrating than getting stuck behind a wheat combine on a straight-as-a-string Oklahoma highway and not being able to trust your car to have the power to pass it.

I probably should've called ahead to make sure John Joe would be in the office, but knowing his aversion to actual work, I felt it was a safe bet he'd be there. Even when he worked cases full time, he spent most of his time behind a desk. Now that he's one of the top brass, I doubt he ever leaves the building.

I hadn't been to OSBI headquarters since the Murray case. It hadn't changed much. I told the receptionist who I was and that I was there to see Chief Assistant Director Heckscher. She called up, spoke to Heckscher's secretary, and with told me to go right up.

The men I rode in the elevator were kidding around and telling jokes; I reckon the high from the Roger Dale Stafford arrest hadn't worn off.

Their high spirits must've rubbed off on me. I began to think I'd actually done the right thing by coming. Except for my clashes with John Joe, my dealings with the bureau over the years have been mostly positive. There were some good people in its ranks.

The door to Heckscher's outer office was open. A middle-aged blond woman greeted me from behind a desk. "Chief Hardy?" she asked.

"That's me."

"Go right in. The Chief Assistant Director is expecting you."

I'd been in that office before, when it belonged to John Joe's predecessor. The décor had been pretty vanilla: small metal desk and shelves, white walls, plain curtains, plain tile floor.

Evidently, John Joe had spruced up the place. The floor was covered in wall-to-wall blue carpeting, emblazoned with the state seal. The metal shelves had been replaced by oak bookshelves. The wallpaper was blue with gold stripes, and the small metal desk had been replaced by a much larger one made out of the same polished wood as the bookshelves.

Heckscher stood and offered his hand. "Chief, good to see you," he said with a smile that didn't seem a bit forced; I guess over the years, we've both gotten better at pretending not to hate each other. The bulge in his lower lip and the dirty paper cup on his desk told me he'd taken up a new habit. He picked up the cup and spit.

"Taken up dipping?" I asked.

"Yup. Trying to quit smoking."

"You're lookin' good!" I said, and it was true. He was still as skinny as a fence post; the lines on his face were a little deeper, and his skin was as brown and leathery as a catcher's mitt. But for a man his age—which is my age, give or take a few years—he looked just fine. Probably better than me, in fact.

"Looks like you've come up in the world, John Joe."

"Actually, Chief, I'm going by J.J. now. Easier for people to remember."

"Ok, then, J.J."

"Yeh, I guess I have come up a little bit," he said, basking in the luxury of his surroundings in a way that encouraged me to do the same. "Solving the Murray case caught the eye of some important people. Of course, you helped with that, and I'm grateful."

I more than helped; I was the one who got to the bottom of it.

"You deserve it," I said.

Today was my day for telling whoppers.

He offered me a chair and sat behind his desk. "What can I do for you?" he asked.

"I've got to warn you," I said. "It's a pretty long story."

"Ah, heck, I ain't on the clock anymore; I'm management. Take your time."

I started out by reminding him of the Murray case, which he'd done some work on. I told him about how John and I had set out on a mission to move Carrie's remains from Peckerwood Hill to a private cemetery, then took the story up to the present—telling him of the research John had done on Carrie's background and that of her family, and how I suspected it might have had something to do with his murder. I covered Fletcher Fluke's arrest for killing John and Chastity, then went over what he told me about Scott Sayre's drug smuggling. I finished by describing my stakeout in great detail, and explained how the events surrounding it had confirmed Fluke's allegations.

"How'd Fluke know about it?" asked Heckscher.

"Someone told Chastity and Chastity told him."

"Who told her?"

"I don't know yet," I said. "What does it matter? It's true. I saw it with my own eyes."

He sat there for a few moments without saying anything, just sucking on his Happy Days and spitting into his cup.

"You sure Blanchard's involved in this?" he said.

"He was right there the whole time the bikers were unloading the drugs. *Of course* he says Fluke's lying. He's involved, and doesn't want to get caught."

"But really, how can you be sure Fluke wasn't the killer?" said Heckscher. "It's possible the two crimes—the drugs and the murders of your friends—are completely unrelated."

"But John Joe, doesn't it make sense that, given Fluke's knowledge of the scheme, Sayre and the rest would try to frame him for the murders—if nothing else, as a way to discredit his account of their drug smuggling?"

He shook his head. "I don't know, Chief," he said with a furrowed brow. "I'd have a hard time taking the word of a druggie over a respected man like Scott Sayre."

His skepticism seemed sincere, but I couldn't tell for sure; it could've been his disinclination to rock the boat if he thought it might harm his chances for advancement.

The optimism I felt earlier was fast fading. "John Joe," I said heatedly, "can you please explain to me why you think I'd lie about seeing one of those bikers pull a brick of heroin out of the door of that pickup?"

He made a gesture meant to calm me down. "I didn't say that, Emmett. I'm just thinking out loud, is all."

"Listen," I said. "I watched one of his bikers take a brick of heroin out of the door of that pickup, ok? Then Sayre put a gun to my head and basically made arrangements to have me killed while I sat and listened. I heard the bullets whiz by my head as Blanchard shot at me. If you think I'm lying about all this, I guess I'll just go to your boss, tell him what I told you, and see what he says about it."

He sucked his cheeks like he was trying to draw the last bit of mint from that pinch of Happy Days. I'd always known John Joe wasn't the brightest bulb on the tree, but this wasn't about that. His inability to see was really an unwillingness to see.

He didn't say anything for so long that I finally gave up.

"It seems plain to me," I said, "but maybe I'm missing something. Anyway, John Joe, I'll get out of your hair." I stood to go.

"Come on now, Emmett," he said, as earnest as I've ever heard him. "Sit back down and let's talk about this."

I hesitated, then sat back down.

"Do you have any idea how much pushback I'll get if I go to my boss and propose investigating one of the most prominent Republicans in the state?" he said. "My boss is a Republican, and h*is* boss is a Republican. Hell, *I'm* a Republican, and I like and admire Scott Sayre. No jury's going to convict a fella like that based on what you say you saw, and hearsay testimony from the mouth of a junkie charged with murder."

"So investigate!" I said. "Find more evidence! It's there, I promise you."

Quietly, he said, "Alright, Emmett, that's what I intend to do, but we have to do this the right way. You understand?"

I nodded.

He thought about it a moment, then said, "How about I do this: I'll assign an agent to work with you. Tell them what you know, and let them look into it. If they think there's something to it, I promise you, we'll take it up with the man upstairs." In case I misunderstood, he pointed at the ceiling and added: "The Director."

The offer didn't thrill me, but it was better than nothing. Heckscher said the agent he had in mind was out of the office and that

I should come back at 2:30. "You're going to like this gal," he said. "I think you might even know her."

Gal? I thought. As far as I knew, the only woman agent they'd ever had was Isabel Cruickshank, and she'd left a few years ago for a job with the FBI. If the agent he assigned me was half as good as she was, I'd be getting a hell of a deal.

I ate lunch at a diner near the state capitol. I took my time, getting back to OSBI headquarters a couple of minutes early. John Joe's secretary buzzed me in at 2:30 on the dot.

Sitting across from John Joe was a youngish woman in a gray pantsuit and an ID card hanging around her neck.

"Chief Hardy," he said, "I believe you might know this young lady."

She did look familiar, but it wasn't until I looked at her identification badge that I realized who she was.

"Bonnie Hubbard!" I said. "You did it!"

"What'd she do?" asked Heckscher.

"Became a cop," said Bonnie with a smile. "Chief Hardy was my first teacher."

CHAPTER TWENTY THREE

She'd changed, of course, but if I looked close, I could still see the young girl who read Truman Capote behind the cash register at her mama's store.

I first met Bonnie Hubbard back in '66. Her mother, Grace Hubbard, owned the Butcherville Store, a small general store not far from Burr. Bonnie worked there on occasion, although she spent most of her time behind the counter with her nose in a book. The day we met, she was trying to fend off customers while trying to read *In Cold Blood*. I'm a pretty big reader myself, so we got to talking about books, especially that one. I hadn't read it yet, but I did later, based partly on her recommendation.

Before they moved to Butcherville, Bonnie and Grace had lived in Wichita. During the brief time they lived in Butcherville, Bonnie was a fish out of water. With her long, straight brown hair and the turtleneck sweaters and blue jeans she always wore, she looked like she'd come to Burr straight from a Greenwich Village coffee house. She and her mother moved to Butcherville after her father ran out on the family. Clyde Raymer—Grace's father and Bonnie's grandfather— owned WestOK Petroleum, a local natural gas processing plant. He wanted his daughter close to home, so he bought the store for her to manage.

Small-town life didn't agree with either of the women, but I'm pretty sure Bonnie hated it more. She and I got along great, however. In fact, other than her mother, I might've been her only friend. She told me on the day we met that someday she wanted to be a cop. Maybe I taught her a thing or two, but nothing I did for her could hold a candle to what she did for me.

First, she helped me nail her grandfather (whom she despised) for conspiracy to murder, then later, she and Karen rescued me from having my brains blown out.

Bonnie and Grace didn't stay in the area for very long. Bonnie had wanted to move to New York City so she could attend John Jay College, a school that prepares folks for careers in law enforcement. I guess that's what she'd done.

I hadn't thought about her in ages.

"Great to see you," I said.

"Great to be seen," she said; I was reminded how she'd always been a little bit of a smartass. But in a good way.

"I remembered Agent Hubbard had lived in your town for a spell," said Heckscher, "and she lives in Norman, which I thought might be helpful." He looked at his watch. "Listen, I've got a meeting to go to," he said, "so I'm going to get out of here and let you two get reacquainted. I've already given Agent Hubbard some background. I'll leave it to you to fill in the details. Now, if you don't mind, I've got to lock the office when I leave."

We were being kicked out. As John Joe strode down the hallway, Bonnie and I lagged behind.

"What've you been up to for the last 13 years?" I asked.

"Wow, has it been that long?" she said. "I'm surprised you remember me."

"I tend to remember folks who save my life."

She smiled shyly.

We walked slowly toward the elevator, making small talk. I asked if she knew of anyplace we could sit down and talk. "There's a diner nearby," she said.

"That's fine," I said. "Do you mind if we take your car? Mine's a rental. I don't like it very much."

"What kind is it?" she asked.

"Chevy Vega," I said. "It only runs downhill."

"My advice is: drive slow," she said. "Those Vega engines have been known to actually melt. The guy who used to run GM tells a story about the first time they test-drove a Vega; the entire front end fell off."

"I'll keep that in mind," I said. "I'd forgotten how well you knew cars."

"I'm not as up on them as I used to be."

In the parking lot unlocked a dark blue Mercedes, a few years old, but in almost new condition. "This is mine," she said. "Get in."

The inside was as sharp as the outside. Bonnie might not have been as up on cars as she once was, but she still knew enough to pick a winner.

It turns out that the diner she had in mind was where I'd eaten lunch. I got a cheery "Welcome back!" from one of the waitresses as we came in.

"I just ate lunch here half an hour ago," I said, by way of explanation.

We sat in a booth far from other customers. I had a Tab, she had a coffee, as we brought each other up to date. She did indeed go to John Jay; after she graduated, the only job she could get was as a town constable in a small village in upstate New York. The work was "soul-crushing"—her words—so after a couple of years, she went back to John Jay and earned a master's degree in criminal justice. Afterwards, she applied to law enforcement agencies all over the country. The only agency to show any interest was the OSBI. She wasn't thrilled to be coming back to Oklahoma, but she didn't have many options, so she accepted their offer. As of that day, she'd been on the job exactly a month.

I gave her a brief accounting of what was going on with me, including the fact that Karen and I had gotten married, which Bonnie didn't know. I cut it short, though, because I wanted to bend her ear about the case. "It's not mine, really," I said. "I just kind of fell into it. John Joe probably told you, I've got no jurisdiction."

"Agent Heckscher says you don't think the guy Norman PD picked up did it."

"There's a lot more to it than that," I said, then spent the next few minutes filling in the blanks. I ended by saying, "I'm not sure how much of it Heckscher actually doesn't believe, and how much he doesn't *want* to believe."

"You're saying he's only pretending not to believe it, but because if it's true, it becomes a problem."

"Exactly."

She stirred a packet of sugar into her coffee. "Listen," she said, "it goes without saying, I believe every word you say. You saw someone holding a brick of white powder hidden inside a car door. What else could it be but drugs? You had a gun put to your head by Scott Sayre, but managed to escape. When you did, a Norman police detective took potshots at you. What's the problem? If it were up to me, I'd raid the place today."

But, as we both knew all too well, it wasn't up to her. "What instructions did Heckscher give you?" I asked.

"He said to listen to what you had to say and determine what, if anything, needs to be done."

"What will you recommend?"

"That we investigate. Obviously."

"According to a gal I know who works there, Sayre's the real owner of Henny Penny's. Cha Cha Mulvaney's name is on the paperwork, but Sayre's the man behind the curtain."

She nodded. "I've heard some things about Sayre since I've been on the job that make me think he's not the fine, upstanding citizen he pretends to be, although it does surprise me that he'd actually try to kill you. On the other hand, he wouldn't be the first guy to launder drug money through a strip club."

"So what's the next step?"

"First thing tomorrow, we should make an appearance at Stop and Go Motors. If nothing else, you should at least be able to get your car."

"I'm not sure it's worth the trouble," I said, "but I agree. Let's do it."

She grinned. "It's your car, plus you're being escorted by an OSBI agent," she said. "What could possibly go wrong?"

***

Bonnie drove me back to the OSBI headquarters so I could pick up my rental car. I'd already decided to spend another night in The Sooner Arms. Better the devil you know. Bonnie lived in Norman, so dropping me off wouldn't have taken her out of her way, but even though I'd much rather have taken another ride in that sweet Mercedes of hers, I needed to get that Vega back to the rental car place.

I just hoped the engine wouldn't melt while it was still in my custody,

The Sooner Arms had a vacancy, praise be. Just like the other times, the little old TV-addicted fella at the front desk gave me Room 12.

I phoned Red first thing. I started out by telling her I'd be staying another night at The Sooner Arms, then segued to a description of my encounter with John Joe Heckscher and how he seemed disinclined to do anything about Scott Sayre. "By the way, John Joe's calling himself J.J. now," I said.

"Ain't that sweet?" she drawled.

"Anyway," I continued, "after all that, he eventually decided to assign an agent to look into it." I paused, then asked: "Guess who he assigned?"

I could practically hear her shrug. "I don't know," she said. "Himself?"

"No, not himself, thank God. You remember Bonnie Hubbard?"

"I tend to remember people who saved my husband's life," she said. "She's with the OSBI now?"

"She is," I said. I went on to sketch out Bonnie's recent history, how she'd only been on the job for a month, and that she believed my story, even if Heckscher pretended not to. "She said she'd raid the place today if it were up to her."

"It's not, though, is it?"

"No, it isn't," I said. "But who knows what might happen? She offered to escort me to Stop and Go so I could reclaim the Honda."

"Is she going to arrest anyone?"

"Not yet, I don't think. We're still in the early stages."

"You sure it's worth the effort, trying to get that car back?"

"In fact, I'm pretty sure it's *not* worth the effort, but we're going to do it anyway, just on general principle. I think she might want to force their hand and see what they do when I show up."

The conversation wound down quickly. Karen filled me in on everything that had gone on in Burr over the last 24 hours, which took about five seconds. We exchanged mushy goodbyes and ended the call.

***

Bonnie and I had arranged to meet at Mary's for breakfast. After we ate, I'd drop off the Vega, then the two of us would drive out to Stop and Go to pick up my Honda.

Things started going downhill right off the bat. Before we even finished eating, Bonnie realized she'd left her OSBI credentials at home and would have to go back to her apartment to get them. First, we dropped off the Vega, then I rode with her to her apartment. I'd had a couple of Tabs at breakfast, so my bladder was full. I asked Bonnie if I could use her restroom. She winced and said, "Ok, but I should warn you, my place is a mess."

Everybody says their place is a mess when they invite someone in. Bonnie's was, but I couldn't blame her. She actually kept it pretty neat, but there's not much she could do about the holes in the sheet rock and the water-stained ceiling.

She grabbed her badge, I did my business, she apologized for her place being a dump, and we shoved off.

We talked about guns on the drive over. She carried a Smith and Wesson Model 22, which is a .45 revolver. "That's a pretty powerful gun for a woman," I said.

Drily, she answered, "Don't worry, I can handle it."

She asked me if I still carried the Colt .45 automatic I'd brought home from the Marines. "I'm surprised you remember that," I said. "I do, but all I got on me at the moment is this." I pulled the Colt .38 Detective Special out of my boot.

"Good to know," she said, chuckling uneasily. "You might need that before the day's over."

A school bus that seemed to stop in at every house slowed our progress. Once, while we were waiting, she blurted: "Do you think Heckscher's just setting me up to fail?"

To tell the truth, the thought had occurred to me, but I'd never admit it to her. Truthfully, I said, "John Joe's a gasbag, but he takes his job seriously. He's not going to put you in a position where you could make him look bad."

She nodded and said, "I guess that makes sense."

We drove onto the lot. I asked her to stop near the entrance, then got out. With one eye on the lookout for Sayre's thugs, I examined the line of cars I'd hidden behind, looking for evidence of gunplay. I found nothing, not a single scratch. I don't know what I expected—of course they'd remove any cars with bullet holes and shattered glass—but it gave me an uneasy feeling.

I got back in the car. We drove past the showroom to the back of the building where I'd parked the Honda.

We then ran into a roadblock. Literally.

A long chain was draped across the narrow driveway leading to the body shop. A "Keep Out" sign hung from the middle. In the distance, I could see the Honda parked where I'd left it.

"That chain looks like it has a lot of play in it," said Bonnie. "You could drive under it if I raised it a little."

"Let's do it," I said.

Nobody was in sight. All the doors, including the overheads, were closed. It appeared safe. I slipped beneath the chain and walked toward my car.

Immediately, one of the overhead doors started to hum. I hurried my pace as it rose. As I reached my car, a fella emerged and shouted: "Just what in hell do you think you're doing?" I started the engine, looked up, and saw three bruiser-types hustling in my direction. One of them was Joe, the wrench-fondling bouncer from Henny Penny's. I put Honda into first gear, waited until I could see the whites of their eyes, then popped the clutch and accelerated. They had to scramble to avoid getting run over.

I reached the spot where Bonnie stood holding up the chain. She was right, there was plenty of clearance. I drove under it, stopped the car, and turned to check on her. The bruisers had resumed the chase. She faced them down with her Smith & Wesson drawn. They barked and lunged at her like mad dogs, but didn't attack.

I hollered out my window, "Let's go!" She holstered her gun and got in her car, with the bruisers hot on her tail. By accident, I shifted from first to third, causing the Honda to stall. Meanwhile, our pursuers were fast closing the distance. I waved Bonnie around. She pulled beside me. "Get in my car!" she yelled, but it was too late. The bruisers were too close.

"Go!" I yelled. "I'll be back!" she shouted, then, with a squeal of her tires, drove away.

My door swung open. A pair of hands reached in, pulled me out, and threw me on the asphalt. A combat boot pressed against my face. There was the crunch of tires, and a car pulled up next to the scrum. A male voice said, "What's going on?"

I tried to see who it was, but the boot kept my head pinned to the ground.

"It's that guy from the other night," one of them said.

The car door opened. There were footsteps. A voice said, "You've got to be kiddin' me." A pair of shiny black dress shoes crept so close to my face, I could smell shoe polish. Their owner stuck his face in mine. "You're back!" he said, like he was glad to see me.

"Good to see you, too, Mr. Sayre. Now, would you mind telling this idiot to take his foot off my head?"

The foot lifted. I raised up to my hands and knees. Immediately, a skinny, bucktoothed young fella stepped forward and commenced kicking me in the stomach. Over and over, he'd chant, "That's some funny goddam *shit!*" in time with his kicks. As I lay writhing in pain, I noticed he had a paperback stuffed in his back pocket: *The Mad Make Out Book.*

At least the boy was exercising his brain.

At Sayre's direction, Joe the Bouncer pulled the bucktoothed fella off me, and turned me over on my back. I'm sure if I'd resisted they would've given me an even worse beating, so I went limp. Joe straddled me and slapped on a pair of handcuffs, while the bucktoothed fella patted me down. He snatched my wallet from my back pocket, then lifted my left pants leg over my boot. "Well, lookie here!" said Mr. Bucktooth, as he showed the group my .38.

"Give it," barked Sayre. The kid handed them both over. Sayre put the wallet in his back pocket and held the .38 on me. With a wave of the two-inch barrel, he said, "Get him up and take him inside." The bikers jerked me up by the armpits and hustled me in through a side door.

As they dragged me down the hallway, we ran into the salesman who'd tried to sell me that little Soap-Box-Derby Mustang on my first visit. Alarmed, he asked, "What's going on, Mr. Sayre?"

"We caught this guy trying to steal a car off the lot," said Sayre. "We'll hold him until the cops get here."

"He's lying—" I said, but that's as far as I got, because Joe kneed me in the groin.

The salesman nodded uncertainly and continued past.

We stopped. Sayre took out a set of keys and unlocked a door. "In here for now," he said. The bikers shoved me into the room, but I managed to keep my feet. Joe the Wrench-Fondler didn't like that, so he kicked my legs out from under me.

I fell and banged my head on the floor. The other two bikers laughed. Sayre looked on, expressionless. "Dipshit," Joe muttered, spitting on the floor next to me.

"We'll be back," said Sayre, who no longer seemed quite so happy to have me as a guest. He slammed the door, a key turned in the lock, and I listened as three pairs of boots—and one pair of dress shoes—tromped down the hall.

Other than the stars I was seeing from the blow to my head, the only light was the thin strip under the door. I managed to get to my feet, crept to where the light switch should be and felt around for it. I found it, but when I flipped it, nothing happened.

I didn't know what I was going to do, but whatever it was, I'd be doing it in the dark.

CHAPTER TWENTY FOUR

I was scared of the dark when I was little; not for very long, but for a while I'd wake up screaming for my mama pretty near every night. There was a gnarled oak outside my bedroom window. Sometimes the moon threw the tree's shadow against the wall, which frightened the bejesus out of me. Eventually, my folks got tired of me jumping into bed with them. My dad installed a window shade, and that was that.

I thought of that as I tried to figure a way to get out of that room.

Jiggling the doorknob didn't do anything. I slid my cuffed hands along the walls and floor, hoping to find something I could use to effect an escape—maybe something I could use to jimmy the door— but the room seemed completely empty.

There wasn't much I could do except hide behind the door and jump the next person to come in. Fortunately, Joe had been stupid enough to cuff my hands in front, so there was a slight chance I might be able to defend myself. Maybe when the door opened, I could use it as a weapon—slam it on a hand or head or any other body part that presented itself. It wasn't much of a plan, but my options were limited.

I stood against the wall beside the door and waited.

I don't know how long I'd been there—could've been an hour, could've been more—when suddenly, from inside the room, a telephone rang.

Somehow I'd missed it, but there was a phone on the wall opposite me. A light on it was blinking. Still feeling the effect of Joe the Wrench-Fondler's knee to my crotch, I lurched forward and reached for the handset. I couldn't see in the dark, so I ended up dropping it on the floor. Finally, I managed to pick it up. I held it to my ear and jabbed at the blinking light. I heard voices but didn't listen to what they were saying. Instead I blurted: "My name's Emmett Hardy, and I'm being held against my will by Scott Sayre in an office at Stop and Go Motors. Please call the police."

There was a pause. A woman's voice said, "I don't know who put you up to this, Glen, but it's not funny."

I could hear running feet getting closer and closer. I dropped the phone and positioned myself behind the door. I heard the sound of a key in the lock, and the door opened.

A figure stepped into the room; a man's voice said, "What in hell—?" I looped my arms over his neck and pulled the chain of the handcuffs tight against his throat.

We struggled. I lost my footing and fell to the floor, pulling the fella down on top of me. It felt like I was being crushed by an elephant, but I kept the cuffs pulled tight against his fleshy neck while he clawed away.

A series of noises came from someplace nearby: shouts, yells, and at least one gunshot. Men in uniform ran past the open door without noticing the life and death struggle going on just a few feet away.

The fella seemed about to lose consciousness. I relaxed my hold. He barely moved. I crawled out from under. As I expected, it was Joe the Bouncer/Wrench-Fondler. He seemed to be having a heart attack.

I rushed to the hallway, searching for help. On one end I saw Bonnie Hubbard striding toward me with her gun drawn, looking very business-like.

On the other end, I saw a handcuffed Cha Cha Mulvaney being led out of the building.

***

A team of paramedics arrived and tended to Joe. I asked one of them if he'd be ok. With a straight face, he said, "He's got a red neck, but he'll survive."

I followed Bonnie out to the showroom. We sat on the hood of a like-new Dodge Charger while official activity buzzed around us. "What's John Joe got you doing?" I asked.

"Nothing," she said, obviously angry. "I'm just the one who called in the cavalry, that's all."

We talked for a while. Thanks to Blanchard's involvement, Bonnie didn't trust local law enforcement, so her first call was to Heckscher. John Joe called the highway patrol, then rushed to the scene to direct the raid.

I described what had happened, from the moment Sayre arrived on the scene, right up to the point of her return. "By the way, you haven't seen my gun and wallet, have you? Sayre took them from me while his thugs were beating me to a pulp."

"Ah," she said, then pulled both from her jacket pocket. "Here you go. They were on Sayre's desk."

"Did you get him?"

"He's not here," she said. "Must've gotten away. Tipped off, probably. We got Cha Cha Mulvaney, though. Heckscher says he confessed to everything on the spot."

"Wait," I said, unsure I'd heard correctly. "Why would Cha Cha do that?"

"What do you mean?"

"Why would he confess?"

"Heckscher says Mulvaney's behind everything."

Just when I thought things couldn't get any weirder. "Cha Cha didn't try to kill me," I said. "Sayre did. With help from Blanchard and those bikers, of course."

She shrugged. "You'll have to talk to J.J. about it, I guess."

"What about Blanchard?"

"Under arrest."

"But Sayre's still free?"

"As far as I know," she said. "All I know is Heckscher considered Mulvaney the target from the beginning."

None of this made any sense.

"Did you find any drugs?"

"Bags and bags," she said. "Heroin, and cocaine, some of it right out in the open. We'll have to get a search warrant, but that shouldn't be a problem."

A male agent shouted something at her from across the room. She sighed. "I've got to go," she said. "You ok to get home?"

"I'll figure something out," I said, and Bonnie went off to do whatever it was the male agent wanted her to do.

Over in a corner, Hecksher was talking to a couple of his guys. I waited for them to finish, then approached him.

"Thanks for coming to my rescue," I said.

"Glad to do it," he replied. "You going to be alright?"

"I'll be fine," I said. "So what's this about Cha Cha Mulvaney being the brains behind all this?"

He said, like I'd asked a stupid question, "Because he's the boss."

"No he's not," I said. "Sayre is."

"I thought so, too, but it turns out that Mulvaney's the registered owner, not just of Stop an Go Motors, but Henny Penny's, too. Not that it matters, since he's already confessed."

"Confessed to what?"

"Everything—the drug-smuggling, the hostage-taking. The whole ball of wax."

"How about killing John and Chastity?" I asked.

"He hasn't admitted that yet, but we'll get it out of him."

"But you're still going to arrest Sayre, though, right?"

"We'll talk to him," he said noncommittally.

My agitation was starting to show. "Listen, John Joe," I said, "Mulvaney wasn't the one holding a gun to my head the other night. Sayre was. It was also Sayre who had those bikers kick the crap out of me."

Heckscher shrugged. "I don't know what to tell you, Chief. Mulvaney's singing like a parrot."

It's sing like a canary, you idiot, I thought.

"Think about it, Chief," he said. "If he didn't do it, why would he confess, knowing that, if he's found guilty of drug trafficking on this scale, he's likely to spend the rest of his life behind bars?"

Loyalty, I thought, yet even I couldn't really imagine someone being *that* loyal ... unless he knew the deck was stacked in his favor and he'd never spend a day—never mind the rest of his life—in prison. Murder would be harder to squirm out of, which is probably why Cha Cha didn't admit to that, as well.

If Sayre wanted a fall guy, he couldn't have done better than Cha Cha—a once famous but now low-profile toady, willing to do any illegal thing his boss commands, and stupid enough to confess without seeing a lawyer.

I asked Heckscher if he needed anything more from me. He said I could go, but asked to make sure Bonnie ("your partner," he called her) knew where to find me. I told her where I'd be and asked her to keep me posted. She said she would.

I walked to the back of the building, expecting to get my car, but a state trooper told me I couldn't have it. the entire lot had been impounded. Normally, I wouldn't let a state trooper hose me down if I was on fire, but I was so tired and disgusted, I was happy to accept his offer of a ride.

Back at the motel, I called Karen to let her know I was ok. She'd already heard about Cha Cha's arrest; it had been the lead story on the six o'clock news out of Oklahoma City. She suspected I'd been involved and, needless to say, was glad I'd come out of it mostly unharmed. I assured her I'd be home as soon as I could get away.

I took a shower, changed into a clean T-shirt and pair of underwear, and—despite everything—somehow managed to sleep.

But not for long.

It was still dark when the phone rang.

It was Bonnie. "I just got a call from headquarters," she said. "They need you in Oklahoma City."

I wiped the sleep out of my eyes and looked at the clock on the nightstand. "It's one o'clock in the morning," I said.

"I know, but this is serious. Cha Cha just killed a state trooper. Now he's holding a gun on Heckscher and says if you don't come, he's going to kill him."

CHAPTER TWENTY FIVE

Bonnie was waiting outside my room within five minutes, ready to drive me to Oklahoma City. Of course, my first question was how Cha Cha could have gotten his hands on a gun. She had no idea; her bosses hadn't told her, and she didn't think it was her place to ask. The only way I could think it might've happened was if Heckscher or the trooper had gone into the interrogation room armed and Cha Cha had wrestled the gun away.

What actually happened was a lot worse.

Mulvaney had taken his own gun into the interview room.

***

OSBI headquarters was in full crisis mode when we arrived. TV news vans lined the curb. Floodlights cast harsh light on reporters ad-libbing accounts for the camera. Uniformed state troopers dressed in riot gear guarded the entrance.

We passed three checkpoints. The last one was set up just past the elevator down the hall from the interview room where Cha Cha was holding Heckscher. An agent named Decker led me into an unused office, but ordered Bonnie to stay behind. She took it about as well as if he'd asked her to kiss him on the lips.

Decker and I sat at a small desk, and he filled me in.

"No one frisked Mulvaney when he was arrested," Decker said in disbelief. "A state trooper—Benton's his name—patted him down when they arrived here but he didn't do a very good job. Mulvaney had a gun hidden in his boot. When they got in the interview room, he pulled it and shot Benton." He shook his head. "Heckscher just choked, I guess. Mulvaney used the trooper's handcuffs to lock him to the table and threatened to shoot him if we failed to meet his demands."

"What were his demands?" I asked.

"That we bring you here."

"What? That's it?"

"That's it."

"Why?"

"He didn't give a reason. He said he'd swap Heckscher for you, but that if we didn't get you, he'd kill him."

"So better me than him, is what you're saying?"

"He promised not to hurt you," he said, then paused and added: "Of course, you can refuse."

I took a moment to consider the possible consequences. I had no overwhelming desire to trade my life for John Joe Heckscher's, that's for sure. On the other hand, Cha Cha seemed like reasonable fella when I spoke with him at Mary's. If all he wanted to do was talk, I reckoned that was pretty safe. And according to Decker, he did promise not to hurt me.

A thought ran through my head: *Promises are made to broken, though, you dummy,* which is undeniably true. But if I could save this fella without getting hurt myself, I reckoned I should at least try. Even though I didn't like him very much, he was a human being, after all.

"Alright," I finally said. "What's the plan?"

Decker exhaled, clearly relieved. "Just go in there and listen," he said. "He said when he's done telling you what he has to say, he'll come out."

"You fellas don't have plans to storm him, do you?"

"Not at the moment," he said, "but if it comes to that, we'll make sure you're out of the line of fire."

"Alright, then, I'll do my best." I reached into my boot for my own .38, removed both the holster and gun, and set them on the table.

Decker winced. "You should've checked that at the front desk," he said.

"Someone should've searched me," I said.

He nodded abjectly. "I reckon you could take it in with you, if you want."

I shook my head. "He'll probably frisk me anyway. No need to antagonize him right off the bat."

"Alright then, let's go."

I followed him down a long hallway lined with cops in riot gear. It seemed like overkill, but I suppose it's better to have too much firepower than not enough.

We stopped in front of a door at the end of the hall. "He's in there," the agent said. "He shot out the closed-circuit TV camera, so there's no way we can monitor you."

"No two-way mirror?"

"We use closed-circuit."

"But it's busted."

"Right."

"So it's just me and him, then."

"It will be, after we trade you for Assistant Director Heckscher. Of course, Trooper Benton's body is still in there."

"Then let's get the show on the road."

Decker knocked. Inside, a voice said, "Who is it?" The agent opened the door slightly. Through the opening, "Chief Hardy's here."

A voice I recognized as Cha Cha's said amicably, "Send him in."

Decker moved aside and let me enter. Trooper Benton was blocking the door, so I could only open it a few inches. I squeezed through and stepped over the body. The room was small—maybe ten feet by ten feet. Most of the space was occupied by a wooden table. Cha Cha sat on one side, facing the door, holding a small automatic pistol. Heckscher sat across from him, handcuffed to a metal loop bolted to the table. He had a sheepish look on his face, like he'd messed his pants. Judging by the room's rank smell, maybe he had. Both men were drenched in sweat. I felt hot air blowing on my face and realized the heat was turned up high. They were trying to sweat Cha Cha out.

A few years ago, Red and I took a trip to the Oklahoma City Zoo— I reckon that was the same trip when I saw that orangutan whose hair reminded me of Scott Sayre's. I remember they had a mountain gorilla locked in a cage too small for him to do anything but sit on the floor— belly out, legs spread, shoulders slumped—and throw his own excrement at the folks gawking at him through the bars.

If that gorilla had been in this room at that moment, wearing the same outfit Cha Cha had on, I doubt I could've told the two apart.

He produced a small key and unlocked Heckscher's cuffs. "Go on, git," he said. Without a word, John Joe jack-rabbited over the dead trooper. He tried the doorknob, but it was locked. In a panic, he pounded on the door with flat palms and hollered, "Let me out!" until the door opened and he was able to scramble out.

Cha smiled and shook his head. "Would you believe that fella's the Chief Assistant Director of this whole deal?"

Nervously, I said, "That's what I hear."

He shook his head. "Lord help us all."

He gestured vaguely with his pistol. "Go ahead and take a seat."

I sat in Heckscher's chair. It was wet.

Cha Cha was wearing the same outfit he'd been wearing when I saw him hours earlier at Stop and Go: a gaudy red suit, with blue and white bald eagles embroidered on the sleeves, and white stars on the shoulders. His boots were a slightly different shade of red, with blue stars and white stripes on the vamps, and Gila monsters stitched on the toes. On his head was a red cowboy hat with the interlocking "O" and "U" logo of the University of Oklahoma on the crown. With his oversized belly, he looked like Santa Claus moonlighting at the Grand Ole Opry.

"So, Mr. Mulvaney—"

"I told you last time, my friends call me Cha Cha."

I reckoned that got us off to a good start.

"If you don't mind my asking, Cha Cha, why am I here?"

"Ain't it obvious?" he said slowly, each word spaced apart from the one before it. "I want to give you some material for your book."

I wasn't writing a book, or at least I hadn't been. The book was John's. How did Cha Cha even know about it, anyway?

I asked him.

He grinned faintly, and said, "I got my ways."

"That's real nice of you to want to help," I said. "I can use all I can get."

He frowned and said, "Where's your notebook?"

"What notebook?"

"Don't you writer fellas take notes when you're interviewing somebody?"

I imagine if I really was a writer, I would've known that. "I'm sorry," I said. "I didn't realize you meant to help me with the book."

"Why in hell else would I bring you here?" he said with a hint of irritation. "Ask them fellas out there to get you some paper to write all this down."

"Tell you what, Cha Cha—I'm not much of a note-taker. I tend to use tape recorders in situations like this."

"Then go find yourself one," he said, making a shooing motion with the gun.

I stepped over the body of the expired trooper and tried the door. It was locked. I knocked lightly and said, "Um, it's Hardy, could you open up." The door opened a crack. I peeked out and saw three or four state troopers pointing rifles at my face. I said, "I need a tape recorder."

The troopers lowered their guns and Decker said, "Get this man a tape recorder," to no one in particular. One his men bolted down the hall and came back with a small cassette tape deck. He handed it to me through the barely-open door and gave me a fifteen-second crash course in its use. "Press 'record' and 'play' at the same time," he said. "Make sure he sits close. This thing has a built-in microphone, but it won't pick him up if he's too far away."

I closed the door, sat back down, and laid the recorder on the table. "You should probably move closer," I told Cha Cha. "They said the microphone doesn't work too good."

He moved so that the edge of the table made a dent in his belly, crossed his arms, and rested them on the table. He was still holding the gun, but it wasn't pointed at me.

"Is this close enough?" he asked.

"That should be fine," I said. I pressed "play" and "record."

"Alright," I said. "We're rolling."

I waited for him to speak, but he just hung his head and stared at the floor..

After a minute, he snapped out of it. "Y'all are from Burr, right?" he asked distractedly. "Ain't that where Burt Murray got shot?"

He'd asked the same question the first time we met.

"It is," I said. For a moment, I felt pity for the man. He appeared completely spent, that's true, but there was something else, a certain heaviness about him, and not just because he was overweight. It was like gravity weighed on him more than it does other folks; everything about him sagged: his shoulders, his cauliflower ears, his double-chins, the bags under his eyes.

I waited some more for him to begin. When he didn't, so I figured I may as well.

I nodded at the body of the dead trooper, and asked, "Why'd you kill this poor fella?"

With a heavy sigh, he replied, "I had my reasons."

That might've been true, but I suspected not even he knew what they were.

I asked, "Did you do it to escape?"

He shook his head sadly. "Nah," he said dully. "I'm all done with tryin' to escape."

More silence.

"How'd you manage to sneak the gun into the room?" I asked.

He gave a mute chuckle. "It wasn't too hard. You'd be surprised what people let you get away with when you're famous."

There's Oklahoma *famous and there's* world *famous,* I thought. Cha Cha was Oklahoma famous. I wondered if he knew that.

About the dead trooper, he said, "Poor bastard tried to frisk me, but that other fella stopped him, whatever his name is."

"Heckscher," I said.

"Right," he said, gradually becoming animated. "Heckscher told that kid, 'Mr. Mulvaney's a well-respected fella,' blah, blah, blah. Shit, it's his goddam fault that boy's dead. If he'd let him search me like I needed to be searched, none of this would've happened."

"Yeh, but Cha Cha, you didn't have kill him."

He shrugged wearily. "I guess not. It just seemed like the thing to do at the time."

Both of us were sweating buckets. He took a handkerchief from his shirt pocket, wiped his brow, and offered it to me. "No thanks," I said.

"The jokes on them if they're trying to sweat me out," he said with a chortle. "Back when I wrestled, the coaches always turned the heat up to 90 or 100 so we'd sweat off the fat." With thick fingers, he daintily folded the handkerchief and returned it to his pocket.

"So," he said, having evidently gotten his second wind, "tell me about your book."

I had no idea how he knew about the book. As far as I knew, he'd never even heard of Carrie Fitzjarrald.

"It started out being about that girl who shot Burt Murray," I said. "John knew her from when she and her boyfriend used to hang out at the convenience store in Norman where he worked."

He leaned back in his chair and rubbed his belly in the spot where it was being gouged by the table. "Carrie," he said, shaking his head. "Poor li'l gal never had a chance."

CHAPTER TWENTY SIX

For the last time that day, I felt genuine shock. From then on, I'd only feel sick.

"You knew Carrie?" I asked.

"I did."

"How?"

"We'll get to that," he said, stern-faced, his turkey neck bobbing up and down. He gestured with the gun. "Tell me more about your book."

I blew air out of my cheeks to calm my nerves. Referring to his gun, I said, "Before I go on, is there any chance you might put that away?"

He blushed, as if I'd told him his red clown suit smelled like cat pee. It did, but I wasn't going to be the one to break it to him. He rested the gun on the table, but didn't let go of it.

"Hell," he said, "you don't think I'd shoot a fella writing a book about me, do you?"

He thought the book was about him. Great.

"It's not strictly about you," I said, trying to be diplomatic. "It's really more about Carrie Fitzjarrald."

"I know that," he said impatiently. "But if it's about her, it's about me, too, at least a little bit. You can't tell her story without tellin' mine."

None of that was true, or at least it hadn't been so far. But I wasn't going to argue with the man. Not under those circumstances.

I told him everything that had happened, from Carrie shooting Burt, then Joel shooting her. I recounted John's phone call, which got this whole thing going, and what he'd told me about Carrie's family name, and her being assaulted by an uncle. I told him about John and Chastity being killed, and my suspicion that their knowledge of Carrie's rape was the motive. I told him how we discovered the Fitzjarralds had lived in Longabaugh County—Flat-Nose, specifically—then described my trip to Eureka Springs to speak with Bazil. I told him everything about the case that I could think of, right up to the OSBI raid on Stop and Go, which of course he already knew about.

When I finally finished, Cha Cha whooped, "Damn, son! No wonder you're writing a book! They could make a movie out of that."

He switched the gun to his left hand and shook out his right, like it had been cramping up. He said, "Now I reckon I owe you my story."

"I'd love to hear it."

"And I'd love to tell it," he said with a big, out of place grin.

***

I wasn't wearing my watch, so I can't say how long I spent listening to him. All I know is that his tale was ridiculous, self-serving and full of excuses from beginning to end.

Or almost the end. I ended up getting something relevant out of him, but it took a lot longer than it should.

The first thing he did was lay his gun on the table. "You ain't going to try to grab this and turn the tables on me, are you?" he said, only half-jokingly.

"Of course not," I said. "I want to hear what you have to say."

"Good." He then clasped his hands behind his neck and tilted his chair so he could rest his head against the wall. "So back in the day, I was a sheriff's deputy in Longabaugh County—"

"When was this?" I asked.

With a wave of his hand he said, "Oh hell, I don't know, back when the Fitzjarrald kids were little, whenever that was." He leaned forward and let the front legs of his chair bang on the floor. Scowling, he pointed a finger and said, "This ain't going to work if you're going to be interrupting me every five minutes."

"I'm sorry," I said. "You're right. Won't happen again."

"It better not," he said.

I was beginning to reevaluate his assurance that he meant me no harm.

He tipped his chair back again, and leaned against the wall. "As I was saying, I first met the Fitzjarralds when I was a Longabaugh County deputy. They were an unholy mess, all of them. Harald was the head of the family, and he was about the laziest man I ever met. Mamie was his wife—Mamie Elendar, her name was. Before they got together, she'd been a whore, same as Harald's mother was." He paused for a second, then, as if it had suddenly just occurred to him, he said, "Oh, I just remembered! That's how Harald and Mamie met; she and Harald's mother Clara worked out of the same whorehouse in Amarillo."

It struck me as a little strange how all of a sudden he "just remembered" how and where Harald and Mamie met, but I reckoned it was plausible.

"Harald was living on a ranch near Flat-Nose with Mamie and their kids. Harald made a deal with the owner where he was supposed to slop pigs and feed the cows, or whatever other chores needed to be done. In return, the rancher offered to pay him a few bucks a week and let them live in a house on the property, rent-free."

Knowing how tight farmers pinch pennies, I found that hard to believe, but I didn't interrupt.

"Well, I'll tell you," he said, "that rancher came to regret that deal. Harald never did a lick of work, and the family just about destroyed that house. One day the rancher called the sheriff's department, wanting someone to come out there and evict Harald and his family. As you probably guessed, it was me who got sent out there."

Who else? I thought. Of course, Cha Cha had to be the hero of his own story.

"I went there with every intention of kicking them out of that house," he claimed, "but I changed my mind when I got there. Those people were living in the worst conditions—trash was everywhere, the toilet was backed up, everything stunk. I prayed on it right then and there, and the Lord told me that I was to help that family get its feet back on the ground. From then on, I made it my mission to help the Fitzjarralds any way I could."

Sure you did.

"Except for when he was ordering the kids around and beating on his wife, all Harald did was swill booze and eat Twinkies. I realized that if I was going to help this family, I had to get him out of there. So that's what I did; I loaded him up in my car, drove to Eureka Springs, and found him a place to live."

I had to speak up.

"Excuse me," I said reticently, "but I thought Bazil was the one who got left in Eureka Springs."

He shook his head. "The fella you talked to was Harald. Bazil's been dead for 20 years."

"But Bazil told me it was Hazil who died."

"Nah, Hazil's still around. Harald killed Bazil himself."

"What?" I said. "Why?"

"Bazil was screwing his sister, Zelda. Hazil told him about it, and Harald killed him."

I believed that the man I met in Eureka Springs could've been Harald, but nothing else about this rang true—least of all, the timeline. If, as Cha Cha said, all this happened when the Fitzjarrald children were little, how could it be that the fella in Eureka Springs had been there only four or five years, as Lulu Baker told me? I could see someone being off by a year or so, but two decades?

Cha Cha had probably been there when Hazil dropped Harald off; Mrs. Baker described the chauffeur as an older man in a red cowboy hat. But it wasn't 20 years ago, as Cha Cha claimed.

But I kept my mouth shut and let him talk.

From there, he told story after story of all the wonderful things he did for the Fitzjarralds, especially the children: he bought them food, made sure they all went to school, even taught one of them to play guitar.

"You play guitar?" I asked.

"I'm no Chet Atkins, but I can play the heck out of just about anything Mother Maybelle Carter wrote."

I doubted that like I did everything else, but I didn't say anything. I just let him ramble on. He went on for a few more minutes, with silly, made-up-sounding stories about teaching Hazil to wrestle ("that's why he was Texas state champ") and driving Mamie into Flat-Nose to buy groceries ("of course, I usually paid for them myself"). The more stories he told, the more excited, and the redder his face would get. It got to where I was afraid he was about to have a stroke.

When he finally stopped to take a breath, I butted in. "I sure could use a drink of water," I said.

He pulled out his handkerchief again and mopped his face. "How 'bout askin' those fellas out in the hall if they could get us some?"

I got up from my chair, stepped over the body of the late Trooper Benton, and tapped on the door. It opened a crack and Agent Decker peeked in. "What is it?"

"Water," I said. He disappeared, then came back with a cold pitcher and two cups. I thanked him and he closed the door.

I re-stepped over Trooper Benton, set the pitcher on the table, and poured each of us a cup. We took turns draining and re-filling them.

Neither of us said anything for a minute or two.

"That's some interesting stuff, Cha Cha," I finally said, "but what I'm really interested in is the connection between the Fitzjarralds and the death of my friends. If there is any. Which I think there is."

He nodded, conspicuously avoiding eye contact.

"There's a flat-out *ton* of things I want to know, and you haven't told me any of 'em. For one thing, I want to know why you're taking the rap for Scott Sayre. And heck, you haven't even mentioned Carrie, and she's the reason I got into all this. I want to know who raped her, and who told Chastity about it. I want to know if that's why John and Chastity were killed."

Cha Cha's long, saggy face turned even longer and saggier. "Chastity's the one who told your friend the story about Carrie being raped, am I right?"

"How would you know?"

"Because I told her."

I let that hang in the air for a bit.

"So you witnessed Carrie's assault?" I said.

His voice broke. "Yes," he said.

"And you didn't do anything to stop it?"

"No."

"Why?"

He sighed. "I can't really say."

"Can't say, or won't say?"

"I mean I don't understand it myself."

"But you know who did it, right?"

He nodded almost imperceptibly

"Who?"

"Who else?" he said, his voice barely audible.

I looked down at my hands and realized they were shaking. Quietly, I asked one more time: "Who did it, Cha Cha?"

Sounding less like the grandstanding storyteller and more like someone overwhelmed by a lifetime of regret, Cha Cha said: "Hazil Fitzjarrald, better known in the State of Oklahoma as Scott Sayre."

With a rueful grin, he added, "It's like Shakespeare said. A piece of shit by any other name is still a piece of shit."

CHAPTER TWENTY SEVEN

It must've been over 90 degrees in that room. I was wearing a flannel shirt, and it was as soaked as if it had been dunked in a bucket of water. Worse, flies had started buzzing around the head of the dead trooper. The room already reeked of every objectionable smell a living human can produce; I was afraid that, before long, we could add the smell of decomposition to that list.

I asked Cha Cha, "How much of what you just told me is true?"

Far from the cocky braggart he'd been minutes earlier, Cha Cha now looked like a little boy who'd gotten caught with his hand in the cookie jar. "Some of it," he said, his voice a near whisper. "I did help 'em as much as I could."

"Were you ever a sheriff's deputy?"

"Not in Longabaugh County."

"Were you ever a sheriff's deputy *anywhere*?"

He hemmed and hawed, then muttered: "No, I never was."

Just as I'd expected.

Now that I'd called him on his B.S., I thought maybe he'd be shamed into telling the truth. Yet I still didn't have the upper hand. I wouldn't as long as he held the gun.

"How 'bout you let me hold on to that."

He held it up and let the harsh overhead light reflect off the chrome finish. It seemed to amuse him. "Nah," he said. "I'll hang on to it for a while."

Abruptly, he began playing with the gun—ejecting the magazine, dry firing it, and twirling it on his finger like a little boy playing cowboy.

My chest tightened; while I'd been assured by both him and the OSBI that he didn't intend to hurt me, Cha Cha was starting to impress me as a nutcase.

I thought it best to get a move on, conversation-wise, if for no other reason to divert his attention from the gun.

"Any chance I could get you to tell me some of those things I was just talking about?"

He nodded ever so slightly. "I guess I might could.".

"I'd be obliged if you did."

"Alright, then," he said. "Where do you want me to start?"

"Wherever you want."

For the next hour or more, it was off to the races.

***

"If you had a bible handy," he began, "I'd swear on it that what I'm going to say from here on out is the truth."

I was and remained skeptical, but I reactivated the old B.S. detector, sat back and listened.

I'll tell you right now: If you've got a weak stomach, the rest of this story might not be for you. Most of what he recounted Cha Cha claimed *not* to have witnessed, but was told afterwards by members of the Fitzjarrald family: Hazil, Zelda, Sheilah, and even Harald himself. He didn't tell it in any kind of sensible order, but just dumped it on me like a 30-gallon barrel of of raw sewage. I put it together later, relying heavily on the recording I'd made, augmented by John's notes, which Red had deciphered by the time I sat down to write this. I'd rather not have to tell this at all—I'd rather not have to ever think of it again—but I've come this far, I night was well. It's a long story, but I'm going to make it as short as I can.

I'll try to make it one of those *Dragnet* deals: Just the facts, ma'am.

***

Harald Fitzjarrald was born in Amarillo, Texas on June 14th, 1910. His mama was a prostitute named Clara Fitzjarrald. He never knew who his father was.

Harald grew up in Amarillo, raised in a kind of half-assed way by his mama, who didn't have much use for him, until he hit puberty, at which time she began taking him into her bed.

When he was little, Clara left Harald mostly on his own to do what he wanted. That did not include school; he only went when the truant officers caught up with him, and eventually even they gave up. By the time he was 11 or 12, he'd stopped going altogether.

Instead of going to school, Harald started hanging around a local pool room. The alcoholics, gamblers, and all-round deadbeats who frequented the place became father figures for the boy—only instead of playing catch or taking him fishing, they taught him how to drink.

Wait. It gets worse.

In his retelling, Cha Cha claimed that, aside from part about him being a sheriff's deputy, most of what he'd said about Harald's teen years had been true. He *did* meet and marry Mamie Elandar. She *was* a prostitute working in the same brothel as Harald's mama, and she *was* closer in age to Clara than Harald.

Mamie was infatuated with the writer F. Scott Fitzgerald and his book, *The Great Gatsby,* so when she discovered Harald had almost the same last name, she decided their love was meant to be, and they got married.

This would've been 1929. Mamie was 29, Harald was 19.

Mamie got pregnant almost immediately. Harald was presumably the father, although there were obviously other candidates.

Within a year, she gave birth to a son, Hazil. Over the next two years, she had two more: a son named Bazil, and a daughter named Zelda.

By the time Zelda came, the friction between Clara and Mamie had become too much for either woman to bear. There was a showdown. Clara won, and kicked the family out.

For a short time, they slept in their car, an old Model T panel truck. One day, a fella from the pool room heard about their plight, and made Harald a proposal: The family could live on his ranch near Flat-Nose, a small town about 90 miles southeast of Amarillo, and Harald would run it for him.

Just barely out of his teens, and knowing nothing about ranching or farming, Harald nevertheless accepted the offer, probably because he had no intention of working, deal or no deal. He even convinced the old fella to kick in a few bucks for groceries.

The Fitzjarralds had a place to live.

Eventually, the rancher caught on to the fact that Harald wasn't going to hold up his end. For whatever reason, he didn't kick them out of their home, but he did stop paying Harald.

With no money coming in, someone had to go to work.

With no kindly sheriff's deputy riding to the rescue ("I'm embarrassed I told you that whopper," Cha Cha said sheepishly), and Harald refusing to do anything remotely resembling work, supporting the family fell to Mamie.

Unfortunately, Mamie only knew how to make money on her back, and there wasn't much of a market for prostitutes around Flat-Nose, so she relocated to Amarillo. She lived in the brothel where she worked, kicking back a portion of her earnings for rent, setting aside a little to live on, and sending the rest to her family.

At first, Mamie would hitch a ride back to Flat-Nose on weekends, but those visits soon stopped. "Can't blame her," said Cha Cha. "Harald would beat the hell out of her every time she showed her face, which was a shame, because she was quite a handsome woman. Pretty, with a good figure."

With Mamie gone and Harald not caring whether they lived or died, the Fitzjarrald kids were left mostly on their own.

Years passed, and the two younger kids grew into versions of their parents: Bazil became a lazy bum, allergic to work; Zelda became a kind but not-too-bright girl with big dreams but neither the smarts nor the imagination to make them come true.

Neither had any desire to attend school, and their father was disinclined to force the issue.

Their oldest son was different. Not only was he smart—Hazil was the only Fitzjarrald to finish high school—but he actually wanted to make something of himself. Every year he earned straight-A's, while also starring on the football and wrestling teams.

From a young age, he possessed the qualities of a born politician—or, as Cha Cha put it, not without admiration: "He always knew who to suck-up to." Those who could do something for him, he treated nice. Those who couldn't, he abused.

Cha Cha related a story about Hazil burning a cross on the lawn of one the few black families in the area.

He told it like it was a joke.

Meanwhile, Harald went downhill. His weight ballooned to 300 hundred pounds, which is what happens when you subsist on a diet of Lucky Strikes, Twinkies, and the bargain-basement bourbon, all of it purchased with money earned and mailed to the family by Mamie.

She might not have been Mother of the Year material, but Mamie was a good provider.

Harald didn't miss his wife. "They hadn't screwed since Godzilla was a tadpole," said Cha Cha—not because Harald had lost his desire for sex, but because he'd lost his desire for Mamie.

Harald had never been with a woman younger than him, a fact that would soon take on a much darker meaning.

A younger woman—a girl, really—lived under his roof: his daughter Zelda, age 15.

Without going into detail, let's say that many of the things Harald did to Zelda would have gotten him arrested, even if he'd done them to an adult.

Soon Harald roped Bazil into sharing his nightly depredations, doubling Zelda's misery.

By now, Hazil was barely part of the family. After Mamie left, he'd gotten a job pumping gas at the Skelly in Flat-Nose and began staying away from home as much as possible.

Cha Cha claimed that, because Hazil was away so much, he didn't know about what Harald and Bazil were doing to Zelda. Personally, I found that far-fetched.

In any case, if he didn't already know, he eventually found out in a fairly predictable way.

Zelda got pregnant.

When Hazil asked Zelda who the father was, she said, "Either Daddy or Bazil." Enraged, Hazil confronted Harald, who denied responsibility ("I always used rubbers," he said) and blamed Bazil ("Your brother never did").

While Hazil may have been justified in taking out his anger on both Harald and Bazil, he ended up venting it on only one.

He grabbed the family's 12-gauge shotgun, hunted down Bazil, and shot him in the face.

***

Now a murderer, and facing life in prison or worse, Hazil devised a plan to fake Harald's death.

Not his own, which would have made more sense.

Harald's.

Zelda got on board immediately. Hazil had become her knight in shining armor.

Harald went along, too, out of fear. He was just plain scared of his oldest son.

Harald built the coffin, presumably because he was afraid Hazil would do to him what he did to Bazil. Zelda carved a wooden slab, Hazil dug the hole, and they buried their brother. Bazil had never had a birth certificate, or gone to school, or even visited a doctor. There was no official record he'd ever existed.

Somehow, Harald escaped Hazil's wrath. Maybe Hazil saved his father's neck just so he could wring it whenever he felt the urge.

Months away from having a child, Zelda began leaning on Hazil. Her gratitude turned into something more. Hazil had become her only refuge. Before long, were sharing a bed.

Indeed, the closer Zelda got to her due date, the more Hazil doted on her. They began acting like a married couple.

Like the father on a '50s TV show, Hazil would leave the house in the morning, only instead of going to work, he went to high school.

Zelda played the role of dutiful wife and expectant mother, cooking, cleaning, and preparing for the birth.

When the baby came, Zelda named her Sheilah.

Hazil showed no affection to the child. Cha Cha had no opinion on why that was, but I suspect it was because Sheilah wasn't his.

Another mouth to feed put a squeeze on their budget. Even with the money Mamie sent, Hazil's job at the gas station didn't pay enough.

Hazil took the bull by the horns. He'd always planned on going to law school, so when a local lawyer advertised for help, Hazil jumped on it. All his butt-kissing over the years made it easy to get good references. He got the job.

Not only was he making good money, he was also taken under the wing of someone who could help him go places.

Hazil went to school in the morning, worked for the lawyer in the afternoon, then returned to school for football and wrestling practice. The lawyer taught him things. The family's financial situation improved.

Hazil worked for the lawyer all through high school, doing everything he could to make himself indispensable. When, at the end of his senior year in May, 1947, Hazil asked for a raise, the lawyer refused.

Hazil figured he'd already learned everything the fella could teach him, anyway, so he quit.

His next job didn't take smarts, but it paid a lot better.

All the weight-lifting Hazil had done to prepare for football and wrestling turned him into the second coming of Charles Atlas. When a local strip club advertised for a bouncer, he applied for the position, and got it.

Between tips and his salary, he began hauling in big bucks—so much that he was able to buy a candy-apple red Ford Thunderbird and loads of presents for Zelda.

For five years, from mid 1947 until early 1952, Zelda had almost everything she'd ever wanted.

Then suddenly she didn't.

***

"Things were going great," said Cha Cha, "then one day Hazil vamoosed, took that new T-Bird and left Zelda and Sheilah high and dry."

That's when Cha Cha entered the picture.

At the time of his disappearance, Hazil had been working at the strip club (located, incidentally, in the abandoned Eagles Lodge I'd seen on my visit to Flat-Nose) for almost five years.

Cha Cha claimed to know Hazil from the club, where he was supposedly a regular customer According to what he told me—which, needless to say, I took with a huge grain of salt—when he got word that Hazil had vanished, he drove out to the ranch to check on the girls. (Don't ask me how he knew where they lived or that Hazil was supporting a "wife" and a "daughter." I asked, but couldn't get a straight answer.)

At this point in our conversation, I think it's important that I quote Cha Cha word for word.

With a wistful smile, he said: "I'll never forget that first time I ever saw that little girl," meaning Sheilah, who was four years old at the time. "She was the cutest, sweetest thing—downy cheeks, soft skin, chubby little legs. Pretty little mouth. I reckon I fell in love with her right then."

I feel bile rise in the back of my throat when I think of him saying that.

From there on out, Cha Cha's story adopted some of the same absurd grandiosity as when he began. He talked about making it his mission in life to take care of Zelda and Sheila, and that he would've buried Harald up to his neck, poured honey all over his head and let the fire ants go at him if he ever laid a hand on either of them.

To be honest, I only half listened to most of it.

My ears perked up, though, when he mentioned how, in 1954, Zelda began getting an extra packet of money in the mail every week, on top of what she continued to receive from Mamie.

The return address said the sender was someone named 'Dan Cody.' Zelda didn't know anyone by that name, but was happy to accept the cash. After several months, the cash made a nice little pile. Most of it, Zelda stashed under her mattress. "She called it Sheilah's college fund," said Cha Cha.

Then Harald discovered her hiding place and stole it all.

Cha Cha vowed to kill Harald. Zelda begged him not to. Harald showed up home a week later. Don't ask me why, but Zelda took him back. I expect it was one of those cases of home being the place that, when you go there, they have to take you in.

Still, the money kept coming. Zelda used $200 of it replace the old Model T, which barely ran anymore, with a 1948 Studebaker Champion, which Cha Cha called "The ugliest damn car I ever saw."

All along, Zelda never stopped mooning over Hazil. She'd cry about how much she missed him, and Cha Cha would try to reassure her, telling her that Hazil would come back someday.

But he didn't believe it.

Zelda's and Sheilah's lives went on without much happening. Sheilah got good grades in school; Zelda gradually accepted that Hazil wasn't coming back. They hardly ever saw Harald except to deliver groceries to his little bunkhouse once a week. Life became normal. Predictable.

Then one day Cha Cha showed up to find both Sheilah and Zelda in tears.

Sheilah was pregnant. Harald was the father.

Cha Cha went looking for him. When he couldn't find him, he camped out on Zelda's couch and waited.

The phone rang at one o'clock that the morning; Cha Cha picked up. The caller identified himself as Dan Cody. He told Cha Cha he knew where Harald was, and that he'd never bother Zelda or Sheilah again. Cha Cha tried to get more out of him, but the fella hung up.

If this happened in 1954 or so, it would've been about the same time Hazil set Harald up in Eureka Springs.

Cha Cha claimed he had no idea how 'Dan Cody' had known Sheilah was pregnant. He also claimed that was the first time he'd ever been in contact with Hazil, but the way he said it gave me doubts.

With Harald gone for good, things went back to what passed for normal in the Fitzjarrald household.

That changed in the summer of 1956, when Hazil made his triumphant return.

Turns out, the reason he left Zelda back in '52 was to seek his fortune. While working at that strip club in Flat-Nose, he discovered how much money could be made running a place like that. He started putting money aside to buy a place of his own. When he'd saved enough, he changed his name to Dan Cody and bought his first club. That was a hit, so he bought another—then another, then another, until, before long, he was the strip club king of the Texas panhandle.

Now that he was a success, he'd come back

"Just like in a fairy tale," sighed Cha Cha.

A very sick and twisted fairy tale.

Eventually, Hazil developed a lucrative sideline: drugs. A lot of the strippers working for him were hooked. He figured he could make big money by eliminating the middleman.

The club made it easy to launder the money. Soon he was rich enough to go legit.

But Hazil's idea of going legit wasn't to sell his strip clubs and stop dealing drugs; it was to put so many levels between himself and his shady operations that no one would ever know about his involvement.

Zelda had raved about Cha Cha and all the help he'd been in the years Hazil was gone. Hazil needed a front man. Cha Cha impressed him. He offered Cha Cha the job.

Cha Cha accepted.

The only problem was, Hazil's business office was in Amarillo, and he didn't want Zelda anywhere near it. She begged to go, but he insisted she stay.

But Cha Cha went.

During the week, Hazil and Cha Cha worked and lived in Amarillo. On weekends they visited Flat-Nose.

I realized that Cha Cha had never mentioned where he was living while he was looking after Zelda and Sheilah. I asked him where he stayed on his visits back to Flat-Nose. "Usually on Zelda's couch," he said.

I said, "I see."

But I didn't.

The situation worked out for a while, until one weekend when Hazil didn't show up in Flat-Nose at the usual time. Zelda called every number she had for Hazil and Cha Cha.

No luck.

In a panic, she drove to Amarillo in that ugly Studebaker, not knowing where he lived or worked, but hoping to at least spot his candy-apple-red Thunderbird.

Still no luck.

It wasn't until she got home the next day that Hazil finally called and told her what happened: A feud with another drug dealer turned out to be too big for him and Cha Cha to handle. They had to leave the state.

Hazil wanted to take Zelda with them.

But not Sheilah. Hazil left his pregnant teen-aged niece alone in Flat-Nose to fend for herself.

Cha Cha didn't like the idea, but he went along with it.

***

"How old was she at the time?" I asked him. "15 or 16?"

"Something like that," he said, his voice a mixture of sorrow and half-hearted rationalization. "It's not like we left the cupboard bare. The cash from Mamie kept coming, and Hazil promised Zelda he'd send her all the money she needed."

"I don't know," I said. "It still sounds damned cold."

"Well, the Fitzjarralds are a damned cold family."

I refused to accept that answer.

"What in the world did Hazil have against Sheilah?"

"I reckon when he looked at her, he saw Harald and Bazil. I know that sounds crazy, but if was up to him, he'd have given her up for adoption the day she was born."

I wanted to scream, *But what about you? If you cared as much about Sheilah as you say, why didn't you do something?* But I didn't; I said, "So you moved to Norman."

Cha Cha nodded. "Yup. Hazil was a big OU football fan, and Norman already had a couple of strip clubs, so we knew the business would fly. Hazil had been operating under the name Dan Cody, but now that Dan Cody was on the run from a rival drug gang, he changed his name again."

"To Scott Sayre."

He nodded. "I'd give you a cigar, if I had one on me."

I summoned up the gumption to ask something else: "One thing I'd like to know before you shoot me, Cha Cha—"

He laughed. "Oh hell, I done *told* you I ain't going to shoot you. Don't know why you'd think I've changed my mind, not after the talk we've had. In fact—" He pretended to look around to see if anybody was watching, before pulling a flask from the inside pocket of his jacket. "I don't know where my manners went," he said, taking a slug from the flask. He held it out to me. I knew I shouldn't, but I took a sip. I figured, What could it hurt? I could be dead by the end of the day. I hesitated for maybe a second, then drained the rest. It went down hot and bitter.

Damn, how I had missed it.

Impressed, Cha Cha said, "You're a drinkin' man, are ya?"

"I used to be," I said. "Like I was saying," I said, the booze already causing my lips to partially disobey my commands, "I do have a couple more questions, if you don't mind."

He nodded. "Go ahead."

Now full of liquid courage, I asked him flat out: "Did you kill John and Chastity?"

Waiting for his answer seemed to take forever, although it couldn't have been more than a few seconds. Finally, he frowned, and, in the voice of a 100-year-old, said: "Hazil wanted me to, but I told him I wouldn't do it. That little gal Chastity was a friend of mine."

I will confess to feeling kind of relieved. For some reason, I didn't want it to be him. Don't ask me why, because I couldn't tell you.

"Who did it, then?"

Again, he took his time answering. "One of Hazil's biker friends," he said, which I accepted at face value.

Of course, I had a buzz on.

"One more thing," I said, trying not to slur my words. "I'm not sure you ever answered me when I asked how it was you knew Carrie Fitzjarrald. About an hour ago, you made it clear that you knew Carrie."

He nodded. "I did."

"But you still haven't told me *how* you knew her," I said. "It sounds to me like you were practically a full-fledged member of the Fitzjarrald family. If Carrie wasn't Mamie's and Harald's daughter, or Sheilah's and Bazil's and Hazil's sister, then who was she?"

His eyes twitched and his chin quivered, like he couldn't bear the thought of saying what he was about to say.

Finally, he gathered himself, looked me straight in the eye, and said, "She was my daughter. Mine and Sheilah's."

CHAPTER TWENTY EIGHT

That one hit me like a blast from a firehose.

"I guess you figured out how I felt about Sheilah," he said sadly. "I knew she was a lot younger than me, but I made sure and waited until she was old enough before we started messin' around."

Waited? Yeh, right. Based just on his own words, he'd been drooling over her downy cheeks and chubby little legs since she was four.

"Then Carrie was born," he said. "The poor little thing had a terrible birthmark on her face, and something wrong with her chin; it hurt to even look at her. I wanted to give her up, but Sheilah loved her so much, I let her keep her." His voice faded to a whisper. "After the baby was born, Zelda convinced Hazil—"

"Just a question, "I said. "By now, Hazil was going by the name Scott Sayre, right?"

"Right. He changed his name from Dan Cody to Scott Sayre when we moved to Oklahoma."

"Got it," I said. "Go on."

"After Carrie was born, Zelda wanted her grandbaby close, so she convinced Hazil to let them come live with us."

"Us?" I said, remembering how Cha Cha answered the door at Sayre's the night I tailed Sheilah.

"Yeh, Hazil wanted us together under one roof, like a family."

Right, I thought. *The Manson Family.*

"It was ok for a while," he said, "then Zelda died, and everything went to hell."

He took a deep breath, and I waited for him to tell me how and why everything went to hell.

He never got a chance.

Suddenly, without warning, the door burst open, but only part of the way; the fellas doing the busting in hadn't accounted for the body blocking the door. The few seconds it took them to push it out of the way cost them the element of surprise. Cha Cha swept the tape recorder and our hats off the table, reached across it, horse-collared me, and put the gun to my head.

The room fell silent. Three armed men trained their rifles on Cha Cha. One of them shouted "Drop it!" I could hear Cha Cha's heart beating like a jackhammer as he held my head to his chest and the gun to my head.

Nobody moved. Nobody breathed.

Then Cha Cha shoved me to the floor, put the gun in his mouth, and pulled the trigger.

***

The bark of the gun stayed in my and probably everyone else's ears for half a minute. As it faded, I heard something *click* beside my head. I jerked, afraid it was a gun being cocked. But it was just the tape recorder. I'd fallen almost on top of it.

The click had been the machine stopping itself when the tape ran out.

As you might surmise, sitting ringside as someone blows their brains out is not as much fun as a having 50-yard-line seats at an

Oklahoma Sooners football game. I lay on the floor where Cha Cha shoved me—on my back, under the table.

Cha Cha's lower half had fallen back onto the chair in a sitting position, like he'd never gotten up. The upper half leaned forward into onto the table, giving me a close-up view of his distended stomach. A button right above his belt buckle had popped off, exposing his hairy navel.

It was an outie, if you're keeping score.

Stars twinkled on the edge of my field of vision, probably from my head having slammed to the floor. I turned my head and looked at the deceased Trooper Benton in time to see him being loaded onto a stretcher. A fella in a white lab coat bent over him, doing whatever it is fellas in white lab coats do.

For some reason I wondered if Trooper Benton's next of kin had been notified. Surely they'd be easier to locate than Carrie's had been.

A voice from above asked if I was alright. For a second, I wondered if it was God looking in on me; maybe I'd been wrong to disbelieve in his existence all those years. Then someone pulled me out from under the table by the ankles, and I saw it wasn't God, but one of the state troopers who'd busted in on us.

"You alright?" he asked again as he helped me to my feet.

"Hangin' in there," I said, which was true, but just barely.

Mostly I felt like I'd awakened in the middle of a nightmare, only to discover that the horror I thought I'd imagined, was, in fact, all too real.

Cha Cha's body was bent forward onto the tabletop, his face and head leaking blood, brains, and fluid like the viscera of a butchered animal. Blood covered the walls, the ceiling, the floor. My face felt wet. I thought it was just perspiration. I tried to wipe it off with my bare hand, but when I pulled it away, I saw it was actually blood—also little pink chunks of gray matter and bone chips from Cha Cha's shattered skull.

I rushed out of the room and down the hall to the first men's room I could find, locked myself into a stall, and heaved my guts out. I took a minute to wash my face and gain some semblance of composure.

I'd probably been through some things just as bad, but I don't think I'd been through anything worse.

When I got back, I found John Joe Heckscher outside the interview room, talking to some plainclothes agents and heavily armed troopers, all of them laughing and self-satisfied. John Joe seemed especially proud, like he'd saved the day, instead of getting one of the men under his command killed.

That's harsh, but it's the way I felt.

John Joe saw me and asked what happened.

"Those fellas broke in, and Cha Cha shot himself." I thought about ripping into him about the clumsy rescue attempt he no doubt had a hand in planning, but I held back.

I'm glad I did.

He looked me in the eye like he was trying to make sure I was in full possession of my faculties.

I don't know what he saw in my eyes, but I'm pretty sure I saw pain and regret in his.

Maybe I'd misjudged the poor SOB.

"This has been a bastard of a day for you, Emmett," he said kindly, with a pat on the shoulder. "How 'bout we get you someplace where you can rest?"

'That'd be nice, John Joe," I said.

He winked, "It's J.J. now. Remember?"

I had to smile. "Ok, J.J."

***

Heckscher found Bonnie and told her to take me wherever I wanted to go. She saw me and her face tightened. "You're not getting into my car dressed like that," she said with a wry expression on her face. "We'd better find you something to wear."

She asked around, and got someone to rustle up a generic police uniform without patches or insignia. I changed into it and threw out my bloody clothes. My boots were a mess, too, so I asked if they had anything for my feet. All they could give me was a pair of hospital slippers. I put them on and threw away the boots. They were just Dingos, and easy to replace.

The sun was coming up as we exited the building. The news vans were still on the scene. Reporters ad-libbed reports on the night's events for the local morning news shows. I'm sure if they had known who I was and my part in what had happened, they'd have swarmed all over us. But they didn't know me from Adam, which was fine by me.

Bonnie asked me where I wanted to go. I felt like asking her drive me all the way to Burr. Knowing her, she probably would've done it. But she had work to do, and I reckoned that that later in the day I'd probably need to talk to Heckscher again, so asked her to take me to the Sooner Arms

Neither of us said much on the drive. I asked her if they'd arrested Sayre. She said they had. I didn't ask for details and she didn't offer any. I must've fallen asleep almost immediately.

Bonnie shook me awake in the motel parking lot. "You sure you're going to be ok?" she asked.

"Yeh, I'll be fine," I said, but I wasn't sure I was.

The half-hour of sleep I got in the car was enough to clear my head a little bit. I would've liked to put what had just happened out of my mind, but that wasn't in the cards.

What bothered me most wasn't Cha Cha blowing his brains out. It was everything he'd said before that point—in particular, the role he and the Fitzjarrald men played in the abuse of the Fitzjarrald women. Now that I knew about it, I reckoned I had to do something.

The trouble was, I didn't know what to do.

I dialed Red. She claimed to have been asleep, but I knew better; her eyes would've been glued to the special news reports on all the Oklahoma City stations. She told me they had disclosed my name to the press. I asked if she was surprised when she saw the guy in the news report was me. She said, "Not too much," then told me she was glad I was still alive and that Mr. Paws missed me.

I knew that meant that she missed me, too. I told her I missed her and Mr. Paws, and we ended the call.

I was so exhausted, I went to bed without even taking a shower.

***

That isn't the end of the story. It's just the end of Cha Cha Mulvaney. Between what he'd told me and what we discovered when Red eventually finished translating John's notes, we learned a lot.

But not everything.

What we knew:

Carrie's last name was Fitzjarrald. The Fitzjarralds were a family of rapists, murderers, prostitutes, pedophiles, drug dealers, and incestophiles. The head of the family, Harald Fitzjarrald, was a degenerate who, among other audacities, impregnated his daughter.

Harald's oldest child, Hazil Fitzjarrald, ran a drug smuggling operation. He also killed his brother in a fit of rage, and had other people killed, whenever it suited him. As a sideline, was a leading figure in one of the state's two major political parties. Oh, and he also raped and tortured his niece Carrie, under the watchful eye of his lackey, Cha Cha Mulvaney, who was the girl's father.

Cha Cha might not have been a Fitzjarrald, but he was as depraved as any blood relative of the clan. He fell in "love" with Carrie's mother, Sheilah (who was both Harald's daughter *and* his granddaughter) when she was still a toddler, and he couldn't be bothered to wait until she'd grown up before he started having his way with her.

Those are just the highlights.

What we didn't know:

If any of it mattered.

Of course, it *all* mattered, morally, at least. What I mean is, would anybody involved pay for their misdeeds?

Not Cha Cha. He took the coward's way out before he could be held to account by a jury.

Not Harald, who, as far as I knew, was dying of syphilis in a burned-out house a few hundred miles away from the scene of his crimes.

I guess that's the karma thing Karen sometimes talks about.

As for Hazil, the fella who now called himself Scott Sayre who was too politically connected to touch, or so he thought.

Was it true what Cha Cha said about one of Sayre's bikers killing John and Chastity?

Would we ever know?

Let's not forget Chief Assistant Director John Joe Heckscher of the Oklahoma State Bureau of Investigation, who failed to ensure that a suspect was disarmed, an oversight that resulted in the death of a state trooper. Would he pay a price?

Again, I had my doubts.

***

I slept all day. I'm not sure how many hours, but it was dark again when the phone woke me. Groggy after being awakened from a sound sleep, I picked up.

"Hello."

There was no response. I said "hello" again. Still no answer. I hung up, closed my eyes and tried to get back to sleep.

A minute later it rang again. "Hello!" I said, much louder this time.

A female voice said, "Don't be mad, Mr. Hardy."

"Who is this?"

Silence.

"Listen, I'm going to hang up if—"

"Sheilah Fitzjarrald," she said, her voice barely audible. "Or Zelda. Sometimes I'm not even sure, myself."

CHAPTER TWENTY NINE

One of the few things I remember about Mr. Shannon's seventh grade science is the idea that for every action, there's an equal and opposite reaction. If I remember right, the fella who first said that was talking about moving objects, but it's also true about the way human beings go about their business.

Something happens, which causes something else to happen.

In this case, the action was Cha Cha Mulvaney killing himself, which, among other things, caused Sheilah Fitzjarrald to call me.

***

"How'd you track me down?" I asked.

"I called the police station in Burr," she said. "I talked to your wife, told her who I was, and said I needed to talk to you."

"About what?"

"About everything."

That certainly covers a lot, I thought.

My car was still being impounded at Stop and Go Motors, so wherever we met had to be within walking distance. I asked if she knew where Mary's and could she be there in an hour. She said she knew where it was and could be there any time.

I hopped into the shower. I'm not even going to describe the gunk I scraped off me. Let's just say I felt a lot better and smelled a lot sweeter when I got out.

Unfortunately, I was out of clean clothes, so I had to put on the generic cop uniform from the day before. I'd thrown away my boots, so the only other shoes I had were those hospital slippers. I tip-toed down the street to K-Mart, where a nice young saleswoman with a '60s style bouffant hairdo sold me a pair of socks and some store-brand sneakers for five or six bucks.

From K-Mart, I walked to Mary's. As usual, the little bell rang when I walked through the door, but instead of the usual uproar, the place was almost deathly silent.

The jukebox wasn't playing. Those few customers who spoke did so in whispers. Even the sweet aroma of fried onions that I'd enjoyed on my earlier visits had an acrid tang.

Mary stood behind the counter, her face glum and smeared by tears and mascara. She went off on me as soon as I walked in: She pointed and screamed, "How *dare* you come in here!" then vanished through the door leading to the kitchen.

People turned and stared to see what kind of monster had caused the world's friendliest café owner to yell at a customer. I tried on a friendly smile, but I don't think it came off.

I found Sheilah sitting in a booth on the opposite end of the diner from the one reserved for Cha Cha.

I sat down across from her. "Looks like I'm not very popular."

"Of course not," she said. "They think you killed Cha Cha."

That's the last thing I wanted to hear.

Jaw clenched, I said: "Cha Cha shot *himself*!"

"I know," she said, "but to them you have blood on your hands."

Without realizing I was doing it, I looked at my hands. Just a half hour before, I'd scrubbed the last of Cha Cha's blood from them.

"That's ridiculous," I said.

I was mad fr being blamed, but I could understand it. These folks felt like Cha Cha belonged to them. I'd taken him away. Not even killing a state trooper in cold blood could move the needle from "Beloved Local Icon" to "Deranged Psycho Killer."

Would their opinion change if they knew he'd molested the young woman sitting across from me when she was a young girl?

Probably not.

I noticed Sheilah looking over my shoulder. I turned to see a burly guy in white pants and a ketchup-stained T-shirt standing over me, arms folded over his chest like Mr. Clean.

"Y'all are going to have to leave," he said.

"What's the problem?" I asked.

"You're disturbing the other customers."

"We've barely said a word," I said.

"I ain't talkin' about her," he said. "She can stay. You're the one's got to leave."

Sheilah eased out of the booth. "Let's go," she said quietly.

I fought back the urge to punch him. "Don't want to stay where we're not wanted," I said, and rose to leave.

Mr. Clean let Sheilah pass but purposely blocked my way. Blood rushed to my head, but reason won over rage. "Excuse me," I said politely. After a long moment, he stepped aside.

"And don't come back!" he said, because he was the kind of fella who if he can't get in the last punch has to at least get in the last word.

On our way out, the chime over the door sounded as loud as a church bell.

***

Sheilah had her car, so we drove to her apartment.

Inside, she switched on the light briefly, then groaned and turned it off. Except for a couple of folding chairs and a few taped-up boxes scattered across the floor, the place was empty. It had a musty smell, like it hadn't been lived in for a long time.

"I'm hardly ever here," she said. "I usually stay at Hazil's."

She invited me to sit. I took one of the folding chairs. She asked if I wanted coffee. I said, "No, I'm not a coffee drinker," then waited in the dark for a few minutes while she puttered around the kitchen and made some for herself.

She returned with a cigarette in one hand and a cup of coffee in the other.

"If you don't mind, I'd rather leave the lights off," she said.

"That's fine."

I couldn't make out her expression. On the phone she's insisted that we talk, but I was afraid that at any minute the walls she'd put up during our previous encounters would go right back up.

"Before I say anything," she began, "tell me what you already know. Or what you think you know."

"First," I began, "I'd like to express my condol—"

Wildly, ahe waved her lit cigarette like a 4th of July sparkler. "Please don't!"

That was my first clue that Sheilah might not feel about Cha Cha the way Cha Cha felt about her.

***

I told her what I'd learned, which at that point was mostly what Cha Cha had told me.

Except for the occasional nearly inaudible moan or groan, she didn't comment. Her first actual words came when I got to the part about her getting pregnant with Carrie.

"That was all my fault," she said dully. "I was all alone when I went into labor and had to drive myself to the hospital. Carrie wouldn't wait. I had to pull over on the side of the road and squeeze her out by myself. The doctor said I must've compressed her skull."

She took a puff of her cigarette. It lit up her face. The hurt there matched the hurt in her voice.

Thinking about how she'd been left alone by her family to face the birth by herself, I said I thought she was being too hard on herself.

She shook her head viciously. "No, I'm not!"

Pitiful, that girl was.

I tiptoed through the rest of Cha Cha's account, ending when she and Carrie joined Zelda and Hazil in Norman.

I left out the part about Hazil assaulting Carrie.

She brought it up.

"Did you know that Hazil raped Carrie?" she said.

"Cha Cha told me about that, too."

"Why didn't you mention it?"

"I reckon I didn't want to upset you."

She laughed maniacally. "Didn't want to upset me? Boy has that ship ever sailed!"

She calmed down and we were quiet for a bit.

"Did you know about that?" I asked.

"About Hazil raping Carrie? Yes."

"And you stayed with him?"

Her chin quivered. "You don't know what it was like."

"What does that mean, 'I don't know what it was like?'"

"Being held prisoner all your life," she said, her voice rising in pitch and volume. "First by your uncle, then by an old pervert like Cha Cha Mulvaney. You don't know what it was like!"

She was right, of course, although I thought I could imagine it—a little girl groomed and probably sexually assaulted by a middle-aged man before she'd even lost her baby teeth. But I couldn't ever really know.

Gazing upon her in the darkness, it suddenly hit me. I realized who Sheilah reminded me of.

Bonnie Hubbard.

Sheilah was a bleach blond, whereas Bonnie had dark hair, and Sheilah was a couple of inches shorter than Bonnie. But their eyes were the same color, and their facial features were nearly identical.

More importantly, both were put through hell by a man—or, in Sheilah's case, men.

Bonnie was a teenager when we first met, newly arrived in Burr after spending her early years in Wichita. From the beginning, she was different from the other girls her age. They all wore dresses and girly shoes and dated football players; Bonnie wore black sweaters, clunky black lace-up boots with thick gum soles and dreamed of marrying

Jack Kerouac. She and I both loved to read, so we hit it off pretty well. Bonnie hated Burr until she met someone who seemed to share her interests.

Unfortunately, that person was a psychopath—the Darryl Martin fella I was talking about earlier. He was a lot older than Bonnie. He was also married, although even if he'd been single, he had no business getting involved with a girl her age. Bonnie thought Darryl was the bee's knees, right up to the point where he killed a few people and then kidnapped her.

I remembered how easily Bonnie had been taken in. I'd almost forgotten how easy it is for older men to prey on young girls. Darryl knew and took full advantage. Bonnie recovered, largely because she had a mother who loved her and treated her right.

But what if she didn't have that kind of mother? What if Bonnie's mama had abandoned her in her hour of greatest need, like Zelda did to Sheilah? What if Bonnie hadn't finally seen through Darryl and rejected him?

I don't know why it took me so long to figure it out.

"You're right," I said softly. "I'm sorry you had to experience that, and I'm sorry if I badgered you about it."

"That's ok," she said.

"No, it's not."

It felt like any barrier between us had crumbled. "That's about all have to tell you," I said.

"Ok," she said. Very deliberately, she put out her cigarette and took a last sip of coffee.

It was time for Sheilah to have her say.

***

"Some of what Cha Cha said was true," she said. "Some of it isn't."

Essentially, all the bad things Cha Cha said about the Fitzjarrald family were true. As I'd suspected, the few things that flattered Cha Cha—or at least didn't incriminate him personally—were not.

"He told the truth about he and I being Carrie's parents," she said. "He was also right about him being Hazil's front man in the strip club business, Cha Cha's name is all over the paperwork, but Hazil's the real owner."

"I figured that's how it was."

Everything Cha Cha said about the family's origins was true—Harald's mother was a prostitute, and so was his wife. Mamie supported the family for years, and was probably still sending money to the old Flat-Nose address. Masquerading as 'Dan Cody,' Hazil did send his sister money. Cha Cha also told the truth about Bazil and Harald raping Zelda. "That happened," she said, then leaned forward and pointed at me with her cigarette.

"But he got one thing very, very wrong," she said forcefully. "*Harald* wasn't my father. *Hazil* was."

My head reeled.

On top of all the other crimes he committed, Hazil Fitzjarrald—or Scott Sayre or whoever he was this week—had impregnated his sister.

Knowing what Destiny had told me that night at Henny Penny's—that Sheilah and Sayre were a couple, I expected it to get worse.

It did.

***

"It wasn't a coincidence that Cha Cha came by to check on us when he heard Hazil disappeared," Sheilah said. "Hazil *hired* Cha Cha to keep an eye on us while he was off making his money."

There was something almost noble and, at the same time, utterly immoral about such a thing.

"How did they know each other?" I asked.

"Probably from that club in Flat-Nose," she said. "That much might actually be true."

"So all that time, Hazil was *paying* Cha Cha to watch over you gals."

"Oh, he did a lot of watching, alright," Sheilah said sarcastically.

In turns out that, in reality. Cha Cha wasn't Sheilah's loving protector, but a source of misery. While he never laid a hand on Zelda—she belonged to Hazil—he wouldn't *stop* putting his hands on Sheilah.

"I belonged to him," she said. Some of her earliest memories were of Cha Cha bringing her new clothes, seemingly for the sole purpose of watching her change in and out of them. Afterwards, he'd make her sit on his lap "to cop a feel," she said.

"Did Zelda know?"

Scoffing, she said, "Of course Zelda knew. She just didn't care! All she cared about was Hazil."

"Pardon me for asking," I said, "but did you ever try to get away?"

"Once," she said, "but I came back. It's your fault I did."

Not understanding, I said, "How could that be?"

"I was working for that friend of yours, remember?"

"Yvette?"

"Right. I found out about her through another dancer. Yvette was nice and looked out for her girls. The job wasn't much fun, but at least I had some freedom." She put out her cigarette in her coffee cup and lit another. "Then Yvette told me a policeman came looking for me."

My stomach turned.

"I reckoned Hazil must've sent you," she said. "I hoped if I went back to him on my own, he wouldn't beat me when I got back."

"Wait a second," I said. "Didn't you go back to Cha Cha?"

She laughed again, wildly. "No, no, no, no!" she said. "You still don't get it! I didn't belong to Cha Cha anymore."

I must've looked confused.

"It's like this," she said slowly. "Cha Cha ... didn't ... like ... women! Cha Cha ... liked ... girls! I ... was ... too ... *old*!" She laughed—at the drama, at the absurdity, at the hurt she must've felt. "Hell, I was already too old when I got pregnant with Carrie. That's why Cha Cha left me in Flat-Nose."

Cha Cha had conveniently left that out.

"I reckon it must've been a relief to be rid of him," I said.

"It was," she agreed, "but it didn't last very long. See, Zelda died, and Hazil wanted me to replace her."

"Didn't Cha Cha have something to say about that?"

"*Listen now to what I'm saying!*" she said, biting off the words like a lion feasting on an antelope. "*By this time, I was a woman, ok?* Cha Cha liked girls! He didn't want me! He sold me to Hazil."

Once again, I was stunned.

"You don't mean he actually paid Cha Cha for you?"

She chuckled, likely because I was coming off as denser than a block of cement. "Oh yes he did, and the funny part is, he didn't even have to. He could've just taken me, and Cha Cha wouldn't have said a word." She puffed on her cigarette. "But no. Hazil wanted to show everybody what a big man he was, so he went out and bought Cha Cha a new Cadillac. He even gave him a card. It said, 'For being such a good friend and employee,' but I knew better." She frowned and looked down at the floor. "After that, I slept in Hazil's bed. Still do."

The sheer depravity of it shocked me into silence.

***

Outside, traffic rushed past. A horn on a passing car played "Boomer Sooner."

"What are you to Sayre now?" I asked.

"His property," she said sadly. "His slave."

I shut up.

***

Something else came to mind, something I'd tried to push away.

"I'm not sure you knew," I said haltingly, "but Carrie was pregnant when she died."

"Oh Lord," she sighed. "I guess you want to know if it was Hazil's."

I nodded.

She shook her head. "Not possible."

That meant, in all likelihood, the father had been Carrie's boyfriend, Leon.

"Good," I said.

There was one more thing. I guess I don't have to tell you what it was.

I was almost afraid to ask. "Did Hazil kill my friends?"

Seconds passed as I listened to her loud breathing before realizing it me.

"He didn't do it himself," she finally said. "But he had it done."

No surprise there.

"Who did the actual shooting?" I asked.

She didn't answer right away. "Surely you know," she finally said, looking at me strangely.

"Cha Cha said it was that bouncer from Henny Penny's."

"He did, did he?" she said. "No, it wasn't him."

"Then who was it?"

"You're serious?" she said, her disbelief plain. "You really don't know?"

"I don't."

The air was electric.

"Cha Cha," she said. "Who else?"

Indeed.

Who else?

CHAPTER THIRTY

When all was said and done, I didn't come close to knowing everything there was to know about the Fitzjarralds. The family was so corrupt, so incredibly rotten to the core, it was almost anyone's guess where the lies ended, and the truth began.

That said, I did believe Sheilah. She'd been hurt too much to lie.

***

The day after I talked to Sheilah, I drove to the OSBI office in Oklahoma City to make my formal statement. I'd expected to meet with John Joe Heckscher, but was directed to one of his underlings instead; Heckscher had been unavoidably detained.

I suspect that what unavoidably detained him was embarrassment over his role in the Cha Cha Mulvaney cluster-you-know-what, but I didn't say that to the fella who interviewed me.

I drove straight back to Burr after we were finished.

***

Later in the week, I turned on the 6:00 news from one of the Oklahoma City stations. The lead story was about a breakdown at some nuclear power plant in Pennsylvania, but right after that came a report about an investigation into Scott Sayre. The reporter interviewed a state official, who said something about crossing their t's and dotting their i's, but nowhere did he mention any specific allegation of wrongdoing. I already knew he'd had been arrested—Bonnie Hubbard was one of the agents who took him in—but for some reason, they didn't mention that.

My phone rang almost as soon as the report was over.

"Chief Hardy, this is Bonnie," she said (I liked that she still called me "Chief"). "I was just watching the news and—"

"Yeh," I said, "I saw it."

"So do you think he's going to get away with it?"

I did, but instead of saying so, I asked her how Sayre had reacted when she picked him up.

"Oh, he was all bent out of shape," she said, "yelling and screaming about government oppression, and how he was going to have the head of the OSBI fired. Something about cutting taxes, I don't know. Bunch of nonsense, really."

"I guess that's about what you'd expect out of someone like him."

"Yeh, well, he'll be talking out of the other side of his mouth once they throw him in jail."

I slipped and said, "*If* they throw him in jail."

"So you *do* think he'll get away with it," she asked.

"I wish I didn't, but yeh, I think he'll manage to squirm out of it. That's what worms do."

Sure enough, that's exactly what happened.

***

Ever heard the saying, "Justice delayed is justice denied?" The case of Scott Sayre/Dan Cody/Hazil Fitzjarrald is a prime example.

In the days and weeks after his arrest, it looked like he might actually go to jail on federal drug charges. The US Attorney in charge of the Western District of Oklahoma was gung-ho about it, and practically had Sayre's orange jumpsuit all picked out.

Unfortunately, the fella above him dilly-dallied until after the next presidential election, a period of almost two years.

Sadly, the wrong team won.

The new president dismissed the sitting US Attorney, and appointed Sayre's former lawyer to the post—a state representative who was also Vice Chairman of the state Republican party. Somewhere along the line, the tape of my conversation with Cha Cha disappeared. That made it easy for them to blame everything on Cha Cha, who obviously couldn't fight back on account of being dead.

Scott Sayre, a/k/a Dan Cody, a/k/a Hazil Fitzjarrald, walked. End of story.

Except that it's not.

Weeks after the case against him was dismissed, Sayre was found dead in his office at Stop and Go Motors. His passing caused quite the uproar. Once again, Bonnie Hubbard was the first OSBI agent on the scene. She found Sayre at his desk, face down in a small mountain of cocaine.

Later, FBI chemists found the cocaine had been tainted, leading to concern within the bureau that he'd been poisoned by a Mexican drug lord he'd been doing business with.

None of that was reported in the press.

The local papers and news shows said Sayre died of natural causes. Not a word was said about his ownership of Henny Penny's, or his previous life as Hazil Fitzjarrald, or the fact that he lived in sin with his sister and, after she died, imprisoned, beat, and raped his niece— who was also his daughter—on a nightly basis. Likewise, nothing was said about how the first US Attorney had him dead to rights, but the new guy let him off without so much as a slap on the wrist.

No one said anything about how he murdered his brother, either, probably because only two people ever knew about it, and one of them was dead.

There was more than enough evidence of Hazil's other crimes to put him away for a good long time, but he managed to run out the clock.

First the charges were dismissed. Then he died.

***

In the end, Cha Cha got blamed for everything—except the crime he actually committed: the murders of John Smith and Thelma Jean Parham, alias Chastity.

As for the man arrested for that crime, Cha Cha was right; Fletcher Fluke hanged himself in his cell the day I visited him. He used his belt.

He wasn't wearing it when I saw him. They'd taken it away.

I guess they gave it back.

***

As for Detective Blanchard, any evidence that he collaborated with Hazil, or had anything to do with Fletcher Fluke's death, was buried. Last I knew, he was still on the force.

***

OSBI Special Agent Bonnie Hubbard could've ripped the lid off the cover-up if she'd wanted to. I assured her that if she did and got fired, she'd always have a job working for me.

But Bonnie's ambitious. She likes her job and probably hopes to run the entire OSBI someday.

She backed off without saying anything.

As you might imagine, I was pretty disappointed by that.

***

Mike Fike, the fella who managed Henny Penny's and performed other nefarious chores for Sayre. I only saw him a few times, notably on that first night at Henny Penny's when I saw him slap Chastity on the rear end. Fletcher Fluke was convinced it was Fike who planted the gun on him, trying to frame him for the murders of John and Chastity. I suspect he was right about that, based on having seen Fike bossing around the bikers, that night I staked out Stop and Go Motors.

Fike disappeared the night Cha Cha swallowed his gun. For a while, he was wanted for questioning by the FBI, but their interest waned after the new US Attorney dropped the charges against Hazil.

***

Joe the Bouncer survived our wrestling match on the floor of Stop and Go, but was later killed in a motorcycle accident, *ala* Harold Stafford, Roger Dale Stafford's brother.

***

Also, Henny Penny's burnt down.

One night, some crackpot, incited by the uproar over State Question 339, squirted gasoline under the box office's money slot and lit a match. Fortunately, the club was closed. However, the fire did claim one victim: the janitor, a middle-aged fella of Vietnamese descent who only a few years earlier had come to Oklahoma as a refugee.

The six o'clock news folks sent a reporter out to talk to his neighbors. One of them said he'd been a doctor back in Vietnam but couldn't practice in the United States. "He told me he was studying to become an American citizen," the neighbor said. The reporter asked if the victim had any friends. "Not that I know of," admitted the neighbor with a shrug. "He mostly kept to himself."

***

Not everything that happened was depressing.

Destiny—the dancer who got me all hot and bothered that first night I went to Henny Penny's—graduated from OU with honors, and enrolled in graduate school, just like she said she would. I never saw her again, but I did call her once to see how she was doing. She'd quit dancing and was now working two jobs: one as a graduate assistant teaching a couple of introductory business courses, the other as a clerk working the graveyard shift at a convenience store—not the Sunshine

Store, in case you're wondering. That would have been kind of poetic, but it's not how it happened. I told her to be careful. She said she would.

I wanted to ask again what her real name was, but I totally forgot.

Maybe it really *was* Destiny.

***

Finally, and most improbably, Mamie Fitzjarrald resurfaced. Turns out she'd been living in Amarillo all those years. She saw news reports about Scott Sayre's death, and recognized him as her son Hazil. For some reason, she contacted me. She didn't seem too broken up by his demise; more concerning to her was that he'd changed his name. "He probably did it for political purposes," I said, but she wasn't buying it. When I asked where she'd been all these years, she said that shortly after leaving her family and going back to work as a hooker, she'd met a nice man and got married.

"Harald and I never wed," she explained in voice like the lady who plays the millionaire's wife on *Gilligan's Island*. "We were just common-law." I told her about my plans to exhume Carrie and asked for her help. She said she'd be happy to, but when I called her a week later, her phone had been disconnected.

I never heard from her again.

***

There were nights right after I'd been held captive that I came very close to drowning my sorrows in one or several bottles of Old Grand-Dad.

For weeks, I was sad and shaky and couldn't sleep. It wasn't nightmares keeping me up; you've got to be able to fall asleep before you can have a nightmare.

Occasionally, on a weekday afternoon, I'd leave Red in charge, go home, and lie down for an hour or so. Some of those times I probably actually did sleep, but mostly I lay tossing and turning and scratching various body parts. I never knew a person could itch in so many places.

The last time I'd slept the whole night through was that last time at the Sooner Arms when I slept almost an entire day.

One night, about a month after my talk with Sheilah, Red and I were lying in bed before turning out the lights. I was apologizing in advance for my nightly itchy acrobatics, when she made a suggestion.

"You know," she said, "you never did do what you set out to do."

"You think I don't know that?" I said. "Hell, I didn't accomplish *anything* I set out to do. I sure as hell never got justice for John and Chastity."

"C'mon now, Emmett, that's not how this started," she said. "It started with you wanting to find Carrie's family so you could get her moved out of that prison cemetery, but now that you can do it, you've been putting it off and putting it off."

"Thanks for reminding me," I said as I scratched a spot behind my left knee.

"You know I'm right," she insisted. "You found her mama so you're out of excuses. Call the Department of Corrections and get it done."

There were other reasons I couldn't sleep, the most obvious being what I'd just been through. Maybe I've lived a sheltered life, but not in a million years could I have imagined a family so depraved as the Fitzjarralds.

But Red had nailed it; I pride myself on finishing what I start, but in this case, I hadn't, even when nothing was really stopping me.

Still, I felt paralyzed at the very prospect. It took Red kicking me in the butt to get me going.

In fact, once I managed to rouse myself from the stupor and actually get after it, the solution proved almost shockingly simple. All I needed was a member of Carrie's family to cooperate.

I called Sheilah, who by then had thankfully escaped Sayre's clutches, and was then living at a shelter for battered women. I told her what I had in mind. She was thrilled.

The Oklahoma State Department of Corrections forced us cut through enough tape to wrap an army of mummies. Fortunately, Karen is an ace at stuff like that, so she handled most of it. Sheilah had either lost or never been issued Carrie's birth certificate, so we had to wait around for the state of Texas to sort that out. Once we had that, the coast was clear.

The state of Oklahoma told us how much the exhumation would cost. Sheilah didn't have the money, so Red and I said we'd pay for it.

Thank goodness for my folks' oil money.

When all was said and done—and I give all the credit to Karen, who was the one who did most of the work—we got permission.

Finally, after all those years, Carrie was going home.

EPILOGUE

Except Carrie didn't have a home.

That's the story of her life.

Sheilah got frantic when I suggested we bury her in Flat-Nose, near where they'd buried Bazil. She hated the place and refused to ever go back. I couldn't blame her, but we had to find someplace.

It was Red who suggested Burr. There was an empty burial plot on Memorial Hill beside the two we'd purchased for ourselves. Folks aren't exactly flocking in droves to be buried in Burr, Oklahoma, so the price was reasonable, although we would've bought it even if it wasn't.

We finally had a place to put Carrie to rest. We cut the Department of Corrections a check. They ran a backhoe out there, dug up her coffin, and transported it to Memorial Hill.

The night before the funeral, I slept like a baby.

The day was overcast, just as it had been when I drove to Noble that day in 1979 to hear what John had discovered about Carrie. I remembered how on the phone he'd referred to her as "our girl," and that I knew immediately who he was talking about.

Sheilah refused to hold the service in a church; she didn't believe in God, and I couldn't think of any good reason why she should. Instead, we held it at Bates Funeral Home, where, when the time came, Karen and I planned to hold our own services.

The casket was closed, needless to say, but the funeral director did contribute a new one, free of charge, much fancier than the pine box she'd originally been buried in. Sheilah asked me to say a few words. I felt strange about it; I'm not sure I ever shed the guilt I felt about her death happening on my watch. But I couldn't refuse. I don't remember what I said, probably because it wasn't very memorable. I did my best.

The funeral procession consisted of four vehicles. In the lead was the department's old black and white Plymouth Fury, which we only cart out on special occasions. The Fury was always Bernard Cousins' car when he worked for us, so I let him drive, accompanied by Joel and Cindy. Behind that was the hearse with Carrie's casket, followed by the funeral parlor's black Lincoln Town Car. The original plan had been for Sheilah to ride in the Lincoln with her grandmother, but when Mamie didn't show up, Sheilah asked me to ride with her. Again, it didn't exactly feel right, but if that's what she wanted, I was glad to do it. Bringing up the rear was Red in her little blue Ford Falcon.

Two years had passed. It was now the summer of 1981. The trial of Roger Dale Stafford had come and gone. He'd been found guilty and sentenced to death for killing that family and those kids, which I reckon he deserved, although I've never been all that comfortable handing over the power of life and death to the government. Still, if anyone deserved to die for his crimes, it was him.

Despite a boatload of evidence pointing in his direction, the fella they arrested for killing those Girl Scouts was acquitted. A couple of months later, he died in prison of a heart attack.

That's karma, as Karen would say.

Scott Sayre—or, as I will henceforth forever call him, Hazil Fitzjarrald—was dead, too, as was his father Harald. I thought about how the new US Attorney had essentially given Hazil a pardon, which the current president (who, I felt, had been elected on a platform of cruelty) might have given him, anyway. Hazil beat the rap, but he couldn't outrun his sins. Death is death, whether it comes at the end of a rope, a jolt of electricity, or a dose of cocaine mixed with cyanide.

The day started with a temperature in the 80s. However, by the time we got to the cemetery, a cold front had hit, and it had dropped a good 20 degrees. Oklahomans know when that happens, there just might be a tornado in your immediate future. We hurried to get things done.

The four of us men carried the casket from the hearse to the gravesite. Karen had wanted to say a prayer, but Sheilah put her foot down. Instead, we stood silently around the casket, buffeted by the wind and about to get rained on, each of us left to our own thoughts. After a respectable length of time, the funeral director—his eyes on the clouds swirling overhead—thanked us for coming, and we headed to our cars.

There are at least two other cemeteries in Burr that the Hardys could have chosen instead of Memorial Hill—which isn't really a hill but more of a plateau, rising only slightly above the surrounding land. But neither of those other places provides the same spectacular views of sand hills on the banks of the nearby Cimarron River, and, to the east, a long ridge made up of striped mesas rising above the land like islands in a waterless sea.

I tend to think that previous generations of Hardys were blessed with restless spirits, since it is to the east—at exactly the point where land meets sky—where trains traverse the horizon, all day, every day. Many is the time I've stood at my parents' graves, watched one of those trains go by, and wished I were on it.

As we got into our cars, a massive freight at least a mile long chugged across the horizon. It approached an intersection and blew its horn. Sheilah stopped and watched.

"Carrie loved trains when she was little," she said, smiling through her tears, in a tone that was sad but optimistic. "I think she's going to like it here."

I sure hope so.

ABOUT THE AUTHOR

Chris Kelsey spent most of his first twenty-five years in Oklahoma before moving to New York City in the mid-1980s. He now lives a few miles upstate in Dutchess County, where he serves as Director of Instrumental Music at the Trinity-Pawling School. An accomplished jazz saxophonist and a life-long educator, Chris is also the proud father of two terrific kids, the husband of one endlessly patient woman, and a dedicated teacher to any young person with a desire to make music.

OTHER TITLES BY CHRIS KELSEY

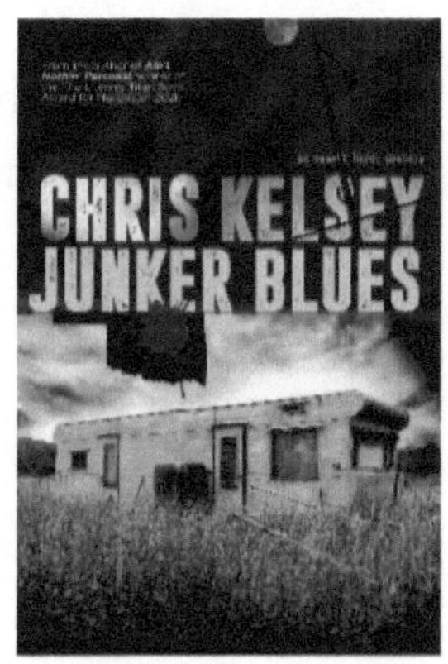

NOTE FROM CHRIS KELSEY

Word-of-mouth is crucial for any author to succeed. If you enjoyed *Somebody, Sometime*, please leave a review online—anywhere you are able. Even if it's just a sentence or two. It would make all the difference and would be very much appreciated.

Thanks!
Chris Kelsey

We hope you enjoyed reading this title from:

www.blackrosewriting.com

Subscribe to our mailing list – *The Rosevine* – and receive **FREE** books, daily
deals, and stay current with news about
upcoming releases and our hottest authors.
Scan the QR code below to sign up.

Already a subscriber? Please accept a sincere thank you for being a fan of
Black Rose Writing authors.

View other Black Rose Writing titles at
www.blackrosewriting.com/books and use promo code
PRINT to receive a **20% discount** when purchasing.

9 781685 137144